Shadows in the Cotswolds

By Rebecca Tope

THE COTSWOLD MYSTERIES

THE LAKE DISTRICT MYSTERIES

THE WEST COUNTRY MYSTERIES

Shadows in the Cotswolds

REBECCA TOPE

Allison & Busby Limited
11 Wardour Mews
London W1F 8AN
allisonandbusby.com

First published in Great Britain by Allison & Busby in 2013.
First published in paperback by Allison & Busby in 2014.
This paperback edition published by Allison & Busby in 2019.

A CIP catalogue record for this book is available from
the British Library.

10 9 8 7 6 5 4 3 2 1

ISBN 978-0-7490-2432-1

Typeset in 10.5/15.5 pt Sabon by
Allison & Busby Ltd.

The paper used for this Allison & Busby publication
has been produced from trees that have been legally sourced
from well-managed and credibly certified forests.

Printed and bound by
CPI Group (UK) Ltd, Croydon, CR0 4YY

*Dedicated to
my long-suffering offspring-in-law –
Andrea and Gareth*

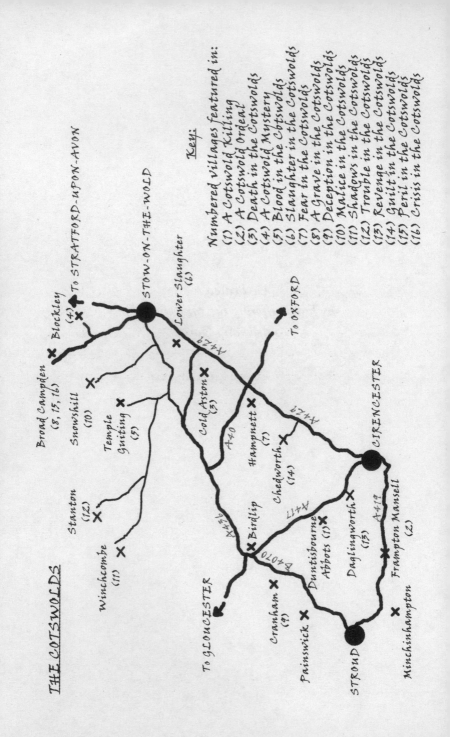

THE COTSWOLDS

To STRATFORD-UPON-AVON

Blockley (4)

Broad Campden (8, 15, 16)

STOW-ON-THE-WOLD

Lower Slaughter (6)

Snowshill (10)

Temple Guiting (5)

Cold Aston (3)

A436

Stanton (12)

Hampnett (7)

To OXFORD

A40

A429

Winchcombe (11)

Chedworth (14)

Birdlip

A417

Duntisbourne Abbots (1)

A419

CIRENCESTER

A4070

Daglingworth (13)

Cranham (9)

Frampton Mansell (2)

To GLOUCESTER

Painswick

STROUD

Minchinhampton

Key:

Numbered villages featured in:
(1) A Cotswold Killing
(2) A Cotswold Ordeal
(3) Death in the Cotswolds
(4) A Cotswold Mystery
(5) Blood in the Cotswolds
(6) Slaughter in the Cotswolds
(7) Fear in the Cotswolds
(8) A Grave in the Cotswolds
(9) Deception in the Cotswolds
(10) Malice in the Cotswolds
(11) Shadows in the Cotswolds
(12) Trouble in the Cotswolds
(13) Revenge in the Cotswolds
(14) Guilt in the Cotswolds
(15) Peril in the Cotswolds
(16) Crisis in the Cotswolds

Author's Note

The layout of Winchcombe is very much as described in this story, but some liberties have been taken with the lower end of Vineyard Street, Castle Street and the former Silk Mill building, for which I hope I will be forgiven. The main house and all the characters are products of my imagination.

Prologue

'Thea? Hello? It's me.'

'Yes, Mum, I know. Where are you? It's an awful line.'

'I'm in the churchyard, so I can't shout. I know it's dreadful of me to be using a phone here, but I wanted to talk to you.'

'Dad's grave?' Thea could visualise the whole scene. 'Have they put the stone up?'

'That's why I'm phoning. They did it last week – at last. You'd think they could have made the effort to get it done in time for the anniversary. As it is, they're a month late.'

'I can't come and see it yet, I'm afraid.'

'Why can't you? What are you doing?'

The answer was too complicated for a breathy mobile conversation. 'I'm busy,' was all she said. Her mother would give her the benefit of any doubt, accepting her second daughter's unpredictable lifestyle with a reasonably good grace. The knowledge that the truth was a long way from the claimed busyness made Thea feel guilty. In reality, she had very little to do for the foreseeable future. She was in fact busy being bored and depressed, with none of the traditional September sense of bracing new beginnings. The onset of autumn was not something she anticipated with any relish at all.

'Phone me again when you get home and we'll have a proper talk,' she said. 'And see if you can make your phone take a photo of the headstone. Then you can send it to me.'

Her mother snorted. 'I can do that quite easily,' she said. 'Damien showed me how, *ages* ago.'

The second phone call came at seven that evening, after a perfect picture of her father's memorial had come through. Its tardiness could not really be blamed on the stonemasons: the family had taken months to decide on the wording. Her father had been dead a year, and everybody still felt the loss in their own distinctive ways.

'Me again,' chirped her mother. 'Did you get the photo?'

'It's lovely. Dad would have been very impressed.'

'You really must go and see it. Are you off on one of your house-sitting jaunts again? It's been a while now, hasn't it?'

'Five weeks. It's not unusual to have that sort of gap. But actually – no, there's nothing in the diary until November. I'm busy with stuff here.'

'Decorating?' came the hopeful reply. 'Not before time. You neglect that poor little house.'

'More the garden, really. I decided to give it a facelift. It's a huge project.'

'You know, darling, I think you need to consider finding a more reliable job. I don't want to interfere, but really, this house-sitting isn't going to go on for ever, is it?'

'It suits me.'

'I can't imagine why. But listen . . . I wasn't sure whether I should tell you this, but I do know a man in Winchcombe who's wanting somebody to mind his house for a fortnight. Starting this weekend.'

A man in Winchcombe sounded like something her mother would never in a million years be acquainted with. 'Who is he?'

'Oh, that's a long story. He's called Meadows. Oliver Meadows.' She said the name in a tone of familiarity, as if it had been coming to her lips daily for decades.

'I've never heard of him,' said Thea crossly. Her mother ought not to be having male friends without her knowledge. It went against the natural order of things.

'I really know his brother, not him. Fraser, he's called. He got in touch with me a while ago, on the email. He found me on Facebook.' Her mother giggled complacently. 'We had lots of nice chats, and I told him about you, and he said his brother needed a house-sitter. I wasn't going to ask you, but somehow . . .'

Your tongue ran ahead of your brain, as usual, Thea thought. 'It sounds very peculiar,' she prevaricated, already bewildered as to which brother was which. Did she want to spend a fortnight in Winchcombe at three days' notice? She looked to her spaniel for enlightenment. Hepzie was managing their boredom considerably better than her mistress was, and gave a small contented tail-wag.

'It's not in the least peculiar,' sniffed her mother. 'The man has a big wild garden full of birds, apparently, and wants somebody to keep up the food supplies for them. And

11

fend off cats and things that might kill them, I suppose. He's a photographer, so it's not just a hobby. He does pictures of the birds for books.'

'I hardly know Winchcombe.' In her imagination it was a large town, very different from the little villages she normally frequented. She remembered something ecclesiastical in its history, and glimpses of medieval streets of heart-stopping beauty.

'It's lovely. Sudeley Castle is right there. Surely you've been to it? At least the gardens.'

'I fear not. Are you *sure* he wants somebody at such short notice? What would he have done if you hadn't said anything to me?'

'I have no idea. Asked a neighbour, cut short his holiday, left the birds to fend for themselves – I don't know. But he's happy to pay the usual rate, and it seems as if you're interested – despite being so *busy*,' she finished sarcastically. 'Let me give you his phone number. There's a chance he's already found somebody else, of course.'

Chapter One

Oliver Meadows had not found anybody else, and after a disconcertingly brief telephone conversation with him, Thea wended her way across the uplands of the eastern Cotswolds and through the heart of the region towards Winchcombe in the west, on the following Saturday morning. The weather was bright and balmy, the roads uncluttered, and the long undulations of the final miles brought to mind the endless unpredictability of the area. She was on the little road from Guiting Power that led crookedly past Sudeley Farm and then instantly into the heart of Winchcombe, which was nowhere near as large as she'd imagined, and even more beautiful.

The road narrowed impossibly as she approached the junction with the town's main street, forcing traffic to be patient and polite as drivers took their turn to negotiate the junction. It was a steep hill up to the high street, and there was space for only one vehicle at a time, with high old buildings crowding in on either side. One was a big pub, the White Hart, she noticed. A large black car was waiting to turn down into the street, which would be impossible until Thea got out of the way. The potential for genuine logjam was plain; all it would take was one impatient driver, or a learner stalling their car on the hill. But everyone seemed cheerfully content to give way and wait for things to sort themselves out. Thea turned left, wondering just how forbearing the drivers would have been if she'd tried to go the other way. She crawled along, hoping she'd remembered Oliver's directions accurately. The town square (which was in fact a long thin rectangle) was full of parked cars, and a white van was obstructing the way ahead. This gave Thea time to look round and try to get a feel for the place – a first impression that she knew from past experience would colour her reaction to Winchcombe from that point on.

To her right was a long featureless wall and a generous pavement. The wall reminded her of the way Snowshill Manor sat invisibly in the heart of the village behind a similar stone barrier. But here in Winchcombe there was merely the ghost of an abbey that had once been of immense importance. That much she knew from her history. Now it looked to be nothing more than a park with large trees and uninviting gates. The eye was drawn back to the buildings and relative bustle on the opposite side. As she manoeuvred around the white van, she saw Vineyard Street a short way to the left, with a sign to Sudeley Castle. That was her destination and she turned down it with a feeling of relief that at least the first hurdle had been overcome. Getting lost in the Cotswolds lanes was a perpetual faint anxiety, although in reality it had very seldom happened. The local authority was blessedly generous with signs, which helped a lot.

Vineyard Street was wide and probably lovely, if she had been able to see past the throngs of cars parked on either side. There were also trees concealing the detail of the houses. A few yards ahead was a stone bridge, just as Oliver had said, and she accomplished the final approach without mishap.

It was far from customary for Thea to feel uneasy as she approached a new house-sitting commission. And yet here she was, her head swarming with worries. The instructions told her to turn left into a disused farmyard. The house, named Thistledown, was to be found beyond the yard, with its own short track and minimal parking area. That much had come easily, but she was still tense. It had all happened too quickly, with no time to get into the right mood. Normally she had weeks or months in which to prepare for a house-sit. She would consult maps and history books and plan some walks and visits. The fact that events all too often sent such plans into oblivion was neither here nor there.

She had, for the first time, agreed to do the job without her usual preliminary visit, which she knew was risky. She was relying on her mother's recommendation, which felt anything but solid. The tenuous link with another Meadows, whose role in her mother's life she still did not remotely understand, was perplexing. 'But who *is* he?' she had demanded.

'He was a boyfriend of mine, before I met your father,' came the unsatisfactory reply.

'But Mum – that must have been fifty years ago,' Thea had protested.

'Yes. Isn't life strange? He remembers all sorts of things that I have absolutely no recollection of.'

'And vice versa, I expect.'

'What? Oh, I'm not sure about that. His memory seems to be a great deal better than mine.'

There was a shadow of embarrassment in the whole situation. Mothers ought not to discover long-forgotten boyfriends. It was hard to see how any good could come of it.

'Where does he live?'

'He's staying with his daughter at the moment, because he's just come back from Australia. He went there when he was thirty-five, and now he's decided he wants to spend his final years in England.'

'Isn't the daughter Australian, then? Why is she here?'

Her mother had sighed noisily. 'Why so many questions? If you must know, the wife brought the child back here, after ten years of marriage. Fraser stayed in Perth, because he liked it there and had a good job. He married again, but that wife died after only a year. So now he wants to get to know his grandchildren. Is that clear enough for you?'

Thea thought of her mother's handsome Oxfordshire house, where she lived alone, and wondered whether this Fraser might have unwholesome designs on it. The idea of her father being replaced in the bed and chair and garden shed gave her a sharp pang. 'Has Damien met him?' she asked. Her brother was now the acknowledged head of the family, to whose judgements his mother and sisters all deferred.

'He has, actually,' said her mother shortly. 'And you're soon to meet his brother, aren't you?'

She met Oliver Meadows for precisely thirty-five minutes before he departed on his urgent business. He gave her no indication as to what that business might be, and offered no contact details. Thea inwardly sighed – too many people thought it was permissable to simply disappear into the blue, and leave their long-suffering house-sitter to deal with all the unforeseen events that very often transpired the moment their backs were turned.

'It's quite simple,' he said. 'You just have to maintain the feeding programme for the birds. I've written it all down here, look. And I've made a list of places you might like to go and see.'

Instead of reading the notes, she looked at him. He was tall and slightly stooped, aged somewhere in his mid seventies, with calm, slow movements. His gaze seemed to be focused at a considerable distance, so she never felt that he saw her at all. He did, however, see her dog. Somehow, nobody had told him about the dog. 'That's a dog,' he said, when she walked up to his door with the spaniel at her heels.

'I'm afraid it is. I always bring her with me. I assumed my mother would have told you.'

'Does it chase birds?'

It was an awkward question. The dog was a cocker spaniel, so called because they had been bred from medieval times to pursue and catch woodcock. And woodcock were birds. Hepzibah, however, had seldom displayed very much of a genetic tendency to plunge aggressively into whatever habitat the modern version of woodcock frequented. She did, however, enjoy a hearty pursuit of waterfowl. She would sometimes dive into icy waters in futile efforts to catch a mallard or moorhen. 'Oh no,' Thea said. 'She's not the least bit interested in birds.'

'Do you give me your solemn assurance of that?'

Experience suggested that it really was best to be honest, if at all possible. 'She's not entirely perfect with ducks,' she confessed. 'But otherwise, I can promise you she'll be no trouble at all.'

'Ducks,' said the man thoughtfully. 'There aren't any ducks. I have been thinking of putting in a small lake, but it never happened. Perhaps when I get back . . .'

A *small lake* sounded ambitious. 'How many acres are there?' Thea asked.

'Four and a half. I planted all the trees myself, twenty-five years ago. It was just open ground before that.'

'Wow!'

They were standing on a small raised patio, a few steps up from the house, looking eastwards across a densely wooded area. Apparently, the birds were in amongst the trees, which were predominately silver birch, willow, and fir – fast-growing species that gave shelter to wildlife where none had been before. 'Come and look,' said Oliver Meadows, with a swift glance at his watch.

The property was situated immediately to the south of Winchcombe's main street and roughly north of the grand edifice of Sudeley Castle. A little river bordered it on one side, and a generous swathe of allotments had been established just beyond the water course. The whole area was busy on this sunny Saturday, with visitors to Sudeley's parklands, as well as the patchwork gardens dense with beans, cabbages and pumpkins. Both sides of the road were lined with parked cars, which Thea had been forced to negotiate as she located the approach to Oliver's house. 'There is a better way, from the back, but it's too complicated to explain,' he said impatiently.

The tour of the acres was rapid and bewildering. In the middle of the woodland, quite invisible from outside, was a large hide, built from logs and thatched with bracken. Inside it had a cupboard full of peanuts, fat balls, mealworms and other food enjoyed by birds; a table; two high stools; a shelf containing binoculars and notebooks; and a large poster displaying all the finches that could be found in Britain. There was also an expensive-looking remote-controlled video camera positioned in the middle of the long viewing slit, which could swivel left and right to track birds as they visited the extensive feeding station ten feet away.

'There's no power out here,' Oliver explained. 'The camera runs on batteries. They have to be replaced every morning. So does the SD card.'

'Is it going all the time?'

'Ideally, yes. I don't want to miss anything, but I can't sit here the entire time.'

'Of course not,' said Thea, feeling relieved that she wasn't expected to do so.

'I understand that your mother would like to come and see the set-up while I'm away. I have no objection to that, so long as you take responsibility for her.'

The idea struck Thea as mildly comical, but she was careful to keep a straight face. 'Let me show you the routines,' he went on relentlessly, with another glance at his watch.

He took her outside and demonstrated the numerous tables, hooks, water bowls, and wire contraptions all intended to hold food for the birds. 'Squirrels are a huge problem, of course,' he sighed. 'They can open almost anything, given time.'

'I hope I don't have to shoot them,' she joked.

'No, but there is a catapult in the hide, which you're welcome to use. It does take a lot of practice, unfortunately.'

She wisely refrained from telling him that her spaniel was more than ready to chase a squirrel, given the chance. She had yet to succeed in catching one.

He led her down a little path to a sudden area of open ground, thronged with long grass and spikes of various meadow plants, long since gone to seed and stripped. It looked like almost half an acre in size. Thea could see a rickety gate at the far side. 'This forms the boundary of my property,' he said. 'You can get out over there, on foot, and turn left to get into town. You come out in Castle Street, which leads into the high street. It's a short, easy walk, if you want to pop out for some shopping.'

The tour was over in no time, and Thea suspected that they were both feeling decidedly nervous as Oliver scrambled into his car. 'I'm sorry this has all been such a rush,' he said. 'If it's any consolation, I would far rather not be going, but I haven't any choice. The exact day of my return is uncertain, I'm afraid. It could be any time next week – but not longer than that. Your mother knows my brother, of course. If you need any help, he might be slightly better than nothing.' He pulled a rueful face. 'Although I suggest you do your best not to need him.'

'I'll be fine,' she breezed. *After all*, she thought, *how difficult can it be to feed the birds? Any eight-year-old could do it.*

In reality, the instructions had been deplorably sketchy. She wasn't precisely sure how to operate the camera, for one thing. Oliver had embarked on a hurried elucidation of how it worked, but then interrupted himself at the sight of a goldfinch swinging on one of the feeders. 'Hey – she hasn't been here for over a week!' he rejoiced. 'I was worrying.' He lapsed into an enchanted silence as he watched the gaudy little bird.

'The camera?' Thea prompted.

'It's not really difficult. Don't bother with the panning, but if you could change the cards and batteries . . . and label the cards with the date, maybe? I hate to miss anything, you see.' He was whispering, his eyes firmly on the finch. 'It is rather important,' he added. 'The records will lose all their purpose if there's two weeks missing, do you see?'

'Oh yes,' she asserted bravely.

As a final thought, he tried to assure her that it was going to be rather a treat. 'You can go out any time you like, of course. There's a lot to see around here. Winchcombe has more history than almost anywhere, right here on the doorstep. And then there's Hailes Abbey and Belas Knap and all that . . .' He smiled encouragingly at her, and started the engine. As he drove off, Thea found herself struggling

21

to feel glad to be there, with new places to explore and bird species to learn. It was easy, she insisted to herself, and there were bound to be distractions.

But the hurried arrangements began to strike her as unsettlingly irresponsible as she tried to find her way around the house, and resolve such urgent issues as what she would eat and where she would sleep. 'Spare room, everything should be self-explanatory,' Oliver Meadows had said carelessly, without even taking her upstairs. Although accustomed to a certain lack of formality in many of her house-sitting commissions, she found this one the most casual to date. All the man cared about were his birds, it seemed. She could neglect the house completely, so long as the feeders were full and the camera doing its job.

Why had she agreed to do it, she asked herself, as she looked round at the dusty interior. The house faced south-west, with trees to the north and east, and a downhill slope to the south. It was shaded from the sun that morning, and as far as Thea could tell, would not get very much light at any time. The windows were small in the old stone walls, and the interior felt chilly. There was no actual garden with a lawn to sit on or a sun-filled summerhouse. The patio was bare of furniture, containing nothing more than two large plant pots in which grew a bay tree and a fig, neither looking particularly robust.

The kitchen offered basic facilities in the form of a gas cooker, fridge and microwave, as well as electric kettle and toaster. It was almost as ascetic as self-catering holiday cottages used to be, with added dust on many of the surfaces.

She felt unreasonably lonely and abandoned. She had not wanted another commission, as she had tried to explain to her mother. She had been busy being bored, she admitted to herself. Bored and rather depressed, thanks to events over the summer. She was forty-four and single, with no clear idea of her future and a growing suspicion that she was not making the best of her life.

And she had no idea at all what, if anything, she should do about Drew.

Chapter Two

She was forced to go out to Winchcombe high street in order to buy some food for herself and her dog. The path at the rear of the property struck her as somewhat uninviting and vague, so she walked up Vineyard Street and out into the centre of the town, with Hepzie on the lead. She turned right and recognised the rectangular Square, dominated by a bank and a pub called the Plaisterers Arms. There was no immediate sign of a food shop, and she braced herself for the discovery that she would have to drive out to a supermarket somewhere to get bread and milk and cheese. There was, however, a butcher, which seemed to be a good start.

With sausages and bacon in her bag, she continued her exploration. Passing a small museum, she turned left into another street of shops, and paused to admire some of the window displays. As in many small Cotswold towns, there were clothes, expensive furniture, jewellery and antiques – lots and *lots* of antiques – to be found, and after a couple of minutes, a well-stocked Co-op which fulfilled all her basic needs and much more besides. She gave the town a mental gold star and began the return walk in a much improved frame of mind. The buildings were old and solid and lovely, with an assured sense of permanence that she found consoling. The settlement had existed for a thousand years and more, with occasional violence and trauma making its mark on history, but in essence a calmly prosperous spot, confident of its place in the scheme of things. Larger than Blockley or Chipping Campden, Winchcombe still hardly qualified as a full-sized town. Shreds of historical facts about the abbey and St Kenelm surfaced, thanks to a previous house-sit in nearby Temple Guiting, and a deepening fascination with the past. This had once been a very important place, she remembered, ten centuries ago. The abbey had been destroyed and its stone used to build Sudeley Castle and parts of the imposing St Michael's Church. The inn had been host to countless pilgrims, and probably millions of Cotswold sheep had passed through the main street, from the Middle Ages until the nineteenth century.

These disparate facts came effortlessly to mind, almost as if she could read them in the stones. Ubiquitous helpful plaques added further information, as she strolled the length of the main street. She tied the dog to the iron gate of the church and popped in for a look, spending much of the time in front of a fabulously old embroidered altarpiece that claimed to have been wrought by Catherine of Aragon, no less. A man approached her and started telling her random facts about the building. 'Have you seen the gargoyles?' he asked.

'Um . . . no, I don't think so,' she said vaguely.

'Well, when you leave, go across the street and look up,' he ordered her. 'They're really something.'

And they were. She wondered how she could have failed to notice them before she went in. She wished she had binoculars or a telephoto lens with which to inspect them more closely. Two large ones sprang from the corners of the big church porch, grotesque figures with big faces. She moved a few yards for a better view, and found the right-hand figure to be truly ghastly in its lifelike appearance. It had bulging eyes and bared teeth, with arms that appeared to be straining to push the creature out of the constraining stone and into the freedom of the open air. It had wings and a muscular chest. She stared helplessly at it, glad of her long sight that enabled her to pick out more and more detail. Furrowed brow; a suggestion of dog-like ears; a great misshapen nose. How terrifying it must have seemed, down the centuries, to anybody pausing long enough for a really good look. It would haunt the nightmares of children, and savage the conscience of a sinner. But she found herself almost liking the beast, and wishing it could succeed in releasing itself from the centuries of entrapment in the high stone wall of the church porch. It would flap cumbersomely around her head, miraculously using the small wings to keep its heavy stone body aloft . . .

Stop it! she ordered herself silently. *This is ridiculous*. But the gargoyle had already endeared her to Winchcombe, by adding something magical and medieval to the atmosphere.

For good measure, she gave the second gargoyle a look

as well. This was more human, with a beard and a resigned expression. Deep-sunken eyes suggested sorrow, or perhaps a cosmic knowledge of the great weight of misery that was everybody's due. 'Thanks very much,' Thea muttered to it and began to walk towards the town centre. The long wall of the church was adorned with more hideous faces, higher up and harder to see. One had his tongue out, and another wore a hat. Probably modelled on real people, Thea concluded.

The weather remained benign, and it was good to be in the open air. Idly, she turned back towards the Meadows house, and after dropping the bags in the hall, went out again and kept on going, heading for the large gateway into Sudeley Park. She could see dogs and children ahead, and the sense of being part of a typical English weekend was irresistible.

The way was bordered with trees, some of them immensely ancient and toweringly high. Beech, chestnut, and one or two exotic specimens she was unable to name. The sense of permanency was familiar to her. She and her former boyfriend, Phil Hollis, had noted the same feeling in Temple Guiting, something over a year before. However much the traffic might increase and people come to rely on electronic gadgetry, these trees and the houses they protected felt as if they would last for ever. The park was freely available to any who wished to feel grass beneath their feet and let their dogs run loose. Whilst a small cynical voice might suggest that all these common people were only here on sufferance, provided they behaved themselves, that was not the overall impression.

Here and there a gate might be locked or a 'Private' sign forbid entrance, but the space was ample enough to be experienced as expansively generous.

Thea let the spaniel off the lead, and watched as she zigzagged off the path and onto the grass between the trees. An exuberant young dog on a lead held by a young woman approached, and duly abased itself before the matronly older dog. It was yellow and soft and, impossibly endearing, it squirmed and yapped in the hope of persuading Hepzibah to play. 'What a sweet little thing!' Thea exclaimed. 'A golden retriever, right?'

The woman smiled, and said, 'Right. She's five months old.' Thea dimly perceived a person in her early thirties, wearing a long cotton cardigan and leggings. The cardigan was a light tan colour and looked expensive. There was a halo of very fair hair above an unremarkable face. The dog was considerably more interesting and appealing than its owner.

'She's adorable,' laughed Thea, bending to fondle the grinning creature. The hair was impossibly soft, the body warm and energetic. Hepzie showed a coolly polite interest, plainly perplexed as to what the attraction might be.

Thea's spirits had been raised by the encounter, her hand still warm from the puppy's coat. The sheer delight in life that puppies displayed always melted her heart. How wonderful the world would be if people could acquire the same approach. She smiled to herself at the absurdity of the notion. After all, even dogs had their share of pain and misery, fear and neurosis.

She thought back over the year since her father had died,

during which she had undertaken several house-sitting jobs, four of them involving deeply unpleasant behaviour on the part of various people. There had been very little cause for celebration during that time. The loss of her father in itself had been a great sadness. A decent, affectionate man, he should have enjoyed at least another decade of life. Rapidly following on from his death, there had been a turbulent episode involving her sister Emily, and then, six months or so later, she had met Drew Slocombe.

And Drew Slocombe was a major part of the reason for her restless, bored, depressed, worried condition. They had become friends and partners in confronting three instances of violent death. They had found themselves in harmony, at the same time as knowing they had to maintain a proper distance between them. Because until six or seven weeks ago, Drew had had a wife.

And with Karen's death, more than his family life had fallen apart.

It was no longer possible to phone him, or send emails or texts or even letters. His profound grief had removed him from her completely, much to Thea's own surprise. He had phoned her to give the news, in a deceptively calm voice, and for fifteen seconds it had felt as if it could be overcome without too much difficulty. They had nothing to feel guilty about; they were balanced adults already well along the way towards a mature relationship. Drew was good and kind and funny and conscientious. He had two children and a business based entirely on principle. She approved completely of everything about him, and believed he felt the same towards her. Only after those first heady seconds did she understand that it was an infinitely great distance from being so simple.

It was silly and sad and complicated. She herself had been abruptly bereaved at a point where she had assumed she'd be married to Carl for another forty years. Drew had been amply forewarned – Karen had been ill for years. On the one hand, Thea knew that if another man had shown interest in her, barely two months after Carl died, she would not even have recognised him as human, in the midst of her stunned and anguished grief. On the other hand, she and Drew had already laid the foundations before Karen died. They had been funny together, and devious in their strategies for exposing miscreants. She had met his children and shared in some moments of danger and disaster.

And now she could not even phone or text or write to him, because all she could truthfully say was that she urgently wanted to be there for him. And she could not say that because Maggs and Stephanie and his mother-in-law and the entire female population of North Staverton were all in total agreement that this could not be allowed. He did not need Thea, they said – a rapacious and irresponsible house-sitter who consistently managed to find herself embroiled in murky murder and mayhem. No, they agreed, Drew was much, *much* better off without her.

So she phoned her mother instead.

'Maureen Johnstone,' came the reply, impressively brisk and businesslike.

'Hello again, Mum. It's me. I'm in Winchcombe. Thanks to you.'

'Oh, Thea . . . yes. Good. Is it nice?'

'It's sunny, at least. Listen – have you ever actually *met* Oliver Meadows?'

'No, I told you. It's his brother who I knew. Fraser. I thought I explained.'

'I suppose you did – sort of. But it all seems rather odd. Were you at school with the brother or something?'

'No, no. I knew him in London, in the early sixties. He lived in Notting Hill Gate and I had a bedsit in Bayswater. He took me to Crufts.'

'Crufts. Isn't that in Birmingham?'

'It is now. It used to be at Olympia. I only went that one time. I remember the poor dogs were all terribly hot.'

'And somehow he's found you again, after all this time. Did you say it was Facebook? I didn't know you were on there.'

'Well, I am. It's great fun. I use it to keep track of Emily's boys, mainly. You'd be amazed the things they say. I feel I know all their sins.'

'What a modern granny! The whole thing makes me feel weak.'

'You're old before your time. I always said that. You were a dreadfully sensible child.'

'And I never made a fuss about food; yes, I know, Mum. There are some people now who might tell you that's all changed. I don't think I was very sensible in Lower Slaughter last year, for a start.'

Her mother groaned. 'Don't talk about that awful time. You did your best. If only Emily . . .'

'Okay.' Thea headed her off. The topic of Emily and the events in Lower Slaughter was a taboo area within the family. After a year, it was still too raw for casual mention. 'Oliver Meadows said you might be here with me for some of the time. Is that right? Where did he get that idea?'

'I'm sure I told you. Fraser suggested it. He says the house is big enough for us all for a few days, and he'd like to explore the area. That'd be all right, wouldn't it?'

'There are only three bedrooms. One's Oliver's and I'm in another.' The appalling notion of her mother and the rediscovered boyfriend sharing a bed in the third room rendered her dumb for a few moments. The woman was in her seventies, for heaven's sake. She had sagging wrinkled skin and mottled legs. Such thoughts were probably proscribed by the demands of anti-ageism, but they were insistent, for all that.

'Whatever are you thinking?' her mother demanded, with a scandalised laugh. 'Fraser can use his brother's room, of course.'

'Are they Scottish?' Thea asked, registering the name for the first time.

'What? No, I don't think so. His accent is perfectly English. They grew up in the East End. He went to the LSE and did that PPE thing they were all doing then. Although, actually, he was a bit ahead of the crowd. Wasn't it 1968 when all that was so fashionable?'

'I don't know, Mum.' She was struggling to keep up.

LSE was the London School of Economics, but she was still puzzling over PPE. 'What's PPE?'

'Politics, philosophy and economics. I always thought it sounded terribly *dry*, but he seemed to think it was something to be proud of. He'd only just graduated when I met him.'

'Did he have a job?'

'Not that I can recall. He seemed to be around in the daytime a lot. I think he might have worked in a cinema – that little one in Hampstead, maybe. I can't remember the name, but it was where they all went. It showed unusual foreign films.'

'It all sounds like the Dark Ages to me.'

'Yes . . . it does to me sometimes, as well. He seems to remember it all far better than I do. Strange as it might sound, it looks as if I made a lot more of an impression on him than he did on me. He says I was his first love and he's never forgotten me.'

'But you've forgotten him?'

'I remember *some* things. He was very young and innocent. I was a bit older than him. But he did know London and showed me around. I know we did a Jack the Ripper tour, looking at all the places where the murders happened. I don't think I've ever been to the East End since then.'

'I hope you didn't break his heart.'

'So do I, but I have a nasty feeling I did. And it feels much worse that I can't really remember him. I mean – he must be so *hurt*. Although obviously I try not to let it be too obvious.'

'Did you keep a diary? Wouldn't that jog your memory?'

'I did, actually. But it just says things like "Fraser phoned again" and "Fraser here in eve" which doesn't help much. I get the impression he was rather clingy and I had to be cruel to get rid of him. I met your father all at that same time, and wanted to be available for him. I get odd flashes of memory, but nowhere near a coherent picture.'

Thea wanted to ask *Did you sleep with him?* but couldn't. Who in the world could ask their mother such a question? The answers that might come spilling out were too awful to contemplate. What if Damien, born ten months after her parents' wedding, was somehow the offspring of this Fraser, for example? The contiguity sounded uncomfortably close. What if her mother had conferred one final sexual favour on the wretched rejected boy, a few weeks into her marriage? It struck Thea as all too dreadfully possible, as she rummaged for impressions of the promiscuous nineteen sixties. Didn't they all sleep with everybody in those distant days?

'And what does he want from you now? Some sort of atonement? Does he seem *angry* with you?'

'Reproachful, a bit. It's hard to explain, but I think there's a natural human wish to relive the past. It gets stronger as you get older. It's some kind of unfinished business for him and he thinks it should be for me as well. He wants to talk about his family and what happened after I stopped seeing him. There was another brother, quite a bit older, who took on the family business from their father. He's been talking about that a lot lately.'

'What was it? The business, I mean?'

34

Her mother laughed again. 'You won't believe it when I tell you. And I had no idea at the time. I'm convinced he never said a word about it.'

'Come on, Mum. What was it?'

'Undertakers. The Meadows family are undertakers.'

Chapter Three

But Drew's an undertaker, she wanted to shout, as if this was a huge and unacceptable coincidence. Other people couldn't be undertakers; that wasn't fair. What if her mother had married Fraser, and he had gone into the family business instead of escaping to Australia? Maureen Johnstone would have been Maureen Meadows and her children would have grown up amongst coffins and pallbearers. The randomness of life, with its insistent alternative realities, was frightening.

But her mother did not know about Drew. Thea had never once mentioned his existence to her, although her daughter Jessica had met him. Jess would not have gossiped to her grandmother about him, she felt sure. She would not have known what to say, picking up on the ambivalence that Thea herself felt. For the first time, Thea understood that Jessica's reaction to her love life was very much the same as Thea was now experiencing about her own mother. The generations repeated the pattern without even realising it. Their fathers were dead in both cases, and the painful resentful loyalty that a daughter inevitably maintained ensured that there could never be a fully acceptable replacement. Of such rigidity small tragedies were made, as well as large sacrifices. Because Drew's young Stephanie and Timmy would be prone to exactly the same jealous adherence to the memory of their mother. The dead cast deep shadows, and there was no avoiding them.

'So when do you think you might come?' she asked.

'We thought tomorrow. Late morning, probably. We can go out for lunch.'

'Provided we don't have to have a Sunday roast,' Thea warned. She had eaten too many tasteless thin slices of unidentifiable meat covered in glutinous gravy to willingly risk it again. 'I've yet to find a pub that makes a decent job of it.'

'You never used to be so fussy. I blame Carl,' said her mother lightly. It was true – Thea's husband had been exacting in his gourmet standards. The meat had to be locally reared and killed, and the gravy made from its juices, with not a grain of Bisto. And he preferred it in chunks, not slices.

'It's not fussy,' she objected. 'It's wanting them to serve something worth eating.'

'We can have a salad in a garden somewhere, preferably by a river. I'm sure you can come up with the ideal spot.'

'I'm sure I can,' said Thea confidently. Then she had a thought. 'But surely Fraser knows Winchcombe? He must visit his brother sometimes.'

'He's only been twice. Oliver is very reclusive, you see. He doesn't encourage visitors.'

'But he does know how to get here?'

'Oh, yes. There'll be no difficulty with that. He's brilliant at that sort of thing.'

She came to the conclusion that she was more pleased than otherwise that her mother would be joining her, as the afternoon slowly waned. It was only three o'clock, and there were two hours at least before she needed to go and check Oliver's birds. She picked up the notes he had left, and saw the lines: 'Cleeve Common is worth a visit, for the views. Drive to Postlip Hall (left turn off the Cheltenham Road that runs past the church and out of town), park just off the road and walk up the track.'

The light outside was likely to be ideal for views, she judged. A thin layer of cloud would ensure there were no stark shadows, but a clear uniform visibility was almost guaranteed.

'Come on, then,' she told the spaniel. 'Let's start as we mean to go on. It might be raining for the rest of our time here.'

She turned left at the top of Vineyard Street and passed the church. The street was lined on both sides with an extraordinary collection of houses. No two were the same, as far as she could tell. She couldn't recall another place, whether in the Cotswolds or anywhere else, that offered such a dazzling variety of styles, materials and sizes. It must be an architectural historian's dream.

There was a left turn within a mile or so, and she glimpsed a sign including the words 'Postlip Mills' and she turned down it, assuming it was where Oliver meant. But there was nowhere to park, and it looked incongruously industrial. Notices directed deliveries and other official business matters, and the road dived rapidly downhill. 'This isn't right,' she told Hepzie. 'It's some kind of factory, I think.'

Nervous of being stopped and interrogated, she hurriedly turned the car and went back to the main road. A second turning quickly came into view, with a sign announcing 'Postlip Hall'.

'Aha!' she breathed, and turned left again.

Immediately she found a fingerpost pointing up a track to 'Cleeve Common'. It was, apparently, half a mile distant. She and the dog could be up and back within forty-five minutes, quite easily.

They set off, the spaniel running free. The way was steep and stony, and Thea found herself considering the possibility that it had once been a significant road, bordered as it was with old stone walls. Somewhere there was a hall, invisible behind the trees on her right. Overhead, the branches met to form a green tunnel, and the path snaked enticingly upwards, renewing the sense of incipient magic that had begun with the gargoyle.

The half mile took ten minutes and left her breathless. A gate marked the sudden emergence onto the common. Hepzie had wriggled through its bars before Thea managed to open it. Ahead was an expanse of scrubby grass, and an abrupt hill boasting a scattering of vegetation that might have been gorse. There was a sign, headed 'Cleeve Hill Common', so badly stained with mildew that she could barely read the depressing list of regulations it contained.

She walked on, turning back every few yards in the hope of a good view of Winchcombe without having to go all the way to the top of the hill in front of her. There were trees in the way at first, but finally she got what she wanted, with the solid square-towered church clearly to be seen.

The town, evidently, was on reasonably level ground, with a considerable escarpment behind it, which after some difficulty she concluded had to be to the east, despite the fact that Winchcombe lay on the very western edge of the Cotswolds. It was not in a bowl, like Blockley or Cranham; instead it had been arranged in the valley caused by the river that she had already realised must have been important, from the number of times the word 'mill' appeared on street names.

The church stood protectively above the jumbled houses, like a shepherd with his sheep, she fancied. The colours were muted greens and greys, and from such a distance it was easy to perceive houses and trees as much the same in terms of their harmonious place in the picture. The town was inconspicuous, unassuming. It made no brash claims, and in the overcast light there were no unnatural flashes of sunshine on glass or metal.

It gave her an overview that she was pleased to have. However important Winchcombe might have been in the past, it was now a tucked-away little town, with no major roads passing through, no claims to power. It was clean and tidy and timeless, and it sold antiques. The woods were full of birds, and the houses were all quite effortlessly individual.

'We like Winchcombe,' she told the dog, which had come to her side after nosing idly in some clumps of long grass.

Later, she took the dog to the bird hide and sat watching a selection of finches picking delicately at the sunflower hearts on their feeding station. She could recognise chaffinches, both male and female, quite easily, and waited in the hope of seeing the colourful goldfinch again. Instead there were a dozen or more blue tits, and something that could only be a greenfinch. A slender little brown bird flitted amongst the branches that was neither a wren nor a sparrow, and brought Thea to an agony of self-reproach at her ignorance. The birds were certainly very entertaining, as they followed a complex dance from tree to table and back again, the little tits so quick and acrobatic amongst the bigger species. According to Oliver's poster there should also be bullfinches and siskins, and possibly even hawfinches and redpolls. She began to grasp how exciting it could be to lure the rarer species into your garden, with the right kind of food and a careful lack of disturbance. She noticed that there were at least three distinct sorts of tits, where she had initially bundled them all under the single heading of blue tit. Hepzie lay peacefully on the rough earth floor, as her mistress indulged her new interest.

It would be even better, she guessed, in the early morning. Birds were at their most lively at dawn – weren't they? There had to be a great many more species out there in the trees; some preferring fat and others seeking seeds. Where were the robins and wrens; thrushes and sparrows? As she mentally listed all the birds she could recall, there was a flurry at the seed table and a flash of red. When she looked properly, there was a sharp-beaked visitor with a comical red skullcap. Anybody could see it was a woodpecker, but Thea was sure she had never seen one so close up before.

It was plainly very nervous, darting rapid glances at the busy blue tits, as well as swivelling to check its back. It was almost too frightened to snatch a sunflower heart, but it remained long enough for a comprehensive inspection. Its front was a soft-looking beige, with a splash of red near the tail. The red was more suited to something much more exotic – like a parrot. Far from the more muted orangey-red of the robin, it was pure scarlet and thus surprisingly exciting. Even without the red, its black and white back was dramatic. 'Ah,' she breathed happily. 'What a beauty!'

As well as the finch poster, Oliver had left a large colourful *Birds of Britain* book on the table in the hide. When the woodpecker had gone, she looked it up, and readily identified the 'greater spotted' variety. The thrill persisted for many minutes; the glimpse of the wild creature had been an unearned privilege that made her feel honoured and awakened to a world she so often forgot. Then she flipped through a section depicting small brown birds, and concluded the answer to that mystery was a willow warbler. She wasn't at all sure she had ever heard of a willow warbler before, and certainly had had no idea what it looked like.

And she should not forget this world of British wildlife, because Carl, her husband, had been an environmentalist, fully aware of the birds of Britain, as well as the badgers and foxes and otters. She had walked with him and seen larks and swallows galore in the open fields, and coots and cormorants in the Essex marshes where they had holidayed. But they had not spent time crouched in a woodland hide watching these little things in such numbers and taking time to admire the soft breast feathers of a woodpecker.

'Well, old girl,' she told her dog, 'I think we might be due for a rather enjoyable stay at this rate.'

Hepzie wagged a slow plumy tail, and Thea felt something that had been in abeyance for very much too long. She could not recall a sense of anticipation in the whole of the previous year, other than for the most fleeting moments. She had enjoyed the big house in Cranham for a day or two, she reminded herself, and the lovely old buildings of Snowshill had raised her spirits, but she had lost her sense of wonder at the natural world, which had been there twenty years ago. Although, of course, she had permitted herself to anticipate each new encounter with Drew Slocombe. The sight of his boyish features and engagement with his witty banter had been the main pleasures in her life since the previous March. A mere six months since she first met him and all she had to show for it was a depressed foreboding that nothing happy would ever come of it.

And now she could rediscover her natural lightness of heart by watching wild birds. It was like tapping into a vein of gold she had forgotten existed; a beam of sunlight to remind her that it was in fact a wonderful world.

It was a shame, then, that her mother was due to arrive the next day, with her mysterious new man. No way would Thea bring them to the hide and share its secrets. She would come down early to fill the feeders and check the camera, and then spend the day being sociable and hospitable, and take them to Winchcombe Church and perhaps Sudeley Castle. No mention had been made of the proposed duration of the stay, but she hoped it would not be more than two or three days. The idea that they might intend to stay for the whole fortnight gave her a nasty jolt. Surely there was no danger of that. Her mother had a short attention span; she would soon get bored, especially if the weather took a downward turn. And the man, this Fraser Meadows – did he not have a life of his own? From what she had heard of him so far, she rather suspected that he had little to distract him other than his long-ago girlfriend, who could barely remember him.

She went back to the house, approaching it from the north-east, so that the whole wall was in deep shadow in the late afternoon. The door, which she had mentally labelled the back door, had a modest porch over it, and opened into a passageway that led through the middle of the house to another door, which she thought of as the front. But the house did not have an obvious facade with which to greet the world. It was much the same both sides, with a door and four windows like a child's drawing. It sat awkwardly on the uneven ground, and the question of an approach drive and somewhere to leave the car had never been properly resolved. Oliver clearly cared little for such details, and had done nothing to address them. It gave a sense of a fairy-tale cottage in the woods, sheltered by large trees and difficult to find.

The large trees, however, cut out the sunlight and reduced the air temperature. Where this might have been desirable in a tropical climate, it was not such a good idea in England, with sunshine always at a premium.

She found the makings of a late-afternoon tea and sat in the dwindling patch of brightness on the bleak little patio, thinking about her mother. On reflection, it seemed obvious that there could be no plan to stay at Thistledown for the whole fortnight. Why, in that case, should Oliver go to the expense of employing a house-sitter? He had mentioned a conversation with his brother, in which an agreement had been made that there would be a visit – but clearly it was only to be brief. From long habit, Thea found herself analysing her own feelings on the subject, only to discover that she already felt proprietorial over the property and its birds. She did not want trampling feet and loud voices to frighten away that lovely woodpecker. She would risk boredom, and even another dive into depression, rather than take responsibility for amusing her mother. Over her various house-sitting commissions she had been joined by sisters, daughter and boyfriend, not always very happily. When she embarked on this way of life, she had envisaged peaceful interludes with her dog, perhaps making new friends in the different villages, but not sharing the places with relatives. Yet somehow an expectation had arisen that she would welcome them; an expectation that clearly persisted.

The awkwardness of the approaches to Thistledown, whether from front or rear, made it difficult for anyone to arrive without warning. And yet neither Thea nor her spaniel detected any advance sounds of footsteps before the visitor appeared. Hepzie looked up as the shadow fell across her, and emitted a low snarl that startled Thea.

'Gosh! How did you get here?' she said, squinting up at the figure standing between her and the sun. The dog's animosity raised no great alarm in her breast – Hepzie had never been a very reliable judge of character.

'I just walked up from Vineyard Street. I knew there'd be nowhere to park down here. You must be the house-sitter.'

'Yes, I am. And you are . . . ?'

'Melissa. Oliver's niece. I think my father is going out with your mother.'

Chapter Four

Put like that, it almost made them sisters, Thea supposed, with an instinctive recoil. She had enough sisters already, and she was already thinking unworthy female thoughts as she inspected this slender, tanned creature who could apparently tread so lightly as to make no sound.

'Oh,' she said. 'Is it you he's staying with?'

'What? Oh . . . no, that's Mo. She's my half-sister. She's twenty years older than me.' She spoke with a strange sort of emphasis, an iambic line that felt rehearsed but seldom spoken. A little laugh added to the artificiality. Thea was faintly alerted to uncomfortable family business.

'So . . . ?' she invited. 'What brings you here?'

'Don't worry, I won't disturb you. The thing is, Uncle Olly's been keeping some of my stuff for me, in the back room, and I came to collect one or two things. I'll be in and out before you know it. What a dear little dog,' she added, with such insincerity, Thea wondered that Hepzie didn't snarl again.

She felt decidedly wrong-footed. Should she ask for proof

of identity? Was she meant to defend the entire house contents against such an obvious scam? After all, anybody could show up like this, with just such a cover story, and make off with all the best silver. The impression that the opening lines had been prepared in advance gave rise to a wariness that bordered on the fringes of suspicion. The reference to the older sister, which had probably been intended to sound convincing, had instead alerted her to something not quite right. Suddenly the name *Mo* re-echoed.

'Mo?' she said. 'Short for Maureen?'

'I guess so. We don't call her that, though. It's terribly old-fashioned.'

'My mother's called Maureen.'

'Yes. Apparently it's no coincidence. Uncle Ollie thinks it's rather sweet.'

'Fraser named his daughter after a girl he'd gone out with for a couple of months? Blimey!' This new light on her mother was surprisingly unsettling. 'What did Mo's mother think about it?'

'Your guess is as good as mine. If he had any sense, he wouldn't have told her his reason for liking the name. He probably said it was some old film star or something.' The young woman was speaking easily, while looking past Thea at something in the shadowy passageway inside the front door.

'Well, I'd better come with you while you collect your things.' At some point, Thea found, she had decided to trust the newcomer enough to let her into the house.

'No need,' breezed Melissa, heading for the door. 'I know my way.'

'Yes, but . . .' Thea got up from the garden seat. 'I think I should. I mean, I only have your word for it.'

The awkwardness was in no way alleviated by the unsmiling stare the young woman gave her. 'Only have my word for *what*? Don't you believe me? That's appallingly *rude* of you.'

Thea felt weak and cross. 'I dare say it is, but try to see it from my standpoint. I'm being paid to stand guard over this house and its contents. That's the whole *point* of a house-sitter. You can understand that, surely?' She seemed to be repeating that word *stand* ridiculously often, which only made her more cross.

The newcomer shrugged. 'It never crossed my mind there might be any difficulty. I just need a few clothes and a memory stick. Come with me, if you must. I've got nothing to hide. I just don't like being suspected of something underhand, as if I was a criminal.'

Melissa marched ahead into the house, and through to a small dark room at the back corner. It had one narrow window, half obscured by a bush. Stacked tidily in one corner were three large cardboard boxes, with MELISSA written in marker pen and parcel tape sealing them closed. Thea had to admit that if this was a heist, it was singularly well planned. The young woman went straight to the middle box, pulling it open carefully and rummaging inside it. She drew out two long-sleeved tops and a pair of jeans. Then she taped it up again, making use of any residual stickiness in the tape. 'The memory stick's in the bottom one,' she said. 'Can you help me?' Together they lifted the top two boxes out of the way, and Melissa repeated the process.

A plastic box that had once held ice cream contained a neat arrangement of electronic gadgets, including a digital camera and something Thea could not identify. The memory stick was plucked from its nest in the corner, and everything replaced as before.

'You seem to know where everything is,' Thea said, in a grudging attempt at an apology.

'I've been living out of these boxes for three years now. It gets to be pretty routine. I'll have to come back again next month for some warmer clothes.'

'Are you homeless, then?' Thea looked at her: aged about thirty, expensive haircut, clean clothes, apparent good health. 'Surely not?'

'In a way, I am. Actually, it's my job. I travel a lot, and stay mainly in hotels. I just carry whatever I can get in the car – laptop, clothes, phone. I imagine you must be quite good at packing up and moving on yourself, doing this house-sitting stuff?'

'Yes, but I've got my own house as well.'

'I've got a little place in Oxford that costs me a small fortune. I sublet it when I'm away, unofficially. Anyway, Uncle Olly's more than happy to keep this stuff for me. It's not much to ask, after all.'

'It's not my business,' said Thea stiffly. 'Can I get you a cup of tea or something?'

'No, thanks. I've got someone waiting for me at the pub. We'll have a meal there and then head off up the motorway. I'm supposed to be in Stoke tonight. I just had to fetch this . . .' she held up the little torpedo-shaped data storage device '. . . it's got some files on it I'll need tomorrow.'

50

'They're clever little things, aren't they?' said Thea vaguely. Despite being in possession of a BlackBerry and a laptop, she felt herself lagging considerably in the frantic developments in digital technology.

As she had half expected, Melissa gave a scoffing laugh, a single high bray that sounded more like a donkey than a person. 'They're pretty antiquated now, actually. It's going to be much easier to just upload everything to the Cloud and access it from absolutely anywhere. Nothing can get lost that way, and no need for all these physical gadgets.'

'Right,' said Thea, even more vaguely than before.

'Bye, then,' breezed the visitor, with scarcely a backward look. Thea watched the jaunty walk, the carefree bounce of someone who trod lightly across the world. By rights, she should approve of such a lifestyle: carrying no baggage, confident that possessions were unnecessary for a fully productive existence. Instead, she felt defensive about her own choices. Somehow she had come second in an unspoken competition; had been in the wrong from the first moments. She had not much liked young Melissa, who had 'someone waiting for her at the pub' and was therefore also ahead in the unavoidable race to find and keep a man, which every woman was expected to enter. Thea had no illusions about her own position where this subject was concerned. She wanted to be half of a couple. She had liked being married to Carl, and would never forgive the cruel fate that had disrupted her assumptions so completely. She wished quite painfully that there was someone waiting for *her* at the pub as well.

It really was close to twilight now. She was confined

to the house for the coming night, whether she liked it or not. The usual strategies for passing an evening would be brought into play, after she had cooked the sausages from the Winchcombe butcher and the small quantity of potatoes she had found in Oliver's vegetable rack. She had located the television, which would pass the hours if all else failed. She could play games on her laptop or listen to the radio. She could read a book or search for websites of local attractions. It was the same set of options that probably millions of single women across the land were considering, as the daylight faded. Or if not millions, then a lot. Those who had not managed to get together with another person for a trip to the pub or the cinema or a nightclub on a busy street. Those whose husbands had died or departed or disappeared into a garden shed or back bedroom. And those who had never possessed a husband in the first place. A silent community of solitary women, all wishing passionately that there was something more engaging on the TV than the nine hundredth episode of *Casualty*.

She got through it readily enough. At ten, she took the dog out of the back door for a final pee, noting that the moon was very nearly full. Something about September moons stirred in her memory – this one was orange-tinted, and not especially friendly. It rose above Oliver's trees like a reminder that the world was full of small and irrelevant concerns. Hepzie threw a bizarre long-legged shadow over the patio as she sniffed idly at something on the flagstones. Everything was unnaturally quiet: no traffic or music or human voices could be heard. She might be fifty miles from the next habitation, instead of fifty yards. There was a house to the north-west, no further away than that, and a whole double row of them not far beyond. Winchcombe itself was within shouting distance. But in this polite little place, nobody shouted very much, even on a Saturday night.

At ten-thirty she went upstairs, with the dog at her heels, and arranged a comfortable night for the two of them. She closed the curtains and turned off all the lights. Outside an owl was hooting, somewhere in Oliver's wooded acres. She consciously counted her blessings, noting that no part of her body was hurting; she had enough money for her needs; and none of her relatives was suffering unduly. (Except Emily, she reminded herself, and even Emily was very much over the worst, a year on from the Incident.)

Sunday morning dawned fair but breezy. The bedroom looked broadly eastwards, over the wooded acres where Oliver fed the birds, and past that to a hill behind Sudeley Castle. She could hear the treetops swishing, like waves on the seashore, but less rhythmic. There was nothing soothing about wind, no hypnotic predictability, as there was with waves. Wind could blow the roof off, or send the chimney crashing down on top of you. All her life, Thea had very much disliked strong winds.

Her mother was coming. And a man who was brother to the owner of this house. There was some peculiar illogical element to this that continued to evade her. It was hard to see exactly what her own role was in the picture – perhaps that was it. She had to feed the birds. She had to provide seeds and fat for creatures who, in September, could perfectly easily obtain their own food. There were berries everywhere, as well as nuts and seed heads. All she was doing was to lure them into staying close by, so that Oliver could photograph them.

Which reminded her of the video camera. She was supposed to set it going early each morning, when the birds were at their most active and interesting. It would run for ten hours or so before closing itself down. She had to replace the little card and keep the early one safe, with the date on it. A simple task, but one that nobody else was going to do.

'Come on, Heps. Rise and shine,' she said.

It was early – just after seven-thirty. The sun was up, but not yet warm. The slight bite in the morning air was a stark reminder that winter was not far off. September was inescapably evocative to any country-dwelling Northern European, with the atavistic urgency that came with it. Firewood had to be collected, fruit preserved, hay stocks carefully protected. The very gentleness of winter's approach could seduce an unwary population into postponing these essential preparations. There would be warm, sunny days for weeks yet, fostering the illusion that winter might be short and mild this year. And then you could get six inches of snow at the end of October and find yourself in all kinds of trouble.

Except that this was the twenty-first century, when mankind had dominated the elements, and simply pumped in more oil for heat and light, to repel the natural forces of darkness.

There was a pleasing paganism to these thoughts, which recalled Thea to the week or so that she and Phil had spent in Cold Aston, making the acquaintance of Ariadne Fletcher, a real and proper pagan. Almost two years earlier, she realised, with a start. Two years in which the passing of the seasons had pressed in upon her in a number of ways. She had been imprisoned by snow, deceived by rain, and disappointed by a reluctant sun. In a country habitually obsessed by weather, the subject had been greatly augmented by large arguments about climate. At least it was never boring, she thought now, with a smile.

Once outside, the wind seemed much less intrusive. Beneath the trees, it was almost calm, all the activity focused on the top few inches of the branches. The leaves on the birches had just begun to turn yellow, but they were not yet dead enough to fall off in the breeze. The overall hue remained a determined green, on all sides, the leaves hanging on for several more weeks, all being well.

She trod the narrow path as softly as she could, hoping to see the woodpecker again, and aware of his extreme nervousness. The dog danced lightly along, a few paces in front, doing nothing that might scare birds away, other than merely existing. They came into the clearing with the many contraptions for holding food, and the well-camouflaged hide, and Hepzie gave a yap.

'Shut up,' Thea hissed at her. 'You'll scare them all away.'

But then she saw the cause of the dog's alarm, and

felt like yapping, or shouting or calling upon divine assistance herself.

Because there was a dead person lying face up on the rough grass between the hide and the feeding stations, as if in a green chamber created by the protecting trees overhead.

Chapter Five

There was an appalling tidiness to the corpse that Thea found almost unbearable. The hands were folded across the chest, the hair immaculately neat, the expression peaceful. The only jarring note was the three items of clothing that had been collected from the box in Oliver's house. They were lying carelessly tossed aside, a few feet away. 'It's that girl!' Thea said aloud. 'What on earth has happened to her?' She nudged an unmoving arm delicately with her foot, in needless confirmation that life really was extinct.

Nobody replied. All the birds had disappeared, apart from one crow, sitting in clear view on the stump of a tree that must have been cut down to make way for the hide. It eyed Thea and the body with calculating interest, its thick black beak slowly tilting from side to side as it moved its head for a better view.

'Go away,' said Thea loudly.

The bird showed signs of asking itself just what it might have to fear from this human being and her dog. At her feet was some very tempting carrion, enough for every friend and relation for miles around. Perhaps, if it waited a while, the upright being would leave the way clear for the early pickings in the form of juicy eyeballs and soft fleshy tongue.

Robotically, Thea grabbed her dog's collar and began to hurry back to the house, hoping the crow would hesitate before beginning its predations. The body had looked cold and stiff, the lips blue-grey and the visible skin drained of blood.

She called the police, and agreed to wait by the roadside to lead the way to the clearing. They knew where Vineyard Street was, and promised to be there quickly. Shutting the dog inside, Thea ran back down the woodland path with a rug she had grabbed from Oliver Meadows' sofa, and threw it over the vulnerable corpse.

Only as she stood impatiently at the end of the little drive did she remember her expected visitors. What was her mother going to say? And – belatedly – it dawned on her that the victim was the daughter of Fraser Meadows, who was also shortly to arrive on the spot. The man would see his dead child, would perhaps wail and sob on her mother's insubstantial shoulder. From past experience, she knew it was perfectly possible for the dead Melissa to lie undisturbed for the best part of the day while the police examined the scene in every imaginable detail. A tent would be erected over her, and TV reporters would probably turn up and film it. The magnitude of the disaster expanded as she gradually overcame the initial shock and considered the implications.

The birds! There would be forensics people and photographers and a police doctor all crowded into the little space and probably wrecking Oliver's careful arrangements. They would go into the hide and examine its contents.

The camera! Excitedly, she realised that there was a chance that the truth of what had happened to Melissa might be recorded on the little digital card. But it could wait until the police arrived. She would calmly show it to them, and invite them to take the card as a prize piece of evidence.

Despite some acquaintance with the local police, she had never met either of the individuals who first responded to her call. They were uniformed officers, a sergeant and a constable, and she felt uncomfortably old in comparison with them both. 'I assure you she's dead,' she said. 'Is there a doctor on his way?'

The sergeant smiled tightly, and made an excessively polite reply to the effect that all due procedures were in train, thank you, madam. If she could just indicate the exact location of the person concerned, they would quickly have everything in hand. She contemplated her choices: she could tell him in plain English that she had done this before, and knew exactly what the procedure was, or she could flutter her eyelashes gratefully and let him get on with it. There were temptations to both options.

'I know who she is,' she said, neutrally. 'And I can tell you that her father is expected here later today.'

'Thank you, madam. That's very helpful. Now, this way, am I right?'

'Not quite, no. She's down that little path, about a hundred yards or so. You won't miss her. I covered her up with a rug. There was a crow . . .'

He made a peculiar sucking noise through his teeth. 'Shouldn't touch anything, you know.'

'I didn't. I just dropped it over her.' Too late, she realised there would now be contaminating fibres, hairs, skin cells on the body that ought not to be there. 'Sorry,' she mumbled. 'I suppose it was rather silly of me.'

The constable spoke for the first time, giving her a supportive little smile. 'You weren't to know,' he said.

Oh, but I was, she wanted to argue, but instead gave him the grateful flutter she had been debating. There was always the faint possibility that they would never find out who she – Thea Osborne – was. There was always the chance that Melissa had died of natural causes, or that someone was at that moment in Cheltenham police station confessing to having killed her. There might not be any sort of investigation at all.

It might have been her lack of hysteria that gave her away; that suggested even to these tunnel-visioned policemen that something was not as usual. A single woman in a strange house – that much they had somehow ascertained – finding a dead body in the early morning woods, should not be so calmly collected. She caught an exchanged look, a raised eyebrow that was beginning to border on suspicion. Here was something unnatural, some story well beyond the obvious, which they felt themselves unequal to. 'This one's for the detectives, right enough,' she heard the sergeant mutter, before he became welded to his telephone, his expression strained.

The constable shepherded her back to the house, and permitted her to answer the familiar questions before he had a chance to pose them. 'Her name is Melissa, surname presumably Meadows. I saw her last night, at about five-thirty. She was cheerful and said she was meeting someone at the pub. I don't know which pub or who the person was. This house belongs to her uncle, Oliver Meadows, who is away for a fortnight. I'm looking after the property while he's away. His brother is expected here later this morning. He's Melissa's father.'

Clumsily the constable wrote it all down, referring to the G5, which would have to be filled in as soon as the doctor had been. He thanked her, bemusedly, before gathering himself to say, 'You've done this before, haven't you?'

'I'm afraid so,' she smiled wanly. 'It seems to happen to me very much too often.'

'And you don't know these people?'

'I never met any of them until yesterday. But my mother knows the brother – Fraser Meadows. She knew him fifty years ago, in London. They've just rediscovered each other.'

This lad was never going to make detective, she judged. He showed no sign of registering the potential oddness, the underlying possibilities in the story he had been given. He was decently bovine, striving to reassure her that she was safe, seeking to offer her sympathy and family liaison services. She was a witness, and witnesses were one step away from being victims. They would be shocked and anxious, their memories unreliable and their emotions fragile. They were to be treated with kindness, and helped to get their facts straight. Nothing from the textbook was fitting this situation and the boy was floundering.

'My daughter's a probationer police officer,' she told

him, in an effort to convey some sort of explanation. At the same time, she hoped Jessica would show more flexibility, more imagination, if faced with the same circumstances.

'Really? You don't seem old enough,' he said, less from gallantry than genuine surprise. Then he remembered that he was supposed to ask her full name, address and date of birth. 'Actually, I ought to get your details,' he said, opening a new page of his notepad.

'I had her when I was twelve,' joked Thea, before realising this was a big mistake. The dratted youth was perfectly capable of believing her and finding it dubious when she explained. 'No, no, forget I said that,' she amended quickly. 'I was twenty-two. Jessica's that age now, actually.' She trusted him to do the arithmetic.

The arrival of reinforcements stirred things up in a number of ways. Neighbours further along Vineyard Street began to realise something was happening and emerge from their houses for a look. With a glance of confused apology, Thea's solicitous constable returned to the scene to convey her story to any newly arrived detectives. She promised to stay in the house and went to make herself some coffee.

She should phone her mother as a matter of some urgency. It was close to nine o'clock, and she wanted to abort the expected visit. If that caused difficulties for the police, then too bad. The prospect of playing host to the distraught father and unpredictable mother was not to be borne. She tried the landline first, expecting her mother to be gradually waking up over toast and tea. She lived sixty miles from Winchcombe – the journey could not take more than an hour and a half. But there was no reply. Quelling any thoughts of a night spent in Fraser Meadows' bed, or at a romantic B&B somewhere, she tried the mobile.

Her mother had taken well to the new method of communication, on the whole. She liked texting, and would make experimental calls from unusual spots – such as her husband's graveside. But she had a dread of draining the battery and switched the thing off much of the time. 'I like to be in control,' she asserted. 'The idea of it going off when I'm in the middle of something is awful. If something's important, they can leave a message. I check it every day or so.' Thea and her siblings had to accept that there was sound good sense in this attitude.

It was off. With no great optimism, Thea left a brief message – 'Mum, something's happened. Please ring me as soon as you get this.' Her own experience of telephones was that they almost always let you down when you really needed them.

So far, her mother had not regarded widowhood as any sort of liberation. She had not taken herself off on foreign trips or circled the country visiting long-neglected friends. She had remained in the house she had occupied for the past twenty-five years and treated herself gently. There was a sense that she was testing herself, pinning down her own identity as a woman alone, and reviewing her options. She discussed these with her offspring, especially Damien, the eldest and the only son. The sudden acquisition of something alarmingly like a boyfriend was impossible to absorb. It had never once occurred to Thea that this might happen. It made it frighteningly difficult to guess the next steps and act accordingly.

She had to accept the strong possibility that her mother and Fraser would arrive at eleven-thirty or thereabouts, entirely ignorant of the drastic turn of events. She wanted to take her dog and drive away somewhere and let things develop as they might, with no input from her.

But then a slim figure appeared in the doorway, trying to focus on the shadowy interior. 'Is it really you?' came a familiar voice. 'Can this be the Thea Osborne I know and love?'

It was Detective Superintendent Sonia Gladwin, and Thea almost threw herself into her arms.

Chapter Six

Gladwin was businesslike and concerned. 'She's so *young*,' she breathed. 'Poor thing. Now tell me everything you know.'

It turned out to be a very threadbare story, with Thea too stunned to recall details. She repeated what she had told the boy with the G5. 'She's called Melissa, and she keeps a lot of her possessions in a back room here. The owner is her uncle – Oliver Meadows. His brother is Fraser, and he's her father. She comes and gets things regularly. Clothes, mostly. She's got a flat in Oxford. She travels a lot for her work, and was due in Stoke today. Or perhaps it was tomorrow. She took a memory stick out of one of the boxes.'

'Where is Oliver Meadows now?'

'I don't know.'

'Who was the woman meeting in a pub?'

'I don't know.'

'Who's her mother?'

'I don't know.'

The memory stick was nowhere in evidence; Melissa

did not have a mobile phone on her; her car had not been located. Gladwin sighed.

'At least you might have something on the camera,' Thea offered.

'Camera?'

'Oh, I forgot to say. There's a video camera in the hide. It works automatically, filming all day, until the battery runs down.'

'Good God. And what time did it run down last night?'

'I don't know. I'm supposed to replace it every morning. The battery, I mean. And the little card. It might have everything you need on it.'

'Come and show me.'

The little clearing was full of people, as well as the gazebo-style tent erected over the actual body. 'It looks as if she was garotted,' Gladwin confided to Thea. 'At least it was quick. Somebody really meant business.'

Thea was not consoled. She fingered her own neck, reminded of what a very vulnerable area of the body it was. People could all too easily do themselves a fatal damage by carelessly winding a tight ligature around their throat. Suicidal prisoners did it; small children got themselves tangled in string and cord; men seeking extreme sexual thrills went too far; the heart stopped long before suffocation, if pressure was applied to a certain spot. Did the killer know that, or did they assume their victim would slowly strangle?

'She was so *blithe*,' Thea mourned. 'Full of life. It doesn't seem possible.'

'Camera,' Gladwin prompted.

Police people had been into the hide, but had not removed anything. If they saw the camera, nobody had made the obvious deduction. 'They'd have thought it was only activated when the owner was here,' Gladwin supposed. 'It's not the usual CCTV arrangement.'

To Thea's ignorant eye, it seemed very much the same thing, but she refrained from comment. She was worrying about her mother, and Oliver's birds and the whole miserable business of murder.

'I can't get hold of my mother,' she whined. 'She and Fraser will be here in an hour or two if I can't avert them.'

'Why would you try? We'll need him to identify the body, anyway. I could accuse you of interfering in a police investigation, if you're not careful. It seems to me it's all rather convenient the way it's going.'

'You don't know my mother,' Thea gloomed. 'I'm going to have to *deal* with her.'

'Come on. She'll be company for you, a distraction. Once this lot's tidied away, you can get on with it here. At least . . .'

'Precisely. You'll have to find Oliver and probably bring him back. I won't be needed any more.'

'I can't believe you let him go off without leaving any contact details. What sort of a house-sitter does that?'

'I know. It was all such a rush. I never even managed to ask him. His brother probably knows where he is,' she added hopefully. 'This was all his idea, indirectly, I think. My mother thought it would be a neat solution – sort of win-win, with Oliver getting away and me getting some work. I had a sort of feeling that I was their proxy – that if I hadn't agreed to it, they might have come here instead.'

'So why didn't they?'

'Too big a commitment, I guess,' said Thea vaguely. 'A fortnight is quite a long time, after all.' She swung a foot like a bored teenager, wishing herself somewhere quite else. 'I'd better try her phone again, I suppose.'

'Weird that Melissa didn't have a phone on her,' said Gladwin, watching the swinging foot. 'Tell me again where she put that memory stick.'

Thea concentrated her mind. 'She had a little shoulder bag,' she recalled for the first time. 'She put the clothes in a plastic carrier bag, that she pulled out of the shoulder bag, and dropped the stick into the first bag. Is that making sense? There might have been a phone in there as well.'

'Car keys? Money? Where were they?'

'In the shoulder bag, presumably.'

'Which is nowhere to be seen.'

'So she was mugged in a woodland garden, outside a bird hide? They garotted her and stole her bag.'

'Looks like it. I hate to sound melodramatic, but I can't help feeling there was something important on that memory stick. Sorry, Thea, but can we go through the whole conversation you had with her, one more time?'

Under the questioning gaze of another plain-clothes officer, who strolled towards them somewhat warily, as well as a team of white-clad forensics people, who all seemed to suddenly have nothing to do, Thea recounted everything she could remember. Very little was added to her original testimony, other than a description of Melissa as cheerful and unafraid. 'You'll want to look through those boxes,' she realised, when she'd finished.

'Right. And we need to get a look at whatever's on this camera card, as soon as we can. And find that car. It must be out there somewhere.'

'She didn't seem to be coming this way,' said Thea suddenly. 'She went off towards Vineyard Street, and this is the opposite direction.'

'Did you watch her go?'

'Yes, for a little way. She must have doubled back after I'd gone into the house. There's some sort of short cut into town through there.' She pointed to the east, where Oliver had said something about Silk Mill Lane. 'Or maybe she wanted to look at the birds.'

'You got the impression she knew her way around? That she'd been here before?' It was going over something Thea had already told her, but she was used to such repetitions when it came to police questioning.

'Definitely. She went straight to those boxes, without any hesitation. She knew just what was in them.'

'Would you have heard her if she'd doubled back?'

'I doubt it. The dog didn't bark or anything. But obviously all sorts of things must have been going on, and I had no idea.' She sighed. 'I hardly even thought about her, once she'd gone.'

'You didn't like her very much,' said Gladwin astutely.

Thea frowned. 'That's putting it rather strong, but no, I didn't take to her, I suppose. She didn't seem to be inviting me to. She never really looked at me. I was just somebody she had to get past, in order to fetch her things.'

'You tried to stop her?'

'Not exactly. I tried to assure myself that she had a right to be there. That's what I'm being paid for, basically.'

'You got assurances from her – is that what you mean?'

'More or less, yes.'

'Thea – this is going to sound insane, and it is, of course. But *I'm* being paid to do a thorough job as well. So, I have to ask you, formally, whether you had any personal involvement in the killing of this young woman. I'll have to order your fingerprints to be taken and an examination of your shoes made.'

Thea's chin lifted bravely. 'There's no reason why I should be immune, I realise that, of course. It's just . . .'

'I know. Just answer the question, there's a love.'

'I did not kill her. I don't know who did.' It was difficult to say, especially in the hearing of the other police officers. The mere act of proclaiming her innocence made the possibility of her guilt feel bizarrely real. 'But my fingerprints will be all over the bird feeders, and my shoeprints might well be exactly where that body now is. But I think I'm too small to have done it,' she added lightly. 'Melissa must be six or seven inches taller than me. Wouldn't that rule me out?'

Gladwin smiled humourlessly and made no reply.

Fingerprints and shoeprints were taken, back in the house, and people continued to come and go. Sensations of trespass and transgression began to overwhelm Thea, as Oliver's paths were trampled and his home invaded. 'This is terrible,' she muttered to her dog. She was hungry and thirsty and defeated. It was a bitter world and her own pathetic efforts to maintain order and harmony counted for nothing.

All further efforts to contact her mother proved in vain, and at eleven-fifteen a young plain-clothes police constable entered the house to tell Thea there were two visitors for her. 'We can't let them come down here just now,' he apologised. 'They'll have to stay out in the road.'

'Oh, God,' Thea groaned. 'One of them is the father of the dead girl. Am I supposed to be the one to tell him?'

'It would probably be best,' he said, with a faint frown. 'Then we'll take him for a look, probably. They'll be moving her soon, though. Maybe he should go to the mortuary?'

'No, no,' came Gladwin's voice of authority. 'She looks okay. It'll be kinder to get it over with here.'

Thea trudged heavily along to the road, and met her mother's eyes. The expression was confused, but only slightly alarmed. The older woman smiled. 'Thea? What's happening? They said there'd been an incident in the woods. Did somebody get caught in a gin trap?'

'Hi, Mum. I don't think they have gin traps any more. Is this Fraser?' She turned to a tall, colourless man standing at her mother's side. Her heart was pounding with dread at what she had to do next. 'Hello,' she said, holding out a shaky hand.

He took it in a moderate grip, and smiled down at her. 'Pleased to meet you,' he said, in an unexpectedly deep voice. 'Are you going to tell us what's going on?'

'Somebody's died,' said Thea. 'Actually, they'd like you to come and identify the body. I'm terribly sorry about this, and I'm sure it's a shockingly harsh way of telling you, but the fact is, something terrible has happened to your daughter.'

His expression barely altered, but he dropped her hand as if it had bitten him. 'Daughter?' he repeated. 'What do you mean?'

'Can you come with me? It's down by the hide. I expect you know your way around. Mum – they'll let you go into the house, I expect. At least . . .' She looked round for assistance. 'Is that all right?' she asked the detective constable.

'Better not,' he grimaced. 'Forensics are going to want to have a look. Just hang on here for a bit, okay?'

But Thea felt a primary obligation to the shell-shocked old man, who had made no move since dropping her hand. 'Listen, Mum. Can you stay in the car for a bit? It's all rather a circus at the moment. As soon as Fraser has . . . well, as soon as it's over, we can go off on our own somewhere, until things have settled down. We'll have to talk about what we do next. And they'll want to contact Oliver . . .'

Her mother took a deep breath and reached for her new friend's hand. 'Fraser,' she said steadily, 'I have no idea what this is about, but I'll wait for you here, while you go with Thea. She's very sensible. You'll be all right with her.'

The accolade was familiar enough to be almost funny. *Thea has always been the sensible one* was a family mantra that contained only a dash of truth. Emily and Damien had possessed every bit as much sense as had Thea, throughout most of their growing up. Even Jocelyn was only sporadically ditzy.

It seemed to be effective now, however, and Thea began a brisk walk down the path towards the woods. Fraser kept alongside her, his long legs betraying the early signs of shambling that overtook tall old men sooner or later. 'I don't really understand,' he repeated in a low voice. 'I can't begin to grasp what's happening.'

'I'm really very sorry. It's all been a complete shock for me as well. I only met your daughter last night, and now she's . . . out here. Well, you'll see. It isn't too ghastly, really. Not compared to some.' She stopped herself. This was no sort of consolation for a man who was about to set eyes on his dead daughter. She must have been the child of his declining years, if he was as old as he looked. Although she thought her mother had said he was younger than her. This man seemed closer to eighty than the seventy-five she had expected.

'Here we are,' she announced, superfluously. 'This is Detective Superintendent Gladwin. She and I are friends, in a way. She'll take over now.'

Gladwin had been talking to a pair of black-suited men by the door of the hide. She turned and smiled sympathetically at Fraser Meadows. 'Hello, sir. I am so very sorry about this. I hope we can make it as quick as possible. It's just for an initial identification at this stage. Of course you'll have a chance to visit her again in the chapel at the undertakers.' She flapped a hand at the two men, who suddenly became obvious as the men summoned to remove the body. 'They're from Maltby and Salmon, in Stow-on-the-Wold. You don't have to engage them for the funeral, but they're available if you do want them. I can give you their number in a little while.'

Fraser blinked and opened his mouth to speak. But Gladwin was ushering him towards the gazebo, where a young uniformed officer stood guard. 'In here, sir. If you'd just tell me . . .'

Thea could not see what happened next, but it all seemed to be over in seconds. Fraser stooped towards the ground, only his head and shoulders inside the tent. Gladwin had disappeared from sight, presumably to lift a cover from the dead face. Then the deep voice of the old man rang loud through the clearing.

'This is not my daughter. I've never seen her before in my life. This woman bears no resemblance at all to my daughter.'

Chapter Seven

Everything instantly changed. The first sensation was relief. It was no longer necessary to feel solicitous for the old man. His expected horror and grief, potential collapse or even worse, had all receded. From a precious daughter to an unknown stranger was a giant leap.

And then confusion rapidly followed. If not his daughter, then *who*? 'But she *said* she was,' Thea insisted. 'Why would she say that?'

Nobody could suggest an answer to that. Gladwin kept her expression studiously neutral, her brain plainly whirring as she ran through the procedures for establishing identity. Find the handbag and the car. Examine the clothes. Publish a picture. Check missing persons records. Thea could readily guess much of the list, from her long-time associations with the police. Was the woman's name even Melissa? She had obviously told at least one lie – there were likely to be others. But why? She couldn't have known she was about to be murdered; she had shown no hint of fear. Thea braced herself for yet another run-through of everything that had been said the previous evening, with a new twist. This time it would be in search of clues as to who this cold, stiff body had been.

'Well . . . thank you, sir,' Gladwin remembered to say. 'That's obviously come as rather a big surprise. You're quite certain this is not a member of your family?'

The implication seemed to hit Thea and Fraser simultaneously. 'I think I would know my own daughter,' he said, huffily.

But would you? Thea thought. How many men were there out there with offspring they knew nothing about? Thousands, at least. Would Gladwin order a DNA test, to establish the truth for sure? In straitened times, such expensive procedures were regarded as a luxury, to be used only when all else failed. But science trumped unreliable human testimony every time, and there seemed to be every reason to expect that it would have to be employed here.

'Perhaps you could go back to your mother now,' Gladwin said meaningfully to Thea. 'Take Mr Meadows with you. We have things to do here.'

Which was code for *We're going to remove the body now, and we need clear access to this entire scene for the rest of the day.*

Thea was opening her mouth to ask if she could just feed the birds first, when she realised that there would not be any birds visiting their feeding area today. Perhaps they had been frightened off for ever, and Oliver Meadows would be the one to suffer the greatest loss from all this. After Melissa's actual parents, of course – whoever they might be. For surely she had some, somewhere, and surely they would soon note her disappearance with growing alarm.

'Right,' she said. 'Let's go and find Mum, then.' She held out a friendly hand to Fraser Meadows, but he did not take it. Feeling foolish, she dropped it again. How ridiculous to think he might.

Her mother was listening to the radio in the car, ignoring the persistent gaggle of curious neighbours who were craning their necks for a glimpse of the Thistledown entrance and the woods beyond. Several walked past, as if heading for Sudeley Park, only to pause self-consciously a little further on, hoping to get a better view from there. Police vehicles occupied a stretch of roadside, with the undertaker's inconspicuous Renault Espace closest to the gateway. Thea wondered whether they would manage to reverse it past her car, but felt unequal to the task of moving it. Escape felt like the preferred option now, and she had no qualms about taking her mother and Fraser to the nearest pub.

'We'd better drive up to the high street,' she suggested. 'They might need this space for something.'

'No, we'll walk,' Fraser said firmly. 'We'd already decided where we want to go for lunch.' He glanced at his watch. 'A bit early, but that'll be all right.'

Thea looked at her mother, bemused by this new person who had apparently taken her over. Perhaps in the circumstances it would be too much to expect him to smile, but there was a dourness to him that was far from appealing. 'All right,' she said. 'I'm hungry, anyway. I never had any breakfast. And if we're walking, Hepzie can come as well, can't she.' It was a statement, made as firmly as Fraser's had been.

'Where is she?'

'In the house. I'll pop back and fetch her. I need to change my shoes as well.' She looked down at herself, half expecting to see blood and other stains on her clothes. There was nothing visible, but she felt soiled, just the same. 'And I think I might change. I'll be five minutes.' Without giving them a chance to argue, she went back up the track to the house.

'Poor old Heps,' she crooned to the abandoned spaniel. 'What a rotten morning you've had.' In fact the dog seemed to feel no resentment. From her point of view, events had been mildly interesting, although there had been an annoying spell in which she'd been shut in the kitchen. 'Never mind, we're going to the pub now with Granny.'

Upstairs she found sandals and a clean shirt that felt more suited to a Sunday lunch in a pub that might well prove to be rather smart. In the Cotswolds, you could never be quite sure of the dress code. There could be mud-spattered hikers, or expensively turned-out celebrities, or a mixture of the two.

The walk did prove therapeutic to some extent. The houses at the upper end of Vineyard Street were sufficiently characterful for comment. They had distinctive porches, which set Thea's mother talking about a porch on the house she grew up in, where a Mermaid rose trailed memorably. 'Funny the things you remember,' she concluded, with a little sigh.

This appeared to refer to an earlier conversation, to

judge from the little laugh that Fraser gave. 'Don't fret about it,' he urged. 'Nobody can remember everything.'

'But it seems so *mysterious*. None of the theories fit. I mean, with other things – like these porches, for instance – it just needs a small trigger for everything to come flooding back. I can clearly see that rose, and a swallow's nest right over the front door, and my father's old walking boots full of cobwebs, tucked under a rickety bench. I find it rather frightening,' she added diffidently. 'As if the only explanation is that parts of my brain have died.'

'Familiarity,' said Fraser with confidence. 'You saw that porch every day for years. Whereas we . . . well, it was all very brief.' He glanced shyly at Thea. 'Brief but intense, at least from my point of view.'

The potential for embarrassment was prodigious. 'You must remember *something*,' Thea said to her mother.

'I told you,' came the curt reply. 'I do, of course. It's just . . . I thought it would come back in more detail, and it hasn't.'

They decided they were still rather early for lunch, so turned left into what Thea gathered was Gloucester Street for a short way before transforming into Cheltenham Road, for no discernible reason other than a fair balance in acknowledging both the two large towns to the south.

Her mother seemed to give herself a silent talking to, before determinedly staring about her at the houses on either side. 'Heavens, Thea – have you had a chance to really look at these?' she breathed. 'They're amazing.'

'I had a good walk yesterday,' said Thea, distractedly. 'I saw the church and its gargoyles.'

'But the *houses*,' insisted Maureen. 'And the roofs.'

'Yes.' It seemed wrong to be admiring their surroundings, when a murder had just taken place, virtually under Thea's nose. 'I know.'

'Fraser,' Maureen appealed to her friend. 'Aren't they wonderful?'

Fraser in turn appeared to make an effort to concentrate. He looked obediently at the row of mismatched houses. 'No two the same,' he observed. 'Must be very unusual.'

'I *did* notice them,' Thea insisted, childishly. 'They're all different sizes.'

But she had not fully appreciated exactly how varied they were. Some had three gables, some two and some none at all. The heights were uneven, and the widths of dramatically different proportions. Some had a door and a window on the ground floor, others a door between two windows. Chimneys were of crazily differing heights and there was not a satellite dish to be seen. Nor a solar panel, she realised. Most were faced with render, concealing the stone beneath. They were of many assorted colours, from white to blue, with creams and browns between. 'It's not so Cotswoldy, is it?' she concluded.

'It is, though,' Maureen argued. 'Just below the surface, there's all that same stonework.'

'Not to mention the antique shops,' said Fraser, with a laugh. 'Oliver thinks they must be a front for other things. He can't imagine how they survive otherwise.'

'We'd better turn back,' said Thea, realising they'd walked almost the length of the town. 'I'm getting hungry.'

The return walk gave them a different vista, with the long

wall concealing the grounds of the erstwhile abbey gaining in prominence. 'Goodness, look at these!' cried Maureen, pointing to a row of almshouses, standing at right angles to the main street. 'What have they done to them?'

'Sold them for millions, if you ask me,' said Fraser. 'Turned them into a gated community.' He put his face to the firmly closed gate of Dents Terrace, like a little boy.

Thea followed his gaze, realising she had not registered the houses previously. 'They can't be very big inside,' she remarked.

'Bijou,' said Maureen. 'Aren't they beautiful.'

'1865,' read Fraser from a circular plaque on the nearest house. 'It's like a film set.'

Thea agreed with him. Perfect little gardens lined the short stretch of private street. Roofs and drainpipes and brickwork were all in immaculate condition. Slowly she began to wonder at the pressures involved in living in Winchcombe. You certainly wouldn't be allowed to let any weeds grow in your front garden.

They were in the square, where Thea had seen the Plaisterers Arms the day before. 'Is this where we're lunching?' she asked Fraser. 'It looks okay.'

'We thought we'd give it a try. There's a garden, if they don't allow dogs inside.'

They went in, and the initial impression was of an unpretentious old hostelry, that would never dream of excluding dogs or offering polenta on the menu. They peered into the bar on the left, finding it empty of customers. Steps led down to a shadowy area boasting a large sign reading TOILETS. They turned back and went through the right-hand door, into a larger bar containing five people, all of them elderly, and a fat old corgi lying under a table. No blackboards offered Specials, or uniquely creative cocktails. A piano had pride of place, looking as if it had been there for the past century or so.

'Very nice,' approved Thea. 'Haven't you been here before?' she asked Fraser.

He shook his head. 'I very seldom come to Winchcombe. Oliver bought the property as a second home, originally. He and I have had shockingly little to do with each other, all our lives. Of course, it was my doing – I was in Australia for most of the time.'

'And he never offered Thistledown to the family, as a place to come for a holiday? I'd have thought it was perfect for a week in the country.'

'We're not that sort of family,' said Fraser obscurely.

They ordered a lunch that was emphatically not a Sunday roast and headed for the garden, passing a shelf of old books that struck Thea as an incongruous attempt to mimic similar displays in other pubs. It was entirely superfluous, given the effortlessly simple atmosphere of plain food and drink and somewhere to sit.

The fact that they had yet to return to the burning topic of vicious murder loomed larger as they waited for their food. Nobody in the pub had seemed to be talking about it, or even aware that something had happened. Thea had encountered this very British restraint before, particularly in Blockley – another small town like Winchcombe. And yet there had been curious onlookers, who must have picked up the basic fact of a sudden death, at the very least.

'Is Oliver very involved with the local community?' Thea asked Fraser. 'Does he belong to a discussion group or bridge club or anything?'

'I think he goes on guided walks now and then,' was the vague reply. 'He isn't a very sociable chap, on the whole.'

At least it was clear that they really were brothers, Thea thought. Same height, same small mouth and loosely attached legs. 'Which one's the elder of you?' she wondered.

'I'm older, but not by very much. But we were never very close. Went our separate ways and so forth.'

'Literally,' Thea remarked. 'With you going to Australia. You don't seem to have picked up much of the accent.'

'I was in Perth. It's all remarkably English there, even now. I guarded my vowels most assiduously, I can assure you.'

The flash of wit gave rise to the first stirrings of liking for him. She looked at her mother in the hope that she could convey some hint of approval. But Maureen Johnstone was obviously not listening. She was picking at the strap of her shoulder bag, with a nervous tension that drew instant concern from her daughter. Had she missed something seriously awry, in her preoccupation with murder and misplaced daughters?

'Mum?' she said gently. 'Are you okay?'

'Oh yes, I'm perfectly all right. We're lucky with the weather, aren't we? It's often lovely in September. Your father always used to say . . .' She interrupted herself with a glance at Fraser. 'Richard was full of sayings about the weather. He grew up in the country, you see.'

'My husband was the same,' added Thea, slightly too heartily. 'It was one of the things they had in common.'

'They got along well, didn't they?' said Maureen, with a soft sigh. 'Such good men, both of them.'

It sounded strange, but it was nothing less than the truth. Carl Osborne and Richard Johnstone had indeed both been good men, and their loss was never going to cease to hurt. 'They were,' said Thea.

'And a good man is hard to find,' Fraser said, even more heartily. His attempt at a twinkling smile fell flat. Thea did her best to credit him with the right instincts. After all, he had just been presented with a dead body to identify. He could be forgiven for losing his bearings for a while.

'Your daughter's name is Maureen – is that right?' she asked, risking the renewed embarrassment this might cause.

'I'm afraid so,' he said ruefully. 'I never told my wife why – which was very wrong of me, I know.'

Thea's mind clicked into action at last. 'So the murdered girl must have known your family. She must have *some* connection. She told me your daughter's name. She knew her way around the house. Are you *sure* you didn't recognise her?'

He bristled. 'Why should I lie about it?'

'No, no, I'm not suggesting . . . only, you were expecting to see your daughter. So when it obviously wasn't her, that might have been all you focused on. If she was somebody you only met a few times, perhaps as a younger girl, you could easily not realise. Don't you think?'

'No,' he said.

'So where's Oliver?' Thea flashed back, following some urge to put pressure on the man.

'I'm not at liberty to say. I promised him I wouldn't

tell anyone.' He avoided her eyes, and ignored Maureen completely.

'You'll have to tell the police. They'll be wanting to speak to him as a matter of priority.'

'Matter of priority,' he repeated, with amusement in his eye. 'Really?'

She gave up and their food arrived. 'Nice,' approved Maureen after one or two mouthfuls.

Thea silently considered all the things that were wrong with the situation. For the first time all day, she wanted Drew. A warmth ran through her at the thought of him, and how he would sit comfortably beside her if he were there, helping her work things out, making no demands, simply offering himself without conditions.

Stop it, she ordered herself. It wouldn't be like that at all. He would be sad and stressed, preoccupied with his children and the fragile state of his business. He would make demands without intending to, as she knew she had herself, after Carl had died.

'We shouldn't be long,' she said. 'The police will want to keep track of us, I expect.'

As if on cue, her mobile tinkled, deep inside her bag. It was still switched on, she realised, after the abortive efforts to contact her mother. 'Thea? Where are you?' Gladwin's voice was almost calm. 'You're not supposed to just wander off, you know.'

'We're at the Plaisterers Arms, in the town square. In the garden at the back, having lunch.'

'Right. Well, come back here afterwards, will you? We're not finished.'

'No – I was just saying.'

'Half an hour, okay?'

'All right.' She felt more than a little like a schoolgirl summoned by a fairly friendly head teacher who nonetheless carried all the authority and might yet turn out to be unpredictable.

'It's *plasterer* not *playsterer*,' came a voice from the table behind them. It took a moment to understand that it was addressing her. She turned to look. A man somewhat younger than herself was grinning at her, one eyebrow raised disarmingly. 'Sorry – but I thought you'd want to know.'

'Thanks.' Her first thought was that he was a journalist, already onto the fact of a murder and cunningly tracking down the main witness. 'I'll remember that.'

'I know you,' he said, not to her, but to Fraser. 'You were here a month or so ago, staying at Thistledown. You drive a big Renault. You had a dog with you.'

'Oh?' Fraser showed no inclination to respond any further.

'And I think my wife met you yesterday, in the park,' he went on, to Thea. 'She was the one with the young retriever.'

It felt like several months ago to Thea. She forced herself to remember. 'How do you know that was me?'

'Spaniel, pretty, friendly. Actually, it's the spaniel, mainly.' Hepzie took no notice of him from her spot under the table. Thea tried to assess the credibility of his claim. Had his wife described such a brief encounter in sufficiently fine detail for him to recognise her and her dog from it? There had been a dozen or more people strolling in Sudeley Park, many of them with dogs.

She cocked her head sceptically. 'I don't believe you,' she said.

He laughed. 'How wise you are, Thea Osborne.' He got up and moved to sit next to her on the wooden bench. 'I assure you it's true. But there's more to it than that, of course. Your reputation precedes you, you know.'

She had been made aware in Cranham, a few months previously, that she had a certain fame throughout the Cotswolds. She had featured in newspaper reports and had made many acquaintances in a sparsely populated area where people were connected by extended family ties in a fashion that had been common a century or so ago.

'Oh?' she said, feeling a chilly hand stirring her insides.

'Temple Guiting,' he said shortly. 'We never met, but I know all about what happened while you were there.'

Temple Guiting had been over a year ago, but it was barely five miles from Winchcombe. Blockley and Snowshill were similarly within walking distance – if you could walk ten or fifteen miles. People did. The entire area was crisscrossed with well-used footpaths. It was not so much a revival of Victorian times as of medieval practices. News would travel from one settlement to another, exchanged in the taverns and marketplaces. As in Cranham, she found it a sinister notion. She did not want to be discussed and observed behind her back. It felt threatening, like being followed from in front, people anticipating her next move and lying in wait for her.

'Who *is* this, Thea?' came her mother's voice, endearingly protective. Like Hepzie should have been. She nudged the dog with a foot, most unfairly.

'My name is Reuben Hardy and my wife is Jenny. We're quite harmless, I promise you. But we are good friends of people in Temple Guiting, as I say, and we actually saw Thea in the shop there, last year, just before all the trouble came to a head. You're not easy to forget, you know.'

It was impossible to ascertain whether or not the man knew there had been a murder close by, only hours earlier. If he did know, he was making an excellent job of concealing the fact – and why would anybody do that? Perhaps if he had come directly to the pub from a house on the other side of town, he could have missed all the activity down in Vineyard Street.

She had forgotten that he had claimed to know Fraser as well. The old man reminded her.

'You say you saw me, too?' Fraser rumbled. 'Strikes me you do a lot of it, watching people instead of minding your own business.'

Right! Thea silently applauded.

Reuben Hardy merely smiled. 'I have a good memory for faces, that's all.'

'And names,' Thea accused.

'True. And I have good ears, as well. I gather the police are wanting to speak to Mr Oliver Meadows. Well, we all know where he is, don't we? I imagine they'll have to await their turn.'

'Please be quiet,' said Fraser, with heavy pomposity. 'My brother's whereabouts are of no concern to you or anybody else.' His glance flicked from Thea to Reuben Hardy and back again. 'Perhaps we could finish our lunch in peace now?' He returned doggedly to his cottage pie. Thea and her mother tried to do the same, but neither of them found eating to be possible. The question of Oliver's location was apparently not so much of a mystery after all. If this man knew about it, Thea felt decidedly aggrieved at being kept in the dark.

'Oh . . . sorry,' said Reuben Hardy, obsequiously. 'I understand. Say no more.' He tapped the side of his nose in a parody of the Monty Python sketch.

All three turned their backs on him then, and for five minutes they maintained their position. Then Thea glanced at him again. His facile grin had faded, and he was chewing a lip while keying something onto an iPhone. One foot was tapping a leg of the table. She thought over what he had said to them, trying to understand his motives in making contact as he had.

'What did you want from us?' she burst out, her instinctive curiosity getting the better of her. 'Why did you speak to us at all?'

'Want?' he repeated, with wide-eyed innocence. 'Nothing at all. I was just trying to be friendly. My wife said you seemed nice. I can see Oliver's bird hide from the window of my flat, so I feel a sort of fellowship, if you like.'

'In that case, you'll know there's been some trouble there today, won't you?' She was hoping to shock him into revealing how much he knew about the murder, if anything.

'Pardon?'

'There's been a lot of coming and going all morning,' she prompted.

'You know – I don't think I've looked out of the

window all day. It's been rather a rush, one way and another. Why – what happened?'

She scrutinised his face for a long moment. His colour was definitely different and he was finding it impossible to meet her eye. But it seemed to her that he was betraying little more than a natural worry that his equilibrium might be disturbed by whatever she might tell him. 'I can't say, I'm afraid. It'll all come out later today, but for the moment it's better not to spread gossip. I'm sure you'll understand.'

His iPhone warbled at him, and he looked down at the screen.

Thea didn't wait for further conversation with him. 'We'd better go,' she said, noticing that Fraser had finally put down his fork. The old man hesitated fractionally, as if resistant to being given instructions by a woman. Thea stood up impatiently, yanking at her placid dog, and marching determinedly back through the pub. She had no reason to rush, nothing enticing was beckoning, but her patience had run thin. She felt irritated with her mother for taking up with these Meadows people in the first place. Seen from that angle, everything was her fault. She turned back, tempted to say something to this effect.

She caught a complicated look passing between the elderly pair. Some kind of warning was being given by him, received with a pleading expression by her mother – an expression that made Thea angry. But there was also an intimacy, an indication that there was something shared, something understood, that softened the apparent aggression. As if he might be saying *Just be careful, you know how important this is.* And she was replying *Yes, I know, dear, but I really don't like it.* Thea felt no need to defend her mother – rather her anger spread to them both. She was being excluded, even possibly *used*. They had engineered her into this house-sitting commission, without telling her why or forewarning her of the hazards. She felt isolated and exploited and childishly rebellious.

Gladwin was in the road talking to a stout woman wearing leather riding boots and a corduroy jacket when they got back to Thistledown. There seemed to be some animosity in the air. 'But I *always* go through here on a Sunday,' the woman was saying, as if for the third or fourth time. 'It's a regular routine.'

'I'm sorry, madam, but today you won't be able to. This is a crime scene now. The entire woodland is cordoned off.' She caught Thea's eye and made a silent *God-help-me* face.

'Well, I think it's a disgrace. It was hard enough to persuade the Meadows man to keep the path open, without this. He's been impossibly obstructive, over the years.'

'You're telling me there's a public right of way through this property?' Gladwin appeared to register this somewhat belatedly.

'Precisely! That's what I've been telling you for the past five minutes.'

'And do people use it?'

'Almost never. We agreed that it should be limited to locals. There hasn't been a signpost up for ten years or more, so he doesn't get stray ramblers scaring his precious

91

birds. The path isn't obvious at all. It leads through to my field, do you see? Where my *horse* is. If I have to go around the road, it'll take me three times as long.'

'Well, I'm very sorry, but I really can't allow it,' Gladwin insisted, albeit with less force than before. Her mind appeared to be making some sort of calculation. 'Although . . . perhaps if you could show me where the path goes, that might be rather helpful.'

The triumph was plain in the woman's eyes. 'Come on, then,' she said, impatiently. 'We've wasted enough time already.'

'Can I come?' Thea whispered to Gladwin, having swallowed back a thoughtless assertion that she already knew where the path led. She was slowly learning that it was generally best to remain silent in the company of the police and potential witnesses.

Gladwin shrugged and said, 'Why not? But leave your relations behind, okay? And the dog.'

Quickly Thea asked her mother and Fraser to take Hepzie into the house. Gladwin reinforced the request by adding, 'There's a detective inspector waiting to talk to you, Mr Meadows. Make yourself comfortable, and I'll send him in right away.'

With impressive skill, the superintendent arranged the interview with three short words. 'Jeremy! Meadows. House.' DI Jeremy Higgins, already known to Thea, peeled away from where he was scrutinising the screen of a Smartphone, and obediently made for Thistledown.

Passing the much emptier clearing in front of the bird hide, the stout woman led the way at a sharp angle to the right, between tall willow trees, in a direction that seemed quite wrong for the centre of Winchcombe. Before Thea could raise a query, another sharp turn, this time to the left, corrected their trajectory, and within two minutes they were skirting the grassy area that Oliver had shown Thea the previous day. There was a stile in the corner of the property, with a narrow but obvious path beyond it. The buildings of the lower edge of Winchcombe were only a few yards away, jumbled on rising ground, a mixture of periods and styles that would keep a historian happy for weeks.

'That way to Silk Mill Lane, and this way to my horse,' explained the woman. 'Can I go now, please?'

'Just leave me your name and address,' Gladwin said. 'I might need confirmation that this was an established path, known to several local people.'

'Priscilla Heap,' came the ready reply. 'Anything I can do to help, just ask.' She added her address, which Gladwin noted carefully, along with a phone number. 'My house is just over there, behind that tree,' she elaborated.

'Thank you,' said Gladwin. 'I'm sorry to have delayed you.'

'Think nothing of it. There's obviously been something ghastly going on – but I'd prefer not to know any details. I've seen enough mayhem in my time. All I care about these days is my horse.'

She had trotted off before Gladwin could say anything further. 'Well,' she turned to Thea. 'It takes all sorts, I suppose.'

'I've come across quite a few of her type over the past couple of years,' said Thea. 'Most of them turn out to be almost incredibly decent.' She thought of a particular instance in Blockley, and gave a small reminiscent smile. Then she thought of other places and her smile faded. 'Although some of them aren't,' she added.

'I wouldn't rely too much on this one,' warned the detective.

'Oh?'

'If she lives here in Castle Street, and her horse is just down there, why does she have to use the path she just showed us? Why does she have to go via Vineyard Street, when all she has to do is walk straight down her own road?'

'Good question,' said Thea.

Chapter Eight

Drew Slocombe was in a dark place into which very few flickers of light penetrated. He endured great gulfs of shame, greater than the sadness and worry. Shame, because he had never for a moment appreciated the true extent of the suffering that many of his customers were enduring. He had buried their parents, spouses, siblings, offspring, friends, with brisk sympathy and hardly a shred of empathy. Shame, because he had comprehensively lost his nerve and buried his wife in another company's cemetery. Maggs had been appalled, accusing him of insanity, treachery, cowardice, stupidity. Timmy had stared at him in absolute horror. 'But – you *said* she'd always be here with us,' he accused. 'You *said*.'

'I know I did, Tim. I was wrong. She won't be. At least – she will, as we remember her. We want to think of her alive and warm, don't we? Not dead and . . .' *Rotting*, he had wanted to say. But you couldn't say that to a little boy of five. 'I'm really, really sorry, sweetheart, but that's how it is. We'll have a grave to visit, but it won't be here at Peaceful Repose. I think you'll understand it better when you've grown up a bit.'

'I *won't*,' sobbed the child. 'I want Mummy here.'

It had been Stephanie who gave him the resolve to make the change, only hours before the burial was due to take place. She had crawled into bed with him at five that morning, shaking and whimpering. 'Daddy, I had a dream. I saw Mummy's head, coming out of the ground. It was all horrible, with worms and bugs on it. Daddy, do we *have* to bury her here, just outside? It makes me feel scared.'

He had suffered a similar dream himself, the synchronicity just another piece of evidence of his closeness to his daughter. 'It's all arranged,' he said. 'Eleven o'clock this morning.'

'I think you can unarrange it,' she said confidently.

He had cringed at the prospect. Karen's parents, friends, neighbours, were all on their way. Maggs had organised it all, with everyone urged to bring flowers and memories of Karen as she had been at her best. Maggs had been a rock, knowing exactly what to say and do, perfect with the children, letting them laugh without guilt, showing them that there was a way through their misery, that life was far from over. Maggs was young and hearty and straightforward.

'I don't think I can,' he said.

But already he had known that he must. The dreams were too stark a signal to ignore. It would be too terrible to have his cheerful good-hearted wife decomposing just beyond their windows. People did it, of course. He had arranged a handful of back-garden funerals, without reservation. He had gone along with them in the belief that it was a perfectly wholesome thing to do. Now he suspected that it was not. It would be like chaining yourself to the past, like having the dead albatross dragging at your ankles. Perhaps it made sense for an old person, after sixty years of marriage, to retain the partner you'd known your whole life. It was almost normal for people to stand their spouse's ashes on the mantelpiece for year after year. But Drew was not yet forty. Even in his very darkest moments, he knew he had another forty years ahead. He knew he would regret, one day, having his wife's grave forever in his view.

Stephanie's reasons were different, and if anything, more powerful. As he had tried to say to Timmy, the children needed to carry their mother within them, her hugs and homilies and habits part of their DNA, the memories untainted by the knowledge of her corpse right outside. Not so much an albatross in their case, as an ogre, a bogey, distracting them from the happy memories. Stephanie had a wisdom and a confidence that came from being unconditionally adored by her father from her first moments. Stephanie knew instinctively what was best, and trusted him to agree with her.

Timmy was different. To his private horror, Drew had not managed to love his son as much as he loved his daughter. Timmy had been cheated in a number of ways. He had been a toddler when his mother was shot and fatally damaged. For the past three years he had received diminished parenting from her, the attention sporadic and incomplete. He had been bossed by his sister, failed by his mother, and bewildered by his father. Drew knew that Timmy knew there was something missing. It broke his heart in the places where there was still space for pain. Guilt made him boisterous, joking with the boy, refusing to confront the truth. He steadfastly included him in every treat, giving him good toys, lavish approval, bedtime stories. But the secret relief when Tim curled up with a DVD or trashy children's television was impossible to ignore. Drew had no desire to listen to the flights of fancy about Thomas the Tank Engine or the Mr Men, which Timmy could indulge in for hours, given half an audience.

And Timmy was betrayed again by Drew's last-minute decision. He phoned Maggs at half past six, his hands shaking, his voice broken.

'I can't do it,' he croaked. 'I just can't.'

'Can't do what?' Already there was a shard of suspicion in her voice, a flash of impatience.

'I can't have her grave here. We had a dream, me and Stephanie. The same dream. It's not right, Maggs. It's romantic nonsense. We'll have to change it.'

'*Dreams* are romantic nonsense, Drew,' she said sternly. 'Of course you'll bury Karen in your own cemetery. You don't have any choice. It goes without saying.'

'It doesn't, though. I can't explain it now, but I've definitely decided. We'll have to call that place in Dorset and see if they can do it.'

'What place is that?'

'The green place, of course. Please, Maggs. Don't make it any harder.'

She sniffed and said nothing, a woman outraged to her marrow. They both knew it was his decision, that he carried all the moral trump cards. But for him to make it so obvious was yet another sort of betrayal.

And so it had all been changed. The mourners were astonished; some of them arrived for a funeral that never happened. Some of those were angry enough that they failed to attend the rearranged burial two days later, in Dorset. Stephanie had quailed at the enormity of what she took to be all her doing. She did not believe her father when he said she had voiced what he had been feeling himself.

'It's the right thing, darling,' he assured her. 'We did the right thing.'

'But everybody's so *cross*,' she wailed.

'I know. But they'll get over it. And it isn't really their business, after all. It's for us, you and me, to do what's best.'

'And Timmy,' she reminded him. 'Was it best for him as well?'

Drew moaned and pulled the child to him, holding her tight. 'We'll both have to be very, very kind to Timmy,' he said thickly. 'I need that from you, more than anything.'

She understood. Her understanding struck awe into him. He had thought for the past year or more that Timmy's best hope, in the long term, lay with Maggs. Maggs had seen how things stood, even before the second Slocombe baby had been born, and resolved to protect him. She had kept to her resolution, but in some opaque way, Timmy had rejected her efforts. It was as if he was saying, *I already have two parents, thank you, and if they can't give me what I need, then nobody can.* And Stephanie saw it all through her wise little eyes. Stephanie and Maggs were soul sisters, in many ways. They respected each other, and colluded in their elevation of Drew to prime position as demigod. Flawed and needy at times, he was still unarguably the centre of their universe. Even Maggs's husband, Den, realised that.

But Maggs had been badly shaken by his extraordinary failure. So shaken that she made terrible accusations that poisoned the air between them – a poison that still hung about, six weeks later.

'It's that Thea woman, isn't it?' she shouted. 'You want Karen swept out of the way, to give you a clear road, you and her. Bloody hell, Drew, you should be ashamed of yourself.'

He *was* ashamed, that much was true. But not because of Thea. Where she was concerned, his conscience was crystal clear. He had controlled himself magnificently, and somebody – preferably Maggs – should give him credit for it. There had been one or two occasions, earlier in his marriage, when he had been far closer to disgracing himself than he had been with Thea. At least . . . he shied away from the memory of a precarious moment in Broad Campden . . . at least he and Thea were both well-balanced adults, mature enough to know exactly what the implications would be.

But the damage had been done. Maggs's accusation had effectively ensured that he could not contact Thea in any way. He could not permit the slightest hint that what she said could be true. When a beautiful spray of flowers arrived at the aborted funeral, bearing the label 'With my deepest sympathy, Thea' he had sorely wanted to keep it in the house, in pride of place. Instead, he had left it to wither behind the office, with a few other superfluous tributes. He had not told Thea of the change of plan. Presumably, she still didn't know about it.

And gradually, as the weeks crawled miserably by, and the children went back to school, to be treated so dreadfully sensitively by their teachers, and Maggs resentfully kept the business alive, Drew did begin to feel ashamed of his feelings for Thea, as Maggs had said. Ashamed, because she infiltrated his dreams, and whispered into his waking ear. He heard her sensible voice, and saw her lovely heart-shaped face, as he dragged through the days. It was as if Maggs had known better than he did himself where his emotions were headed. In his tormented dreams, Maggs became an avenging angel, barring gates and wielding swords and constantly shouting at him.

But today was Sunday and he was responsible for the well-being of the children. Stephanie had a sore throat, which was apparently getting worse. If she had to be off school next day that would cause difficulties, because there was a burial due at midday. The business was sliding so drastically that he had been forced to apply for state benefits simply to survive. The children got their school dinners for free, and there were vouchers for milk. He knew the money was his due, but even so, the poverty only added to his feelings of shame.

He spent far too much time in the big bedroom he had shared with Karen. A big old wooden chair had always been part of its furnishings, and he had taken to sitting in it, trying to read diverting fiction, or more often, simply brooding over his situation. He was there now, while the children watched TV downstairs.

He would have to get them their tea, before bed. Scrambled eggs, baked beans, a pinch of grated cheese and apples from their own trees was the meal he envisaged. He had cooked for the family most of the time over the past year or two, as Karen became progressively more erratic. He had no objections to so doing, but he did hate the shopping and the endless need to make decisions as to what to provide.

'Daddy!' Stephanie was calling. 'That lady's in the news. That lady friend of yours.'

He knew already who she meant, and clattered down the stairs in the hope of catching the item. He caught the final seconds of a report of a murder in the Cotswold town of Winchcombe. A police officer was being interviewed on an old stone bridge, where behind him, amongst a stretch of woodlands, a body had been found. As the camera slowly panned, a woman and a dog came into focus, part of a small knot of people. 'There!' shrilled Stephanie. 'That's her.'

It was unmistakably Thea and her spaniel. She was trying not to be caught on camera, turning sideways and bending to the animal – which only seemed to impel the camera operator to hold his lens on her for some extra seconds. The police spokesman was asking the public to help with identification of the dead woman, without showing a picture of her.

Drew had little doubt that Thea was yet again involved in a house-sit where something had gone badly wrong.

'Oh, yes,' he said. 'How clever of you to remember her.'

Chapter Nine

After his preliminary interview with Higgins, Gladwin took Fraser Meadows off to compose a formal statement in the hurriedly set-up incident room in a hall on the other side of the high street, and Thea seized the chance to talk to her mother alone. They were in the living room at Thistledown, the house having been declared no longer part of the police investigation. The assumption was that the visitors would stay overnight as originally planned.

'Have you ever met Oliver?' Thea began. 'I've lost track, after everything that's been going on.'

'No. I spoke to him on the phone when Fraser suggested you could house-sit.'

'Before or after you spoke to me about it?'

'Um . . . I'm not sure. Does it matter?'

'Not really. But you did tell me you'd dismissed the idea at first. Why did you? Was there something fishy about it?'

'No, no. I just didn't want you to think I was interfering. I know how independent you like to be.'

Thea sighed, wondering as always why she felt so

chafed whenever a family member claimed to understand everything about her. She didn't regard herself as unduly independent. She'd never been tempted to emigrate to Australia to get away from the family, or keep her life a dark secret from them. She looked at her mother – the white hair and wrinkled neck, mottled hands and stiffening knees. The woman was old by any standards. The fact that there were now innumerable women twenty years her senior still up and running should not obscure this truth. Her mother had been alive for a long time, and her brain and body might be expected to show some signs of wear. Ought they to be taking the apparent memory lapses more seriously? Were they shortly to be faced, as a family, with the dreaded horror of dementia in their parent?

'Have you met Maureen, then? Your namesake. Isn't Fraser living with her? Did you stay there last night?'

'Um . . . Mo. You mean Mo. They never call her Maureen. Yes, I have met her. She's very dark. Her mother was Spanish.'

'Was?'

'She died about ten years ago. They'd been divorced for ages, of course. Absolutely ages. They went to Australia, and then she came back.'

'Where were you this morning? I tried to phone you at home and there was no answer.'

'I was at Damien's,' came the surprising reply. 'Fraser collected me from there after breakfast, and we came here. It isn't very far.'

'So Damien has met Fraser?'

'That's right. I said that on the phone, days ago.'

Thea had forgotten, or paid no attention. Somehow it came as a relief to know her brother had met and presumably accepted the mysterious boyfriend. She still felt in need of more information. 'But you said Fraser married again, didn't you? Did they have any children?'

'No. I told you that, as well. She died tragically, only a year after they were married.'

Thea recalled to mind the murdered Melissa, who had betrayed no trace of an Australian accent. If she had been Fraser's daughter, she might be expected to have been conceived and raised in the Antipodes – although there could be numerous alternative scenarios.

'But you don't really remember him at all, do you? From the nineteen sixties, I mean. He remembers it all, but you don't.'

'I keep trying. You'd think his *eyes* would remind me, wouldn't you? People's eyes don't change.'

'I suppose not.' Thea tried to imagine the stretch of time between the two encounters. Over fifty years was a huge span, the idea of accurate recall almost ludicrous. But there were constant proofs that the human memory could bridge it effortlessly. War veterans cheerfully described battle scenes in vivid detail; ancient women talked about nineteen fifties domestic routines as if they were last week. But Fraser had already explained these – repetition created much firmer memories, and the heightened stress of war would sear it deep into the brain. A fleeting romance in a crowded London life might well fall into oblivion. The real question, surely, was why did Fraser seek now to rekindle it? What could he possibly hope to gain from it? And the answer came again – Maureen Johnstone's house and pension. The man wanted a hearth to call his own and a solicitous partner for his declining years. And yet he had a daughter who was apparently willing to give him a home.

'Does he get on all right with Mo?' she asked.

'Oh, yes. But she's busy – out all day, and most evenings. She hasn't got much time for him. And she's just got a new boyfriend, so Fraser feels rather in the way.'

'How old is she?'

'Almost fifty. Two months younger than Damien.'

'Has she got a husband? Presumably not.'

Her mother shook her head. 'Divorced, seven years ago.'

'Any children?'

'Three. All girls, born within four years. The last one finished university this year.'

These responses brought a distinct sense of progress, of a picture coming into focus. Maureen Junior was wanting her freedom, now her daughters were off her hands. The arrival of an ageing father on her doorstep could not have been welcome. Therefore the prospect of a new girlfriend for him must have been thoroughly appealing. 'I bet she really likes you,' she said.

'Why shouldn't she?' her mother said, with a grin. 'What's not to like?'

It was a reminder of earlier times, when a rare flash of wit would brighten the moment for the whole family. As a mother, she had been no better than adequate, focusing more than necessary on the duller aspects of her role. She complained about scuffs on the furniture, possessions strewn untidily around, coffee mugs in bedrooms and socks adrift from their brothers. She made her husband and her offspring impatient with such trivia. Not one of them ever accepted that it mattered whether or not the cushions were straight and the washing-up done within seconds of the meal being finished. 'It's me that's the normal one,' she said, more than once. 'Without me, we'd be living in chaos.'

It was probably true – certainly the bit about being normal was. But Richard Johnstone and his four children all rejected, one way or another, the lure of normality. Even Damien, with his passion for religion and charitable works, was unusual. Damien could not find a matching pair of socks if his life depended on it, and he had chosen a wife who had a PhD in numerology, which was definitely profoundly abnormal. She told people she had married him for his name, which fitted with a highly significant numerical sequence that made no sense to anybody but her.

What's not to like? echoed in Thea's ears. Not just the sentiment, but the way it had been expressed, made her laugh. 'Right,' she said, with an affectionate pat on the mottled hand.

She had more questions, but the sensation of turning into an inquisitor kept her from voicing them. Instead, other queries were becoming increasingly persistent. *Who killed Melissa?* What was her connection with the Meadows family? Why was there a growing sense of careful background planning leading to her, Thea, being here at Thistledown at such short notice? Where was Oliver? Questions bred more questions, swirling around in her head, each one more worrying than the one before. She found herself feeling glad she'd have company that night.

But that led to another question, which ought to have been settled before now. 'Er . . . Mum? You and Fraser? Do you want to be in the same room? He seems a bit frail to be sleeping on a sofa. He can have my bed, if necessary, and I'll be down here.'

Maureen Johnstone blinked confusedly. 'I thought we settled that. Aren't there three bedrooms?'

'Not really. The bed in the third one is piled high with junk. The room's full of photographic stuff and a computer and books. Why? Did Oliver tell you differently?'

'He can't have done. I just thought . . .' Worry deepened grooves around her mouth. 'No, I don't want to share a room with him. Please, Thea – don't make me do that.'

Before Thea could properly respond to an alarmingly urgent plea, the front door opened and Fraser came in, looking almost as stricken as his new friend did.

The women both stared at him, while he squared his shoulders and forced a smile.

'What happened?' demanded Thea's mother. 'Why do you look so distraught?'

'Delayed shock, I think,' he said ruefully. 'It hit me, all of a sudden, that a lovely young woman, in the prime of her life, has been wickedly killed. All I could think before was that she was not my daughter. But now I understand that she was *somebody's* daughter, somebody's desperate tragedy.'

It sounded to Thea as if he'd been rehearsing the words before uttering them. Not that there was anything wrong with that, she told herself. She remembered how she'd done it herself – searching for words to convey her feelings, and finding them woefully inadequate.

'Yes,' she said. 'It does take a while to absorb, I know.'

He met her eyes. 'The police woman wants me to give you a message. She says to tell you that they now know where my brother is, and that there is every likelihood that he'll want you to stay here at least for the rest of this week. They will interview him in . . . where he is, but he won't be able to come home for some time. He still wants the birds to be fed. Is that all right?'

She had no choice but to concur, despite a feeling that the birds might have been deterred from coming to the feeding station for at least the coming week. Then she had a thought. 'The camera!' she said. 'Have they found anything on the camera?'

'They didn't say, but my suspicion is to the negative. I detected an atmosphere of dogged plodding, rather than any excitement as to leads or hard evidence.'

'What did they ask you?' Maureen wanted to know.

'Oh, the obvious things. Whether I was sure I'd never seen the woman before, where my brother was, how often I came here. Nothing unexpected. I think I made a fairly good witness, though I say so myself.'

'Witness to what?' Thea asked, in puzzlement.

'Sorry – wrong word, I suppose. Provider of background information, I mean. Family connections and so forth.'

'Did they take a DNA sample from you?'

Fraser flushed. 'They did, as it happens. I wasn't very happy about it, and insisted they destroy it as soon as the case is closed. I strongly disapprove of the tendency to store people's personal data, against all reason or legality.'

'So do I,' said Thea, in heartfelt agreement. For the

first time, she felt a flicker of actual liking for the man. 'But they've got to confirm that the dead girl wasn't your daughter, I suppose. After all . . .'

'Yes, yes, you don't have to be delicate. I know there's a theoretical possibility that I had a daughter without knowing it. But if she's the age they think – around thirty – then I can solemnly declare that I was at that time in a prolonged period of self-imposed celibacy. My wife had not long left me, taking my very much loved daughter with her, and after the calamity of my second venture into matrimony, I was most emphatically scared off the entire female half of the species. I was working in a very male environment, helping establish a new mining industry in the Pilbara. It was sufficiently exhausting for me not to feel any sense of deprivation.'

'Pilbara?' Thea repeated.

'It's in the north-west, the middle of nowhere. Massive iron deposits. It's currently ensuring the Australian economy has very little to worry about for at least two or three decades.'

'Blimey!' said Thea. 'I had no idea.'

'It's not important. It was a long time ago.'

Jumbled quotes ran through Thea's head: *And besides, the wench is dead* was the chief one. And *The past is another country; they do things differently there.* Neither seemed to have much relevance, except to reinforce the impression that where her mother's happiness and well-being were concerned, the past did have some significance.

'So the DNA results will come back negative?'

'If they come back at all. The woman said they'd only

110

do a test if they couldn't identify the body in the next day or two. They expect to find her car any time now. They've put little notes on all the ones parked out there, in Vineyard Street, asking the owners to call in and eliminate themselves from enquiries. Rather clever, actually. I've never known that to happen before.'

'You've been involved in this sort of thing before, have you?' Thea was sharper than intended, and she heard a small squeak of protest from her mother. 'Sorry,' she quickly amended. 'That wasn't meant to sound so . . .'

'Competitive?' he suggested with a forgiving smile. 'Think nothing of it. Actually, no, I can't claim to have been questioned by the police about a murder before. It's not a pleasant experience.'

'And not one you'd forget,' said Thea's mother softly. But soft or not, the comment effectively put a stop to the conversation.

'Let's have some tea and then go for a walk,' said Thea a few minutes later. 'We can go and look at Sudeley House from the outside. There are some lovely old trees. And we can't just hang about here. There's nothing to do.'

The TV camera caught them totally unawares. They emerged onto Vineyard Street and turned left, before realising that filming was taking place. Assuming it would not concern her, Thea led her visitors towards the park, before finding herself in the camera's line of fire, as it slowly panned across the allotments and the Thistledown acres. Instinctively she shrank from it. When it passed she breathed a sigh of relief and continued on in the original direction. But then, a minute later, after a brief consultation between the cameraman and a person with a clipboard, it began the same process again, starting with the barely visible roof of Thistledown, and drawing back to include the foreground, then the road, and finally the people in it. This time, Thea bent down to fiddle needlessly with her dog's collar, hoping to keep her face averted. But she stood up too soon, and once more found herself staring down the barrel of a large lens.

Chapter Ten

Oliver Meadows had begged for a police safe house. 'Witness protection,' he said. 'I need to feel safe.' He looked out at the busy London street and shuddered. 'I never feel safe in London.'

The reaction had not been favourable. 'I don't think the situation calls for that, sir,' said the liaison officer he had been allocated. 'We're not dealing with drug barons, after all.' *And besides, aren't you just an old nonentity, who nobody's going to care about enough to offer any threat?* was the subtext.

'But my testimony is going to ruin a man's lifelong reputation. A pillar of the community, almost literally. He won't take it quietly.'

'Indeed not, sir. But don't you think that if he was going to attack you, he'd have done it before now? Just get yourself a little room in an anonymous hotel – one of those near Paddington would be ideal – and nobody's going to find you.'

Oliver could see the sense in this, but the tariff of seventy pounds a night gave him pause. Nobody had mentioned anything about covering his expenses. He had volunteered himself as a witness almost a year earlier, and assumed this meant he'd have to pay his own way. The trial could last for two weeks, he had been told – possibly more if there were absences and delays, as very often happened in the legal system. He might be asked to remain within call for much of that time. He pined for his birds and the fresh country air. London gave him a headache. On arrival at Paddington the previous afternoon, he had booked himself into a hotel chosen at random in Norfolk Square, telling nobody at all of his whereabouts. He would hole up until Monday morning, using the time to steady his nerve.

It was Sunday afternoon, and he was due to present himself the following day. The trial had been going for three days already, with tedious introductory detail that he had not been permitted to attend. His input would be significant, but not exclusively so. There were others, of all ages, finally finding the courage to speak out. It was by far the most terrifying experience of his quiet reclusive life – that is, since the original crime against him, sixty years before.

The hotel room was very small, designed for the use of tourists who would be out all day seeing the sights. It had a bed, table, mirror, wardrobe, television and minute shower room. His suit was hanging on the rail in the wardrobe and a carrier bag of food sat on the table. He had been to the Marks & Spencer in the Paddington Station complex and bought a pork pie, two apples, mixed salad, a carton of milk and a bottle of wine. He could make tea and coffee with the tiny paper packets provided by the hotel. In the morning they would give him as big a breakfast as he could eat for no extra charge.

He turned on the television, braced for it failing to work. The night before, it had flickered and faded unbearably, the colour turning to monochrome at sporadic intervals. But today it seemed to have recovered, and he anticipated a soothing episode of *Countryfile* with something approaching satisfaction.

He was early. They were showing the news. The news was reporting a murder in a small town in Gloucestershire called Winchcombe. A murder of sufficient interest to find a slot on the national news, on a quiet September Sunday, it seemed. He watched with a sense of totally detached disbelief as his own front gate appeared on the screen, followed by the woman he'd employed to feed his birds. He knew it was her – he recognised the dog, as final confirmation. He had been worrying about that dog.

He also recognised his brother Fraser, at which point his detachment turned to extreme rage. He had taken consolation from the idea that he could keep his Winchcombe life quite separate from the sordid events in London. Now, it seemed, they were set to collide, thanks to his blundering brother. He should have known better, he thought furiously, than to agree to a house-sitter already known to Fraser.

The whole country, it seemed, had been watching the news that evening. The sheer caprice of it annoyed Thea the most. Some arbitrary decision by a television editor had turned what would normally have been a fleeting local story into a national headline. The fact that the victim was a pretty young woman made all the difference, of course. Thea already knew the consequences of a child being murdered and had no illusions as to the persistent power of the press, but this came as a surprise.

The stroll around Sudeley Park had taken just over an hour, spent arguing over tree identification and letting Hepzie run loose. Somewhat to Thea's amusement, her mother had collected a pocketful of conkers from beneath a huge chestnut tree. 'They're for Noel,' she said defensively.

'I don't think they let them play conkers any more,' Thea said.

'Maybe not, but he can plant them and grow new trees, can't he? That's what he does. He's got a proper little copse established already, didn't you know?'

'Has he? Where?' Her sister's garden was modest in size, and her five children had ensured that nothing but the most robustly prickly plants would grow in it.

'He keeps it a secret. It's common land, apparently. He gets them started in pots and then puts them in the open ground. According to Jocelyn, he's got an amazing success rate. Noel is an amazing child,' the fond grandmother added happily.

'You're not supposed to have favourites,' Thea said sternly.

'Too late. As the youngest of six grandsons, I think it's permissible, anyway. He's liable to get lost in the crowd.'

There was little that Thea could say to this. In truth, young Noel was her own favourite of all the nephews and nieces, as well. Carl had similarly favoured him. 'If we could order one like him, I'd be tempted to have a try,' he said, with a wary smile. He had accepted that it was for Thea to decide on the size of their family, but sometimes he let slip his hope that one day it might swell to two children, rather than one.

'Me too,' she'd replied lightly. 'But we'd just get a bad-tempered girl who wanted everything in her life to be pink.'

'That would indeed be dreadful,' her husband had laughed.

Conversation on the walk was fragmented and inconsequential. Fraser strolled slightly apart, hands clasped behind his back, eyes mostly on the ground in front of him. He seemed neither cheerful nor miserable, but content to let events swirl around him, without any active involvement on his part. The fact of a large park practically on the doorstep gave Thea a sense of obligation. Whatever happened, she ought to make the effort to enjoy it. The towering trees, with the edges of some leaves crimped with the first signs of autumn, had clearly been there for at least a century. The general layout was reminiscent of even earlier times – she had read that there had been a deer park around the castle since at least the fourteen hundreds. The usual complicated history of destruction and rebuilding made it impossible to pin down precise dates, but she could very well imagine Jane Austen's contemporaries taking the air on these very swards of well-kept grass, pausing on the same stone bridges for brief flirtations.

Queen Elizabeth I had visited, even earlier. Then it had come to grief during the Civil War and languished until Victoria's time. All this Thea dredged from her sporadic researches into the history of the Cotswolds, finding scraps of knowledge she had scarcely known she possessed. Whatever fate had befallen the castle, it seemed clear that the park had survived, if much diminished in size. The familiar sense of continuity struck her – the idea that human feet had walked the same spot for more than a thousand years. The fact that those feet might have belonged to Good Queen Bess, and other monumental figures, gave her a frisson of excitement.

'Can't we see the castle properly?' her mother asked.

'Apparently not. Just the roof, I think. There's a wall round it. You have to book a tour if you want to see inside. I think it's only weekends.'

'Today is Sunday,' her mother reminded her. 'Can't we give it a try?'

'Feel free,' Thea said. 'But they won't allow dogs. I'm not really in the mood for it, to be honest.'

'You have to book in advance,' said Fraser, with authority. 'They call it a connoisseur's day, or some such thing. I'm with Thea. We can come back some other time.'

Maureen shrugged and accepted defeat. They walked on, past even bigger and more exotic trees. By the end of an hour, Thea could see that her mother was limping slightly, one knee starting to ache. Various friends had mentioned the possibility of a replacement joint, which filled Maureen with horror. 'It's nothing like bad enough for that,' she protested, and made every effort to conceal the inexorable degeneration of the bones. When she bent to collect the conkers, she did it from the hip, making an angular figure, feet apart and the effort of straightening considerable. Thea could hardly bear to watch.

When they got back, her phone had accumulated four missed calls, all of them from more or less predictable people. The realisation that she had already appeared on television and been recognised came as a shock. The callers all said it was their reason for phoning. They were, in order, her friend Celia in Witney, from whom she had drifted away in the past few years; her brother-in-law James, from whom she had also felt very distant recently; her daughter Jessica, who never watched television, but had happened to be at a friend's flat when it was on; and her sister Jocelyn. Against her inclination, she called them all back to assure them she was fine, that the police had finished their questions, and she would remain in Winchcombe for at least another week.

One person had not phoned: a person she knew watched a lot of television with his children, who would recognise her from the most fleeting glimpse. There was no message from Drew Slocombe.

Oliver's landline was busy, too. It rang five minutes after they got back to the house. Unsure of the protocol as to who should answer it, Thea left it to Fraser, who seemed unsurprisingly reluctant. 'This is a nightmare,' he groaned. 'What am I supposed to say?'

In the event, he had no difficulty. 'Oh . . . Mo,' he said. 'Yes, I'm afraid so . . . What? For heaven's sake, don't even think of it. There's no space here for you to stay.' He cast a wild look at Thea, who tried to retain a neutral expression. 'Well, if you must but there's absolutely no need . . . That would be better, I suppose . . . What does it have to do with him, anyway? He doesn't even *know* Oliver . . . Yes,

yes, I know you are. You're very kind, dear. I'm sure you're awfully busy . . .' The conversation tailed off into monosyllables and he replaced the receiver. 'That was Mo. She wants to come and see for herself what's going on.'

'When?' asked Maureen. 'Not tonight, surely?'

'Fortunately not. First thing tomorrow. With Jason, God help us.'

Thea felt the familiar sensation of being at the mercy of whoever chose to call at her appointed house-sit. She was a captive, forced to remain at her station and endure whoever might come and harangue her. There was, however, more than a flicker of curiosity about this Mo, this child of a Spanish mother who had been named for Maureen Callaghan, as her own mother had once been called.

But before she could worry about the next day's intrusions, there was a knock on the front door that gave her good reason to concentrate on the day in hand.

Chapter Eleven

Two people and a smiling young dog stood there. The golden retriever and its people, she realised. The man was much the same as he had been in the pub garden: insincere smile, calculating eyes. The woman's hair was all Thea could recognise of her. The dog seemed much as before. 'Hello,' said the man. 'Reuben Hardy – remember? And this is my wife, Jenny.'

'What can I do for you?'

'We've just caught up with what's been going on, probably the last people in the Cotswolds to realise. We're *horrified*, quite honestly. We came to see if we can offer any help, in any way. I mean – we only live two hundred yards away. We feel *involved*.'

'It's a bit more than that, Reu,' his wife corrected him. 'We're in the silk mill building, actually,' she addressed Thea. 'I don't know whether you've seen it?'

'I don't think so,' said Thea, still resisting any pressure to admit them into the house. 'I was intending to explore properly today. Only—'

'Of *course*,' gushed Reuben, and Thea began to wonder whether he might be a minister of religion or something of the sort. He had the same unusual delivery and assumption of a kind of entitlement. 'We *do* understand.'

'I don't expect you do,' came Thea's mother's voice from behind her. 'It has been a long day for us all, and we were hoping for a quiet evening. Exactly what you think you can do is a mystery to me – especially as you appear to have a dog with you.' The animal was rubbing noses with Hepzie, amidst a lot of tail-wagging and sideways jumps. It was distracting, to say the least. Thea gave her mother a long admiring look. Plainly encouraged, the older woman continued, 'The police have everything under control, and I'm sure you understand that we have been strongly discouraged from gossiping with anybody about the details of the terrible tragedy.' She was improvising magnificently, since she had not exchanged a single word with a police officer, as far as Thea could recall.

'Yes, I'm sure that's so, but you must be feeling very much under siege. And being strange to the area, and so forth . . .' The man was babbling, and Thea began to wonder about his sanity.

'We were settling down to a quiet evening, hoping not to be disturbed,' her mother repeated relentlessly. 'There's nothing we need to know about the area, thank you.'

At least we haven't let them in, Thea thought grimly. Once inside, she doubted they would ever leave. There was something very unsettling about them, with the woman at her husband's shoulder, as if urging him on. Thea took a deep breath and took over from her mother. 'This is ridiculous,' she said. 'You haven't explained why you're here, you ignore our requests for privacy. What do you *want*, exactly?'

'We want you to know how vulnerable you are,' said Reuben earnestly. 'We were *worried* about you. That girl must have thought she'd be perfectly safe walking through the woods, when all the time . . .' He swallowed painfully, and his eyes seemed to sink back into his head.

Behind him, his wife nodded agreement. 'The poor thing,' she said. 'Poor innocent creature. Just minding her own business.'

'Well . . .' Thea struggled to voice her unease at this assessment. 'We don't really know, do we?' she finished feebly.

'Know what?' The question was uttered with wide-open eyes and a slight smile.

'What she was doing in the woods. Where she was going. Who she was meeting.'

'Was she meeting somebody, do you think?' Jenny had somehow taken over from her husband, stepping forward into the light, while he faded out of it.

'She said she was, yes.' Thea felt tricked into revealing something she should not have done. 'At least, I think she did. I only met her for a few minutes.'

'Of course, there are evil people everywhere. That's what we wanted to come and say to you. You have to be careful. Whoever killed that poor girl Melissa might still be out there, waiting to do it again. He's probably mentally ill.'

'Well . . .' Thea floundered even more deeply. 'I don't think that's very likely,' she managed.

'We're worried about you,' said Reuben softly. 'That's why we came.' His manner seemed to have changed slightly, from the brashly grinning person he had been to a more nervous individual. 'It's a terribly shocking thing, after all,' he added.

'Yes,' endorsed his wife. The puppy, which had been sitting watching Hepzie, suddenly jumped up and pawed at its mistress. 'Oh, Blodwen, all right. You've been a good dog,' she said, laying a loving hand on the animal's head. 'A very good dog.'

Reuben seemed to sigh, and Thea wondered whether the animal might have replaced him in Jenny's affections. It wouldn't be very surprising, if so, she concluded wryly.

Could it be true that the couple really did have their welfare at heart? Were she and her mother being outrageously churlish in their reactions? She looked back into the house for Fraser. As the closest person to the owner of the house, he had a right to be heard. But he was nowhere to be seen.

'It's kind of you to come,' she told Reuben. 'But honestly, we'll be perfectly all right.'

'Let me give you our numbers,' he said. 'I've written them down, look.' He proffered a piece of paper with three telephone numbers on it. 'Landline, and both our mobiles,' he explained.

Thea took them automatically.

'I expect we seem a bit pushy to you,' said Jenny. 'The thing is, we've recently taken over the Neighbourhood

Watch – chair and secretary – and we want it to have some bite. If we can't take a serious role when there's been a murder, what use are we? That's all it is. Obviously, we've never been faced with a situation like this before and we're probably doing it very badly. But we honestly do feel worried about you.'

It was a seductive speech and Thea for one was seduced. 'Oh, gosh,' she breathed. 'Now I understand. I'm sorry we were so frosty.'

'Think nothing of it. You must be terribly shocked and confused. I mean – just who *was* the woman who got herself killed? That's what everybody's asking.'

'I'm sure they are. Now if you'll excuse us . . .' Thea's mother took control and began to close the door. The Hardys stepped back uncertainly, and Thea called a final 'Goodbye and thank you' and they disappeared from view.

'Mother! Weren't you rather hard on them?' she hissed.

'Hard on the Hardys? Possibly. But I don't trust them – do you? They wanted something, and I don't see why we should give it to them. As far as I can see, they're just ghouls, wanting to hear all the dirty details. That Neighbourhood Watch nonsense was just a fabrication, I bet you.'

'It did come as a bit of an afterthought,' Thea said slowly, disliking the implication that her mother was a substantially better judge of character than she was herself. 'He was pretty obnoxious at the pub, wasn't he?'

'Exactly. You seemed to forget that.'

'I did,' Thea admitted. 'But I liked her yesterday in the park. She was perfectly friendly. And that was before there was any hint of a murder.'

'Oh well, they've gone now. Where's Fraser? What's he doing?'

Fraser was in the back room, looking confused. 'Why does it seem so empty?' he asked Thea. 'There was more in here.'

'The murdered girl's boxes,' she said readily. 'The police have taken them all. There's a good chance they'll find something to identify her. I shouldn't wonder if they know just who she is by now.'

'Was,' he corrected huskily. 'Poor girl.'

'Right. Plus they probably have the whole attack captured on film, so they'll know at least what her killer looks like. And then they'll find her car, which will tell them a lot more about her.'

'Let's hope so.' The old man sighed and drifted back into the main living room. 'What a dreadful day it's been.'

'I suppose Reuben's right there, at least. We are all suffering from delayed shock, I expect. We should go to bed early and see if everything's better in the morning.'

'Bed?' He looked at his watch. 'It's only seven o'clock!'

'I didn't mean *now*. We have to have some supper first. I can make something with the bits and pieces there are here. We could open a tin of soup or beans and add some eggs and potatoes. But I suggest we disconnect the phone and see if we can get a decent sleep.'

'Thea!' gasped her horrified mother. 'We can't do that! What if something important happens? You can't just disable the phone.'

'We've got mobiles. You can leave yours by the bed, if you like.'

Bed! They still hadn't settled where everyone was to sleep. Thea felt weak at the prospect of reorganising all the rooms. 'Um . . .' she began. 'Fraser – I don't think that bed in the third room is going to be useable, is it?'

'What?' He frowned at her in bewilderment.

'Sleeping arrangements,' she said. 'How are we going to work it? Who's having Oliver's room?'

'Maureen is. The sofa turns into a bed. I'll have that. I'll get up early and put it all back before either of you are up.'

'Oh. Right.' She felt foolish for worrying when there was such a simple solution. 'Thanks.'

'Mo's coming in the morning,' he reminded her. 'I'm not sure that's anything to look forward to. She can be rather hard work, I warn you.'

'Not to mention Jason,' Thea laughed. 'I know it's awful of me, but I can't help visualising a truck driver or bricklayer, with a name like that.'

'You're not far wrong. He runs a caravan park in the Chilterns. He's decent enough, from what I can make out. I've only met him a few times. But he's what they call a rough diamond, all the same. All those faceless people coming and going, up to God knows what – it's a strange way to make a living.'

'And things are a bit turbulent in the Chilterns these days,' Thea remembered. 'With that stupid new railway going through.'

'Stupid? Is that what you think?'

'Of course. Don't get me started. I haven't heard a single credible argument in its favour.'

Fraser put up his hands. 'Let's not squabble over

that,' he begged. 'Although I'm not sure Jason would share your views.'

'I suppose he thinks he can provide accommodation for the navvies who build the thing,' she said sourly. 'Short-term profit and long-term devastation.'

'Something like that,' agreed Fraser mildly. He glanced again at the empty room with a little frown. 'It's what they've been saying about the Pilbara for a while now. I must admit, they have made a pretty fine mess of it.'

His work in Australia, she remembered, thinking how very far away and irrelevant it must seem to him now.

Thoughts of supper were the next preoccupation, and Thea constructed an acceptable meal from available provisions. Fraser went out to his car and returned with a bottle of red wine. 'The police are out there again,' he reported. 'Checking the cars, I imagine.'

'And door-to-door enquiries,' said Thea knowingly. 'Now that people are back from their days out.'

Her mother shivered. 'It's very horrible, isn't it? All that police business going on out there, without us knowing about it.'

'That isn't what's horrible,' Thea disagreed. 'What's horrible is that somebody is dead when they shouldn't be. Although when you think about it, there are all kinds of ordinary little killings happening all the time.'

'Ordinary killings?' Fraser repeated. 'What do you mean by that?'

'Oh – don't you ever think about all those animals out there, getting on with their lives regardless of us? Foxes, birds, rats, even cats – all busily fighting and breeding and hunting, while we remain completely ignorant of what's happening.'

'You sound like my brother,' he said.

'You mean with his birds? That's why he sets the camera going. So he can know something of what they do when there's nobody watching. I can well understand how fascinating that must be.'

'His fascination starts and ends with the birds. My brother prides himself on his ignorance. He has no desire to involve himself in anything beyond his four walls – apart from the birds. The birds are safe, you see. And I suppose everybody has to take an interest in *something*.'

Thea concentrated on the food for a few moments, trying not to think about anything else. But when the silence became too much, she burst out, 'Safe? Your brother needs to feel safe, does he?'

Fraser shrugged. 'Doesn't everybody?'

'Not the way you seemed to mean it, just then. As if he's usually frightened.' She thought about the man she had met so briefly. Had he seemed timid or nervous? She found it impossible to judge. 'And why won't you tell us where he is?' she demanded again. 'What's all the mystery?'

'He asked me not to. Besides, I honestly don't know where he is at this precise moment. I do know where he'll be tomorrow, and I told the police where that is. If you don't mind my saying so, I think that's all I'm required to do.'

'He's right, Thea. You shouldn't be so curious. It isn't your business,' said her mother, not especially gently.

Thea took it graciously. 'You're right, of course. I'm just a nosy cow. Everybody says so,' she laughed. But there were two burningly inescapable questions at the forefront of her mind:

Who was waiting for Melissa in the pub, the previous evening? And what was on that memory stick?

Chapter Twelve

When the doorbell rang at eight-forty on Monday morning, Thea's first thought was that Mo and Jason were disgracefully early. Fortunately she had been up and dressed for over an hour, worrying about Oliver's birds and a number of other things. Fraser had been as good as his word, and risen at seven, restoring the sofa to its original state. When Thea went into the kitchen, it was because she'd been enticed by the smell of coffee that had filtered up to her room at seven-thirty.

She pulled the front door open with every intention of being less than welcoming.

'Not too early for you, am I?' breezed Gladwin. 'I didn't think I would be.'

The senior police detective stood there like a waif, thin and tired, her clothes rumpled and an angry pimple on her chin. Thea knew she had two boys at home, who saw far too little of her, and a husband who seemed to be some sort of ghostly saint. Thea had never seen him, but was aware that he provided the energy and support that made everything possible.

'You take too much for granted,' Thea told her. 'I might have been in my dressing gown.'

'Come for a little walk with me,' Gladwin instructed. 'We have things to discuss.'

'Can I bring the dog?'

'If you must.'

It was cloudy outside, but reasonably warm. The detective led the way out into Vineyard Street and turned right. 'We're going into town?' Thea asked. 'Is that wise?'

'I want to show you something. It'll take us twenty minutes or so.'

Thea had a sense of being generously included in an investigation that she had no official claim to be involved in. She was simply the person who had found the body; traditionally, such a role was given very little status. But Thea's connections with the police did not adhere to tradition. From the start, she had been privy to more than the general public ever were. Her husband's brother was a senior police officer; her daughter was a police probationer. And she had found herself in the midst of a number of violent deaths over the past two years. 'Must be important if you can spare so much time for it,' she said.

'I'm engaging you as an expert witness,' Gladwin said, semi-seriously. 'Another eye on the matter. Keep that dog close to you – I don't want it causing any distractions.'

That dog was a bit wounding. Gladwin was good with animals, Thea had discovered, but had never entirely warmed to Hepzibah. Such a failing was inexplicable.

They turned right at the junction and walked along the

section of the main street known as Abbey Terrace, with Thea making a few remarks about the long-demolished abbey that had dominated the town. Gladwin hardly replied, but kept up a brisk pace in an easterly direction. Before long, the shops had finished and small terraced houses took their place. 'It does have a certain symmetry,' Thea remarked.

'What?'

'Winchcombe. We walked along the street, the other way, yesterday. Cheltenham Road. All the houses are different. And it's the same this way. Have you noticed? It must have been deliberate. It's almost against nature, when you think about it. It would have been far easier to just build a terrace of identical two-up-two-down like most places. Think of the Welsh valleys, with those rows and rows of miners' cottages, all exactly the same.'

'Mm,' said Gladwin.

'Come on,' Thea urged her. 'It's . . .'

'Gorgeous. Yes. It's history right here in front of us. That's a Tudor house, and two doors down there's a Georgian one. Yes, Thea, it's amazing. It makes you wonder who built them all, and how it was decided and planned.'

'Yes.' Thea was admiring the black and white house that Gladwin had identified as Tudor. It had an overhanging upper floor, with three handsome windows, making it one of the biggest houses in the street. An incongruous-looking bay window protruded at one end of the ground floor. 'I bet it's fabulous inside.'

'That's the first satellite dish I've seen,' Thea pointed

a bit further down the street. 'I thought they must have been banned.'

'They'll all be at the back,' said Gladwin. 'Where nobody can see them.'

'I must be getting old,' Thea sighed. 'Because I actually think that's rather a good idea.'

'Come on, we haven't got time for this. It's along here somewhere,' Gladwin urged.

'What is?'

'There's an alleyway, apparently. It leads down to Silk Mill Lane, and from there you can get onto the path that goes down to the woods where you found the dead girl.'

'And why are we interested?' Thea was panting slightly, with the effort of keeping pace with Gladwin's long legs.

'No real reason. It's just . . . a hunch, I guess. Aha! Here it is.'

The alleyway's entrance was a closed-in tunnel between two houses, the path itself sloping quite steeply downwards. 'Murder Alley,' said Gladwin.

'What?'

'I'm told there was a murder here a century ago. More than a century, actually. Rather a good spot on a dark night. Jack the Ripper territory.'

Thea tried to imagine it. The alley did feel deserted, with no windows overlooking it, high blank walls on both sides. Possibly nobody would hear you scream. 'So?' she asked, in puzzlement.

'Nothing specific. It's a short cut, from the town to the river. It's marked on the map in the main street. We've found some evidence that whoever killed that girl headed this way afterwards. It's a bit dubious, now we know that horse woman uses the path regularly, but it makes sense. If you turn right here, you get back to the high street and that big White Hart Inn on the corner. I'm wondering if the person waiting at the pub might have been in there, rather than the Plaisterers Arms.'

'Which might explain why she headed through the woods and not back up Vineyard Street.'

'Right. And then she'd come out into this road, look.' Gladwin pointed to the end of Silk Mill Lane, where it met Castle Street. 'There's even a way down to the river just here, so you could creep through the undergrowth and hop up here with virtually no risk of being seen. It's all completely speculative, of course. But it does explain one or two puzzles.'

'Small ones,' Thea was bold enough to remark with some scepticism. 'I don't really see how this is helpful. What about the camera in the hide? The memory stick? The contents of those boxes? Haven't they helped at all?'

'The camera ran out of battery at six twenty-seven on Saturday afternoon. By that time nothing interesting had happened. The memory stick has disappeared, and the boxes only contain clothes and jewellery. There's a teenage diary, which is full of references to people called Tony and Sally and Jax, but no mention of the school they went to, or any surnames.'

'Did you find her car? It must be here somewhere, surely?'

'Seems not. Every single one has been accounted for, in an area of half a mile. It was an interesting exercise, actually. Took three constables twelve hours to track them all down, even with it all on computer, but they did it. One or two people took exception to being phoned at midnight to be asked if they owned a blue Suburu parked ten miles from where they lived. But they all had good explanations.'

'So she and the person in the pub must have come here together, and he drove away again. Which implies that it was him that killed her. That's most likely, isn't it?'

'On the face of it, yes. Nobody in either of the pubs can come up with a credible individual, sitting alone at about seven o'clock on Saturday.'

'So she made it up? She lied to me?'

'We know that already. She wasn't Fraser Meadows' daughter, for a start.'

'Mm.' Thea's thoughts were circling unproductively. 'What did you think of him? Fraser, I mean.'

'Slightly too good to be true, maybe. Presented as very eager to help, but was depressingly short of facts. He didn't seem to know anything about his brother's life these days. They almost never see each other.'

'And he doesn't know why a young woman should leave her possessions at his brother's house?'

'He did go a bit thoughtful about that, but said he really had no information to offer.'

'He told me he knows where Oliver is, but he's not allowed to say. Did you ask him that?'

'He asked to be excused from that particular question. We didn't press it, for now.'

'You think he was holding something back?'

'It's possible.' Gladwin shrugged. 'It can take two or three attempts to persuade people that we really do want to hear the whole story. And I'm not sure I entirely get what's going on with him and your mum. They knew each other – what? – fifty years ago? Seems a bit of a stretch to think they'd get along after all this time.'

'It's extremely weird,' Thea burst out, only then realising that this was her primary anxiety, and had been for nearly a week. 'I'm not sure she entirely believes it's really him.'

'Really?' The police detective's expression changed to maximum alertness. 'Can't he prove it to her somehow?'

'She scarcely remembers anything. A clever man could persuade her, I imagine.'

'And why would he? What's he after?'

'Her house, probably. She's got rather a nice house and he's homeless.'

'It must be possible to check.'

'DNA,' Thea suggested, with a wry grin. 'Isn't that the answer to everything these days?'

'It's very overrated. Useless unless you have something to compare it with.'

'You took a sample from him, though. Are you planning to compare it with the dead woman?'

'Eventually we might have to. He went very tense when I asked for it. But a lot of people do. They instinctively dislike it.'

'Obviously,' said Thea, knowing there was no need for her usual rant about personal privacy. Gladwin had heard it already.

'It's horrible when you don't know who the victim is,' Gladwin complained. 'Not just because it thwarts any effective investigation, but you can't tell the family, who just think everything's fine, when it isn't.'

'Unless they did it.'

'Cynic. They'd call her Jane Doe, in America. Any unidentified female is a Jane Doe. It hasn't caught on here, for some reason.'

'Too glib?' Thea suggested.

'No, not really. It's rather nice, in a way.'

'I didn't much like her,' Thea said softly.

'I know. You said. But you didn't kill her. We've been over that already. It doesn't matter, does it? You only saw her for ten minutes.'

'But you didn't see her at all, and you care more about what happened to her than I do. What does that make me?'

'Normal,' Gladwin shrugged. 'You probably do care more than you think, anyway. You look pretty miserable to me.'

'Do I?' Thea sighed. 'I wasn't too happy before all this, actually. It hasn't been a very pleasant summer, on the whole. In fact, it's been bloody horrible since Easter.'

'You've had some grim experiences, I know,' Gladwin sympathised. 'You should probably have stuck with Phil Hollis. Everybody thinks so.'

Everybody was the team of Gloucestershire police detectives, Thea presumed. Hollis was another detective superintendent, who had been her lover or boyfriend or significant other for a year or so. It had ended quite badly, and he now had a new partner. And Thea had almost forgotten about him.

'Everybody's wrong,' she said. 'He didn't bring out the best in me.' *And Drew Slocombe does*, she silently added. She knew with absolute certainty that she would never treat Drew as badly as she'd treated Phil Hollis.

They were standing in Silk Mill Lane, speaking in low voices, the dog patiently waiting for further progress. Gladwin waved aside the tribulations of human relationships and pointed the way over the river and back to the Thistledown acres, through a rickety-looking gate that led to the eastern edge of the allotments. 'Or, as I say, you could follow the Windrush Way for a bit and then cross the river. It's passable when the water's low.'

'Do we have to wade across it?' Thea was concerned for her shoes. 'Is that part of this odd little walk?'

'No, no. What's odd about it? I just wanted to have a look round and chat with you at the same time. We can go back through the woods.'

'Hang on a minute.' Thea looked up Castle Street, where a tall house stood close to the road. Behind and above it loomed a substantial chapel. 'Isn't that lovely! So much character! I wonder what its story is.'

'Go to the museum and ask, why don't you?'

'I just might do that.'

'The woman we met yesterday lives here, doesn't she?'

'Priscilla Heap,' Thea remembered. 'I suppose she does. I wonder which house it is.'

'She gave me the name. Something Cottage. That isn't a cottage, is it?'

'A "House",' judged Thea. 'Definitely a "House".'

They walked down the hill, passing a tiny dwelling entitled the Coach House, which Thea privately thought added substantially to her abiding impression of Winchcombe as a place created by magic and existing in some kind of alternative fairy-tale reality. Even the rickety gate that led into the allotments carried a suggestion of ageless mystery to her overactive imagination.

They found the route into Oliver's woodlands, where Gladwin pointed out signs of recent use. 'It's like a Western,' Thea laughed. 'Looking for bent grasses and snapped twigs. We need an Indian tracker.'

'It's very much like that,' Gladwin agreed. 'But it doesn't actually get us very far. I expect you could have done some of this yourself.'

'Me?'

'Didn't Oliver bring you out here on Saturday?'

Thea looked behind her, seeing the view from a different angle. 'Not quite this far, but he did show me this clearing, from over there.' She pointed to where she thought the bird hide must be. 'I think,' she added feebly. 'Are we on his land now?'

'Apparently so. It goes right to this fence.'

'Yes, that must be right. He keeps this part clear for birds that like grasses and meadow flowers. I imagine he comes out here with his camera sometimes, even though there's no hide.'

'There's a sort of flattened area, with marks that

140

suggest a tripod, so I imagine that's exactly what he does.'

'Can I feed his birds again yet?' She had abandoned her responsibilities all too readily, she felt. If she was to stay there all week, and perhaps beyond, she ought to try to get things back to how they had been. 'Is the hide still taped off?'

'Yes it is, but you're free to put stuff out for them, on that feeding station thing. That's the trouble with feeding wild birds – they get to rely on you, and you really shouldn't stop.'

'Even at this time of year, when there must be loads of stuff out there for them?'

'As I understand it, yes. Besides, a lot of the seeds and berries are almost finished now. It's July and August when the real bounty happens. I'm no expert, but I think they'll be feeling the lack of your fat balls and stuff.'

'So I can't go into the hide, but I can go to the feeding station?' Thea clarified.

'Right.' Gladwin patted Thea lightly on the shoulder. 'Now, what are we going to do about your mother?'

Thea was silenced by this abrupt change of subject. She opened her mouth and closed it again. Did the police believe her mother was a suspect? How was that possible. 'Er . . .' she managed.

'I mean, with this mystery man from the past. She's got to establish beyond doubt that he is who he says he is. There must be some way to do that.'

'Are you offering to help?'

'I might be. When all this is over.'

'But you don't think there's a connection?'

'There's the same connection that we've encountered before,' sighed the police detective.

'Oh?'

'You, Thea Osborne. Once again, the connection is *you*.'

Chapter Thirteen

Mo and Jason were only slightly early, arriving at ten, which meant that Thea had nearly an hour with her mother and Fraser, in which they talked awkwardly about trivial matters. Thea asked Fraser to describe more of his years in London before going to Australia, in a vague attempt to establish his credentials. He answered cordially, explaining that he had become a land surveyor, scoping out likely routes for new roads and railways, operating such equipment as theodolites and mastering advanced geometry. He had married Domenica, who came from Toledo, after knowing her for only three months. She was fiery and adventurous and wanted to see the world. Going to Australia had been her idea. Mo had been three when they set sail in classic migrant fashion, and another baby was on the way. 'It miscarried on the ship,' he said briefly. 'It was really dreadful for poor Nica. She took years to get over it.'

'And you never had any more?'

'We never did,' he smiled sadly.

On the face of it, he was being open and frank, answering

the questions in a relaxed easy manner. Only when she thought about it did Thea spot the gaps. Where exactly had he worked? Where had he grown up? She tried to flesh out the picture. 'Do you remember the war?' she asked. 'You must have been about five when it started.'

'I was exactly five years and one month,' he responded. 'And I was just shy of eleven when it ended. I remember it very vividly, of course. I'm sure your mother does as well.'

'Were you in London all the way through?'

His expression hardened slightly. 'Oliver and I were evacuated for a few months, but we both behaved so abominably that they sent us back. My mother was even more traumatised by it than we were, I think, looking back now. Even those few months disrupted our family so violently that we were permanently changed by it. Oliver more than me, I believe. He felt she had deliberately betrayed us, and I think he held it against her for the rest of her life.'

'That's tragic!' Thea exclaimed with genuine distress. 'People do such terrible things to each other, don't they? In the name of the greater good, and all that.'

'It was certainly well intentioned,' he nodded. 'And life in the Blitz had its own ghastly consequences. We saw things that small boys ought not to have seen. The worst thing, actually, was the dog.' He gave Thea's spaniel a look, as if being deliberately reminded of something dreadful.

'Dog?' Thea encouraged reluctantly.

'It was the domestic pet variation on evacuation, in a way. They had them put down, in case there was an invasion and the Germans tortured them. That was what my mother said, anyway. We had a golden spaniel called Spike. My brother adored that dog – you know how boys can be about their pets.'

'So she really *did* betray you,' Thea summarised furiously. 'How could a mother do such a thing?'

'As you said – she thought it was all for the good. She thought that was what she had to do. People will do the most appalling things for the most flimsy of reasons. They're very suggestible.'

'Stupid, I call it,' said Thea flatly. 'Just plain stupid.'

Fraser Meadows showed signs of exasperation. 'You can't judge if you weren't there,' he said. 'That isn't fair.' Then he brightened. 'But it was different for your mother. She was living in leafy Oxfordshire and never heard a bomb.'

'Not entirely true,' corrected Maureen. 'We saw a lot of bomber planes, and one or two let their bombs drop not far from us. Nobody seemed very worried about it, though.' Her eyes glazed as she relived those distant days. Seventy years ago, Thea calculated, near enough. To her it was like a completely different world. With different ideas of right and wrong, she suspected, as Fraser had implied when telling her about poor Spike.

The conversation had strengthened her appreciation of her mother's dilemma. Fraser Meadows was almost entirely credible. But then conmen always *were* credible. That was the whole point. They had a knack of making you like and trust them. Fraser was sometimes obviously trying hard to be nice, but at other times he seemed to be genuinely relaxed and spontaneous. There was no hint of calculation in his eyes. He seemed concerned for her mother's well-being, and mildly embarrassed by his lifelong fondness for her. But as acting parts went, it had to be a relatively easy one to play. A few basic background details, which Maureen had almost certainly given away on Facebook or Friends Reunited, careful listening as she chatted about family, and one or two inspired guesses, and he could easily be convincing. Bodies changed dramatically over a lifetime, after all. Accents, even mannerisms, modified. And if he was fooling Maureen Johnstone, he must surely be fooling Oliver Meadows, and his own daughter, as well. Or was Mo another impostor, sharing the deception?

'Reuben Hardy said you had a dog,' she said suddenly. 'Last time you were here, visiting Oliver. Reuben said you had a dog. Where is it now?'

'It wasn't mine.'

'So whose was it? Mo's?'

'No, no. Mo never liked dogs much. Takes after her mother in that.'

'So . . . ?'

'It's a long, irrelevant story.'

Thea felt a great desire to push it and demand every detail, but her mother repressed her with a look. It probably was, after all, irrelevant.

Mo turned out to be a faded beauty. She had silver streaks on her temples, a startling dead tooth at the front, and thick black eyebrows. The tooth was the most disconcerting feature. It was dark brown and looked alarmingly loose. It made Thea think of Albanian peasants or Moroccan crones. The woman looked as if she was about to emit a loud cackle or curse. Jason was almost equally surprising, with a pot belly and dense grey beard. As relatives – or near relatives, in Jason's case – of the very civilised Fraser, they were entirely unexpected in every respect.

But they both spoke with standard English accents, seemed impressively concerned for the welfare of all three people at Thistledown, and duly acknowledged Hepzie. The spaniel took to them immediately, and curled up at Mo's feet when she sat down on the living room couch. As far as Thea could see, the woman nursed little or no animosity towards this particular dog.

'So, who's this woman that got herself killed?' Jason demanded, within the first five minutes. 'Have they worked it out yet?'

'Not as far as we know,' Thea said cautiously. 'She told me she was Fraser's daughter.'

'Well, that's me, and I'm not dead,' said Mo, emphatically. 'No other daughters out there, eh, Dad?'

'I think I can safely say not,' he asserted. 'I thought to begin with they were telling me you'd been murdered. I didn't know what to think. I mean – I'd only seen you a day or two before.'

Mo snorted, and began a close inspection of Thea. 'So this is my stepsister-to-be,' she said cheerfully, greatly to Thea's alarm. 'Pleased to meet you.'

'Um . . .' Thea floundered, throwing her mother a pleading look, and recollecting for the first time that Melissa had made her think something very similar. 'I . . .'

Maureen forced a laugh, from the doorway. 'Not quite,'

she demurred. 'That is, nobody's said anything . . .' She took a step backwards, towards the kitchen, as if trying to escape.

Fraser coughed self-consciously. 'Steady on, Mo,' he advised. 'You're not getting rid of me that quickly.'

'Aw – shame!' grimaced the woman, with self-mocking exaggeration. 'Still, worth a try, I suppose.'

Mo, Thea reminded herself, had grown up in Australia, despite the absence of an accent. That might explain the brashness, the complete lack of shyness or hesitation. She had a loud laugh and used it often.

'I gather you've got three daughters,' she said, when the conversation flagged.

'Too right,' agreed Mo. 'For my sins.' Then she laughed. 'No, they're good girls, all of them. Never caused me any grief. Give them a few years and I'll be a granny two or three times over, I shouldn't wonder. That'll be a thing – Granny Mo.' She laughed again.

'And great-granddad Fraser,' Thea pointed out, hoping to draw him back into the centre of things. Somehow the whole exercise felt as if it centred on him; as if it was designed to explain something. The stepsister remark could have been it, perhaps. If so, it was very much not what Thea had wanted to hear.

'Yeah,' Mo muttered, as if that was hardly relevant.

Thea's mother had appointed herself maker of coffee, and she came in with a laden tray, dispensing mugs of perfectly brewed real coffee. When it was finished, which took all of a minute and a half, Jason slammed his mug back onto the tray and gave himself a little shake. 'Well, if you good people will excuse me, I'm off for a look at the railway museum they've got here.'

'Is it open on a Monday?' Thea wondered. 'They often aren't.'

'I don't mean the actual *museum*,' he corrected. 'I mean the station and trains they've got preserved, out on the Gretton road. I'll drive up there and have a look round, see what they've got. Always like to see the big old steam engines, every chance I get. Lovely things!' he sighed nostalgically. 'Wish I'd been around when they were operating.'

'I gather you're in favour of the new high-speed abomination,' Thea accused, before she could stop herself.

He visibly resisted the challenge to make it a serious argument. 'I sure am,' he said in a joke American accent. 'Have to move with the times. And the engineering's going to be a miracle. Imagine it – it'll be like flying through the countryside.' He spread his arms, and made a whooshing sound. 'It's great that trains are still going to be around, right through this century. Pity the Yanks haven't got the same idea.'

Thea was torn. Obviously trains were easier on fossil fuel consumption, and altogether less of a hassle to use than planes. But she completely failed to see much, if any, environmental benefits to a slashing new line carving up the hills and vales and woodlands of Middle England. 'I think it's horrible,' she asserted, with her usual emphasis. 'Absolutely horrible.'

'That's what they always say about new things,' he dismissed. 'After a couple of years, everyone'll wonder what the fuss was about.'

'Well, I for one still think it's never going to happen. Too many powerful people are against it.'

'We'll have to see, then, won't we?' said Jason calmly.

'I'll be dead by then, anyway,' said Fraser, as if the idea held quite an appeal for him.

The stark word brought them back to the present reality, and Thea's mother sighed. She looked at Thea. 'Presumably they still don't know who she was – you'd have told us if they did.'

Nobody pretended not to understand what she meant. Mo raised her eyebrows for a moment, but lowered them again, as if the details were unimportant.

'Thea saw the police detective in charge of the case, earlier today,' Maureen explained. 'They went off somewhere, just the two of them.' There was a thread of reproach in her tone.

'They haven't identified her yet,' Thea confirmed.

'Not even found her car?' Fraser asked.

'Nope. They worked late into the night on it, but nothing's come up.' She met his eyes, silently acknowledging that they both had to be careful. There were elements of their exchanges with Gladwin that they were not supposed to disclose – Fraser perhaps more so than Thea. The knowledge was divisive, preventing a cohesive discussion of all known facts. There was no sense of a team diligently assisting the police. Rather, they were flotsam, scrappily floating around the periphery of the investigation, waiting for light to dawn and explanations to be given.

'Well, I think you should come home with us,' Mo suddenly said to her father. 'It's not nice here, with a murder just outside. Uncle Oliver's just a crazy old hermit, living in a place like this.' She looked at Thea. 'You've been given the short straw, seems to me. What's the sense of asking somebody to come and feed birds, anyhow? Why not just close it up and go home? That's what I would do. That's what we came to tell you.'

'You don't like this place?' Thea repeated. 'But it's lovely. The town is utterly beautiful. It's *all* beautiful.'

'Can't see it myself. Seems dark and gloomy to me, with all these trees. And the people – most of them with more money than's good for them. We came past that Stow place – all antique shops and American tourists. It's not *real*.'

'Well . . .' Thea attempted. 'It's old-fashioned, I suppose, compared to the Home Counties. But you've got all that terrible traffic, ruining the towns. And so many houses everywhere. This is still so unspoilt. There's so much *space*.'

'Pity the new train can't go through here, then,' said Jason, who had yet to go and look at his steam engines. 'If there's plenty of space.'

Thea looked at him as if he'd uttered a terrible blasphemy. He laughed at her. 'Only joking,' he said. 'Even I can see the engineering would be a nightmare. There's hardly a level mile anywhere in the Cotswolds. There'd have to be about a dozen tunnels.'

'I'm not coming home with you,' Fraser told his daughter. 'Maureen and I are staying here another night, and then we'll go back to her place for a few days. We've got it all decided.'

Thea looked at her mother, who was nodding placidly. 'When was this decided?' she asked.

'Oh, all along, wasn't it? Isn't that what we said?'

'I didn't think it was definite. I understood you were only here for *one* night.'

'I'm off,' Jason announced, finally putting his words into effect, with a glance at his watch. 'I left the car in a little backstreet.'

'Oh?' Thea frowned at him.

He grinned. 'Habit,' he said. 'Had a little disagreement with the insurance people, and like to keep it inconspicuous, if I can. Not easy, with all these cameras and gadgets they've got these days. But I knew the rozzers might be hanging around, so I just took a sensible precaution.'

Thea met Fraser's eye, and remembered his 'rough diamond' remark. Jason's careless disregard for the law was both startling and oddly endearing. 'Anyway,' he went on, 'just give me a couple of hours and I'll come back in time for lunch. Are we going to the pub?' He looked brightly around at the four people, like an expectant dog waiting for its dinner.

'We went to the pub yesterday,' said Thea, daftly. Then she corrected herself. 'But there's no food here, so I suppose we'll have to. We'll probably be at the Plaisterers Arms at about one, so you don't have to rush.' The prospect gave her no pleasure at all. She found herself wishing they would all go away, including her mother.

Conversation was no easier without Jason, although they tried. 'Nice dog you've got,' said Mo, evidently touched by Hepzie's unsolicited attention.

'I gather you don't really like them,' Thea said.

'I don't mind either way. I like *some* dogs, but there are a lot of horrors out there that'd bite you as soon as look at you.'

'Your dad had a dog, apparently, last time he came here.'

Mo looked at Fraser with a little frown. 'Oh – yes! That scruffy little stray. He picked it up on the motorway, the old softie. Could easily have got himself killed in the process.'

'Really?' Thea gave Fraser a long appraisal. 'That sounds quite heroic.'

'I couldn't leave it, could I?' he defended. 'It was desperate, dashing in and out of traffic. It must have only just been dropped by someone. All I did was stop on the hard shoulder, and open the door. It came right away, as soon as I whistled. Jumped in the car and went right off to sleep.'

'And where is it now?'

'I took it to Battersea. They said they'd rehome it in no time, nice little thing like that.'

'Fraser – you never told me about that,' Maureen accused. 'How lovely of you to do such a thing.'

The old man shrugged diffidently. 'Anybody would have done it, in the same situation. I was just there at the right moment.'

The modest dignity of the story gripped Thea's heartstrings, and she found herself hoping hard that Fraser Meadows really was who he said he was.

Meanwhile, the question of exactly why Mo and Jason had come in the first place seemed no nearer a credible answer. There was an air of impatience, even in her mother. Something wasn't happening that ought to be happening, and nobody appeared to know what it was or how to expedite it. Thea resented the feeling that she was the one who was expected to establish Fraser's credentials; and that she should be finding out whether he was a safe companion for her mother. Gladwin had implied as much, only an hour or two before. Because, presumably, if he was *not*, then a whole lot of very unpleasant things were possible. Things to do with a murdered young woman and a missing memory stick and a mysteriously absent younger brother.

Chapter Fourteen

It was Mo who finally got things going, after a slow morning of increasingly desultory conversation and rather too much coffee. 'We can't stay cooped up here,' she announced. 'Let's go for a walk. We've got an hour or so before we're due to meet Jason. I know somebody who rented one of the Sudeley Cottages last year, and I'd love to have a look at them. Sounded really nice, they did. Not something Jason would appreciate, of course. They must be just here somewhere – right?'

'About two minutes' walk,' Thea confirmed. 'We can go the back way.' Only then did she remember that the back way involved walking past police tape and the scene of a very recent murder. But it was too late to change tack, and she led the group down the path, skirting the clearing with the bird hide, with minimal comment, and plunging down the barely visible track out into the bottom of Castle Street. 'It all connects up, you see,' she said. 'These ancient towns generally have alleyways and footpaths linking the major buildings and thoroughfares.'

'Like Tewkesbury,' said her mother, surprisingly. 'I love Tewkesbury.'

'Really?' Thea said. 'When have you been there?'

'We had a holiday there when Damien was a baby. Hired a cottage beside the river and spent a week exploring. It was utterly idyllic.'

'First I've heard of it,' said Thea uncomfortably. What hope was there of getting any sort of objective view of her mother's early life, when things like this could happen? Anything was possible back there in those far-off days. Something like ninety-five per cent of it had obviously been forgotten; lost without trace.

'We can go there again,' said Fraser to his long-lost girlfriend. 'Whenever you like.'

'You can see Tewkesbury from that hill, on the road past the church,' said Mo, to Thea's surprise.

'Really?' she said. 'How do you know that?'

'We were a bit early this morning, so we went out there for a look. There's a house called Tewkesbury View. It gets very high up there.'

'I know. I walked it on Saturday afternoon. All I could see was Winchcombe.'

'You need to look the other way,' laughed Mo. 'Tewkesbury's west of here.'

'For that, I'd have had to climb another hill, and I didn't have the energy.'

They found the cottages, which were indeed enchanting, if perhaps somewhat too close together for a truly peaceful and secluded holiday. Ideal, though, for a large family or collection of friends to use, taking all of them together. Thea imagined a variety of scenarios where this might happen, although only one of them fitted her personally. In that one, her brother, daughter, mother and sisters gathered together for a week over Christmas and played old-fashioned games while snow and gales swirled outside. It wouldn't work, of course – Jocelyn's five children would never fit into any of these little dwellings. And the strain on the in-laws might be excessive. When all five Johnstones gathered together, there were in-jokes and age-old stories, and childish hilarity that excluded spouses, even of twenty years' standing.

'Where now?' asked Mo, as if Thea had become the leader. Thea glanced at Fraser, wondering how much he knew of the hinterland of Winchcombe. She was still unclear as to just how closely he was connected to his brother and why he visited so infrequently.

'We could have a look at Silk Mill Lane,' she suggested hesitantly. 'There's not very much to see, but we can make it a circular walk, more or less. That's always better, don't you think?'

Mo said nothing, but appeared amenable enough. She did not strike Thea as a person who often went for walks of any sort. She scarcely looked around her, but talked of unrelated things, such as Jason's business ambitions and the terrible man her middle daughter had taken up with. She virtually ignored her father, which Thea was increasingly aware of as odd. In her experience, daughters of all ages almost always flirted with their fathers, claiming the man as her special possession. She had certainly done it with her own beloved dad, and had enjoyed seeing Jessica do it with Carl, from the age of about twenty minutes.

Opposite the turning into the lane, Thea looked again at the very handsome old house facing the street, built in the ubiquitous Cotswold stone. It felt like only a few minutes since she had been there with Gladwin, and this second walk struck her as singularly aimless and surplus to requirements. She had no desire to behave as a town guide. Precisely why they had come out at all was obscure to her. But she had little choice except to do her best to remain on good terms with these Meadows, now they seemed inextricably linked to her mother. She stopped her companions a few yards after the turning, and ordered them to look back. 'Isn't that fabulous!' she enthused, quickly persuading herself that there was, after all, something to draw their attention to. 'I never get tired of these amazing places. It's as if they've always been here, survivors of far-distant centuries. Just think what this one must have seen.'

'Silk mills, for a start,' agreed Mo, pointing to the name of the lane just to their right. 'Must have been noisier then. And smellier.'

'It's certainly quiet now,' said Thea's mother. 'Not a soul to be seen.'

'It's always like this,' said Thea. 'Some of the smaller villages seem to be completely deserted for most of the day. Even at weekends, there's hardly anybody about. It's part of the Cotswolds atmosphere. Everywhere's beautifully kept, lovely gardens, fresh paint, immaculate roofs – and no sign of the people.'

'Where are they, then?' Mo was puzzled.

'At work, mostly – earning the cash to pay for these places. And a lot of them are second homes. It's a very affluent area.'

'Yeah, but that should mean there's gardeners and cleaners and all that. Somebody must be looking after it all.'

'True,' agreed Thea. 'But I never seem to see them.'

'Weird,' concluded Mo, with a little shudder. 'Me, I like a lot of people around.'

'Not me,' said Maureen. 'I think this is nice. Where are we going, Thea?' All three women looked at Fraser, as if to check that he had no objection to being escorted rather than deferred to. He showed no sign of caring, either way, so Thea simply carried on walking along Silk Mill Lane for a distance that felt longer than during the walk with Gladwin. She began to worry that they'd gone too far when finally a small opening revealed Murder Alley on the left. 'Look, Mum – another alley for you,' she laughed. 'You don't have to go to Tewkesbury to find them. Gladwin and I came down here earlier this morning. I don't expect anybody's used it since then.'

They had not seen a single person in the lane, but now they heard a car start up, further along. Automatically they stepped into the alley, to leave space for the vehicle to pass. 'We go up here, anyway,' said Thea. 'It comes out at the end of the high street. We'll get to the pub in the square just at the right time for lunch.'

'What's that?' asked Thea's mother, on a note high enough to alert her daughter. 'Up there, look.'

The alley sloped upwards, the further end in shadow. It was narrow enough for two abreast to be uncomfortable, and for one person to obstruct the view of those behind. 'What? Where?' said Thea.

She found out soon enough. 'It's a person!' shrilled Mo. 'Lying on the ground.'

Something like fifteen yards ahead of them, there was indeed a person on the ground, lying on his back, hands folded peacefully across his chest, eyes closed.

Thea looked down at him, keeping her dog back as she did so. 'Bloody hell,' she said with some force. 'It's that Reuben.' She looked at her mother. 'Remember him from yesterday? It's Reuben bloody Hardy.'

Quite why she felt so angry was obscure, but she experienced a strong temptation to kick the man's body as it lay there dead in Murder Alley.

Chapter Fifteen

Throughout Monday, Drew thought of Thea, recapturing the images on the TV screen and wondering what trouble she might have got herself into this time. The report had not specifically identified her as being involved in the killing of a young woman, but knowing her as he was beginning to, he could only assume that she would sooner or later become involved, even if only as a helpful spy for the police.

His routines for the day entailed the usual juggling of children and work, heavily reliant on Maggs for continuity with their customers, and clouded with worry for the well-being of Stephanie and Timmy. On some days they seemed quite relaxed and cheerful, secure in the rituals of school and meals; at other times, one or both would be pale and silent and averse to all suggestion of food. This was a relatively good day. Stephanie's throat seemed to have settled down, and she got herself and her brother dressed in clean clothes, then they both ate some cereal and toast. Drew had slept through much of the night, despite the reappearance of Thea, and was giving at least half his attention to a rambling story that Timmy was trying to tell him. They were all in the car in good time, and to all appearances, both children went in without reluctance.

Maggs was a bigger challenge. There had been a phone call at four in the morning from a nursing home, requiring immediate removal of a body, before the other inmates woke and realised what had happened. Since Drew could no longer participate in these call-outs, having no wife at home to babysit, a standby person had been enlisted to go with Maggs. This was a school-leaver called Jackson, broad in shoulder and narrow in outlook. His employment was strictly unofficial, being paid in cash, with no retainer for being perpetually on call. He had no objection to handling dead bodies, but no ambitions to join the business on a full-time basis, either. 'It's just till I get sorted, with a proper job,' he told Maggs and Drew. From what they could see, this might well take a decade or two to achieve.

'I had to go and bang on his door,' Maggs complained. 'He said he never heard the phone.'

Drew clucked sympathetically.

'He's a dead loss, Drew, honestly,' she went on. 'I know I'll get there one of these days, and he'll be out somewhere for the night. Then what?'

'Then we fire him. I dare say there are plenty more where he came from.'

'Dream on! Anyone else'd want all the perks and paperwork, which we'd never have a hope of affording. It's hard enough to scrape up the twenty-five quid for Jackson every time we use him.'

'I know, Maggs. What do you want me to do about it?'

'Sell the field and house in Broad Campden. Consolidate. It was never going to work out, and now it's just a weight around your neck. The whole thing's a lot more trouble than it's worth.'

Broad Campden was where he had first met Thea, six months earlier. Since then, there had been a protracted and inconclusive attempt to open a second burial ground in the Cotswolds. It could have worked – if Karen had been alive and well and Maggs had been more amenable to the idea. As it was, it had never stood much of a chance. He had been left a house, as well, although the legal ramifications were still some distance from being resolved.

'Just sell the damn thing,' Maggs said again.

'I suppose I will, but it seems a shame,' he agreed. 'I'd rather struggle on a bit longer, and see if we can manage. I could put tenants in the house, and bring in some income that way.'

She puffed out her cheeks in a sceptical grimace. 'Who wants to rent a house in a tiny little village?'

'Plenty of people, I imagine. It's convenient for lots of bigger places.' A week ago, he wouldn't have had the energy to argue with her, he realised. Was it possible that a flicker of normality was finally returning? Could it be that the story of a murder in the Cotswolds, with a number of intriguing elements, had revived his spirits where daily life had thoroughly failed to do so? A new puzzle to solve might be the very thing to kick him out of his despondency.

'Well, there's a funeral to arrange, anyway,' Maggs said, with some emphasis. 'They'll be phoning us any time now. It's a Mr Orridge, aged ninety-five, who read about Peaceful Repose when it first opened, and put us in his will, there and then. Wouldn't it be nice if more people did that?'

'A nice surprise,' he agreed. 'Just shows you can never predict what'll happen.'

'If the nursing homes would just be a bit more proactive in recommending us, things would be a lot better. Three-quarters of their inmates have no idea we exist. I think it's a dereliction of duty. They ought to have posters up about us.'

'That'll be the day!' he laughed. 'When they do all they can to pretend everybody's going to live for ever. You're not allowed to even mention funerals.'

There had been several moments during the past six weeks when Drew would have loved to avoid all mention of funerals. He despised himself for it, convinced that other undertakers had no such difficulties. They would take the disposal of their own relatives in their stride, with calm competence – not floundering and changing their minds as Drew had done. But he had not been born to the work, as most in the business had. It was often a service that passed down the generations for centuries. Originally builders and carpenters, only burying the dead as a sideline, they had gradually become specialists. Drew had been a nurse in his twenties, only moving to funeral work on a whim. There were still several arcane details that he ignored or got wrong. There had always been elements he disliked – particularly those involving money. He had rapidly come to the conclusion that undertakers made too much profit from people in no position to haggle. Not only did he campaign for more ecological burials, but he kept them cheap. And as a result, his family had lived on the poverty line ever since Peaceful Repose had been set up.

The phone interrupted their desultory conversation. It was Fiona, his old friend from the council. 'Drew, this is your lucky day,' she began. 'We've got two funerals for you!'

'Blimey!' he said.

'Totally unconnected. One's an old dipso we've had an eye on for months now. She's been found dead in a doorway, poor thing. We'll have to go through the motions, but I can safely say she's got nobody who cares what happens next. And the other's a migrant, we think. We've had him nearly a month, trying to track down his origins. He died of a brain haemorrhage, in the street, no papers at all. The police have done all they're willing to, so now it's down to us.'

Drew felt a wash of sadness at the lonely deaths. 'They must have an *idea* of where he came from,' he said.

'Somalia is the best guess. It's chaos there, you know. Nobody has proper documentation. It's impossible to identify somebody like this. He's black, tall, young, thin, and he died of natural causes. Frankly, Drew, with things as they are, it's never going to get top priority. All these investigations cost money, you know.'

'Okay. We'll give him a decent burial.'

'Usual rates, then. That should put a bit of bread on your table.' Fiona knew most of the details of Drew's life, having been attracted to his way of doing things from the start. It was she who had ensured that his burial ground got all the council funerals, of people homeless and adrift who died in the streets and ditches across Somerset. She justified the decision easily enough to her superiors by pointing out that Drew charged a hundred pounds less than other undertakers.

Even so, the eventual cheque would indeed buy some welcome bread – or shoes. Timmy had been fobbed off with cheap temporary footwear at the start of term, and would need something a lot more substantial before the winter set in.

They established the time frame for the two new burials, and Drew rang off with an unfamiliar sense of incipient well-being. 'Busy!' he said to Maggs, who had been hovering at his shoulder, trying to listen in.

'Hallalujah!' she crowed. 'Maybe we won't starve after all, then.'

'They'll both be on Thursday morning.'

'Yes, I heard. Is Fiona coming?'

'Probably. She usually does.'

'She's a good woman.'

Drew eyed Maggs thoughtfully. Did she mean anything by that remark? Was she amenable to the idea of Fiona replacing Karen, but not Thea doing so? If so, why? Fiona was forty or thereabouts, divorced, plump, good-hearted. Thea was forty-four, small, slender, impetuous and nosy. Drew was in no doubt as to which of the two would be more fun.

'She is,' he said.

When the phone rang again at eleven o'clock, it was

to give details of a fourth funeral. Drew could hardly believe it. An inmate of the hospice had just died, leaving clear instructions that she wished to be buried at Peaceful Repose, as her friend had been a year before. Yet again, it was someone Drew had never heard of, a funeral he had been unable to anticipate. It was as if some great oak door had suddenly been opened to admit light and sweet fresh air. As if he had come to the top of a cosmic list and the gods had decided to confer a few small blessings onto him. Because to be busy was a welcome change, a timely test of his powers to concentrate and provide a decent service. He would have to remember how to behave with the newly bereaved – at least in the case of Mr Orridge and the new hospice lady. He would have to attend to details and not leave everything to Maggs.

Irrationally, with a secret inner smile, he associated the abrupt change of fortune with the glimpse he had had of Thea on the TV the previous night. If the gods had begun to smile, then possibly, just possibly, they would find a way of linking him once more with the woman whose image lurked in his mind, nearly all of the time.

Chapter Sixteen

Thea's anger against this second corpse made her feel guilty. She ought to be appalled, enraged at the violence and the sudden death of a healthy young man. Instead she simply wanted to run away and forget the whole messy business. She felt personally attacked, the body set down carefully just where she was about to walk. But how could anybody know she would be coming this way? She and Gladwin had already been down the alley that morning – when there was definitely no dead man obstructing the way. The fact of him now was ludicrous. It was the stuff of fantasy.

'Good Christ!' Fraser Meadows exclaimed, after a lengthy delay. He had stared blankly at the body for what seemed like several minutes, while his daughter uttered high wordless squeaks and Thea's mother stepped back and turned away, acting out something of what Thea herself would have liked to have done.

'Has anybody got a phone?' Thea asked. She had left hers at Thistledown.

Mo produced one like a magic trick, and held it up. '999?' she asked.

'No, we should call Gladwin direct. I know the number.' She dictated it, and then snatched the mobile when Mo said it was ringing.

Gladwin answered her own mobile phone on the third ring. 'Who's that?' she asked suspiciously. 'This is a private number.'

'It's me. Thea. I'm standing in Murder Alley, with the body of a man. I know who he is. He's dead, Sonia. There's been another murder. It's the same as that girl. Everything's the same.' Her voice was rising dangerously and she paused for breath.

'I don't believe it.'

'Yes you do. And it means he must have known who the girl was. They must be connected somehow.'

'Who, Thea? Who is he?'

'He's called Reuben Hardy and he lives right here, in Silk Mill Lane. He's got a wife and a puppy. It's a sweet puppy.' Somehow the puppy loomed largest in her mind, which she knew was daft and embarrassing, but the mind did that sort of thing in a crisis.

'What do you mean, it's the same? What's the same?'

'The way he's lying. On his back, with his hands folded on his chest. Like an effigy on a tomb. It's ghastly.'

'Can you stay there until I reach you? Fifteen or twenty minutes, okay?'

'There'll be people. There are already people,' she noticed, looking up the alley to the street at the top. 'What should I say to them?'

'Say you've called the police and they've asked you to keep everybody away. Are you there on your own?'

'No,' said Thea tightly. 'And that isn't really a lot of help. There are four of us.'

'Send them away, then. Sorry – I'm ringing off now. I'll be as quick as I can – and I'll send a squad car. It'll probably get there before me.' The urgency in the detective's voice went some way towards placating Thea, who was still experiencing some sense of personal outrage.

Her mother inadvertently contributed, too, by saying, 'Poor man. So young! Doesn't he look peaceful, though? Isn't death the strangest thing!'

'It is,' Thea sniffed, caught unawares by sudden emotion. 'I don't think anybody really understands it.'

Fraser and Mo had retreated back to Silk Mill Lane, speaking in low voices and ignoring the others. Thea called down to them, 'Go back to the house, will you? If Jason comes back, you can tell him what's happened. I can manage here.' Evidently, the couple were unsure as to whether or not to obey her. They stared all around them, as if seeking another opinion. Then they slowly moved out of sight and she forgot about them.

Thea had spoken too soon about managing. Before she knew it, a red-faced person was shouting at her, demanding answers to fatuously obvious questions. It took Thea a few moments to recognise the woman of the previous day who had shown her and Gladwin the path through Oliver's woodland. Heap – that was her name. 'Have you called an ambulance?' she shrilled. 'For God's sake, why are you just *standing* there?'

'The police are coming,' Thea said tightly. 'It's all under control.'

'*Control!* How can you say that, with two killings in twenty-four hours? What the hell is happening here? We're not safe in our beds, that's obvious.'

The woman had every reason to be hysterical, Thea told herself. She could understand it perfectly well. The madness of it was making her feel rather hysterical herself. 'I know,' she said. 'It's terrible.' It was a feeble word for the circumstances, but words always *were* feeble when somebody died. Mo's inarticulate cries had been more fitting.

But why Reuben? His superior smirks and subtle insinuations had been annoying, admittedly. Perhaps he had worked out who killed Melissa and challenged the killer. That seemed a viable explanation, even if he would have had to move extremely quickly. Everything had been so *fast*. 'The police are coming,' she said again. 'Don't let those people get any closer.' A knot of townsfolk were hovering at the end of the alley, perhaps having sent the red-faced woman as emissary. 'Go and tell them they have to stay back.'

Somewhat to her surprise, her order was obeyed, but only after Priscilla had bent down and given the inert face a swift stroke with her fingertips. 'I just wanted to make sure,' she mumbled. Then she was gone and Thea was left with her mother and a dead man. Maureen stood straight-backed against the stone wall, watching and listening, but saying nothing. Her dilated pupils gave Thea some cause for concern. 'Mum? Are you all right?'

171

'Of course not. Only a psychopath could be all right, just at the moment.'

It was the sort of thing her father would have said. He had encouraged an open acknowledgement of emotion as a good rule to live by. 'Don't bottle it up,' he would say, when one of his children was miserable or angry or frightened. 'There's no shame in having feelings.' Their mother had been the repressed one, clamping her lips shut against tears or rage. Her feelings leaked out in a trickle of complaint and sighs.

'I'm sorry,' Thea said, limply. 'You don't have to stay. They'll be here in a minute.'

'I'll stay. You might need reinforcements.'

It was reassuringly close to being a joke. 'I might,' she agreed, with a glance at the band of onlookers.

The alley was longer than she remembered it from earlier that morning. It began as a tunnel, the roof closed in, and then opened into a lane with plants sprawling over the walls, and a modern concrete block addition at the lower end. Reuben Hardy lay at the narrowest point, about halfway along. How was it possible that his killer could have been sufficiently calm to arrange the body, in broad daylight, and make an unnoticed escape only yards from a town centre? The answer was not difficult to find. Winchcombe on a Monday morning was far from busy. There was little expectation that the alley would be used more than once or twice a day. It was at the eastern end of town, beyond the shops, where few people would be walking. The opening to the alley was narrow and shadowy. Nobody driving past would have time to look in and focus on an object lying on the ground. If you had the nerve for it, then it was probably not such a risky enterprise after all. Somehow this made Thea feel sadder than ever.

At least they had an identity for this one, she thought, with a wife they could interview and a life they could dismantle in the search for a reason for his murder. And it was highly likely that a link would be discovered with the other victim, arranged in a similar funereal attitude. The neatness of it was repellent, suggesting something cynical and cold. She thought of Drew, gently settling his people into their coffins, and shuddered at the difference. Being placed like this in the open air, prey to birds and other scavengers, was dreadful. The lack of blood, the closed eyes, removed much of the violence associated with murder, and replaced it with something even worse.

At last, the police arrived, in a single car, without fanfare. It drew up in Silk Mill Lane, some distance past the bottom end of the alley, having failed to notice it. 'They don't know where we are,' said Thea's mother. 'I'll go and fetch them.'

They were two uniformed policemen, who herded the local people away and ran tape across the upper opening to the alley. They eyed Thea and her mother uncertainly, confused as to their precise role. Thea recognised them as having been present the day before, and they quite certainly recognised her. She quailed beneath their glances, aware that they were thinking dark suspicious thoughts.

Gladwin was there in another five minutes, arriving with two other plain-clothes officers. She questioned Thea, her manner intense and jittery. There were no smiles or jokes.

The profound seriousness of the situation could not be avoided. 'We were just *here*,' she burst out. 'Less than four hours ago.'

'Yes,' said Thea. 'I know.'

Chapter Seventeen

In London that morning, they told Oliver that things were progressing more or less as expected, and that he should prepare himself to be called either late that afternoon or first thing the next day. He would not be permitted to observe the proceedings or hear other people's testimony. He was free to leave, of course, but it would be appreciated if he would return by three o'clock. It was then ten-thirty. The intervening hours stretched emptily before him. 'What am I meant to do until then?' he asked plaintively.

'Go to a gallery? A film? First showing's around midday in the West End. It's a nice day. Sit in one of the parks, perhaps. Go and see the rose garden – it's lovely at the moment.' The official was briskly sympathetic, leaving an impression that she had made this identical set of suggestions a thousand times before. Oliver felt helpless. He was reminded of one of his favourite novels – *The Warden* by Anthony Trollope – where Mr Harding was forced to pass several hours in central London while he waited for a very similar appointment to Oliver's own. He had walked up and down the Strand, just as Oliver felt constrained to do, pausing for a long slow drink in a coffee shop. The parallel was disorienting and by midday he was resolved to break it.

There would be birds in the parks, he presumed, if only town sparrows and pigeons. His interest in birds had blossomed over twenty years into a passion. He knew every detail of their bone structure, the way feathers grew and beaks were adapted to different food types. He knew about their social patterns, and which species dominated which. He knew the songs and calls, and the size of their broods. Now and then he dreamt he was an eagle, soaring high and watching the world's puny affairs unfold far below. He understood that he had been in that detached mode for the greater part of his life, and that it was both desirable and deplorable.

But instead, here he was, embroiled in something so repulsive, he still could not find words for it. His own motives were opaque and fragile, the compulsion to testify in public an astonishment from which he still had not recovered. For a while he had assumed it to be revenge, pure and simple. That would be easy to understand and relatively easy to live with. But it was infinitely murkier than that. He lingered on the word *testimony*, suspecting that the clue lay within it. A setting straight, an exposure of a reality that was in many ways banal, but which had done extreme damage. For a man to escape into fantasies of becoming a bird, because normal human life was impossible for him, was at best a waste. Every life should engage in some ordinary interaction with other members of the same species. He would have enjoyed being a father, and all the sociable exchanges that family life involved, if he had been allowed to develop into the person he expected to become when he was still young and innocent.

He had been betrayed and worse. He had been *damaged* beyond repair, and the truth of it could not remain hidden any more. There was a basic morality to it that the world had, much to his amazement, come to recognise so powerfully that proceedings such as he was now participating in were commonplace. With great trepidation he had presented himself, never expecting to be embraced as a key element, to be treated with such gentle respect. His age had only increased the sympathy, it seemed. 'The law pays no regard to the passage of time,' they said, and reminded him of senile Nazis and derelict tyrants, facing their accusers in the final moments of their lives.

Faces filed through his imagination, as he sat in St James's Park, watching pigeons with deformed or missing toes. Faces that belonged to another part of London altogether – the sooty ghettoes of the East End, in the calamitous decade that had been the nineteen forties. His father, craggy and aloof, in the Victorian costume that his profession demanded. A grand old man by any standards, living to the age of ninety-nine, energetic to the last. His death had come less than a decade before, his presence still real for a great many people. There had been women fawning over him right to the end. His mother was infinitely less memorable: the younger second wife, colourless and eternally exuding a faint disgust with everything around her. She had been dead for so long that the only lingering details were that little pucker of her lips and a scent of lily of the valley. And looming over it all, he could not evade the image of his older motherless brother, Cedric, who had been capable of anything. It still made Oliver breathless to remember what Cedric had been capable of. And finally Fraser, the rebel, whose motto, after all the bereavements wrought by the war, was *there's nothing more to lose*. In his way, Fraser, too, had been capable of anything. It was mere good luck that his nature was essentially benign, and his adventures accordingly harmless and ordinary. A near-forgotten bereavement brought another blurred and wispy face to mind. Their baby sister, Joyce, with her huge eyes and tiny hands. Joyce had died when she was two, choking and resisting to the end. Oliver remembered her little white coffin more vividly than he remembered the child.

Later, a new generation slowly emerged. Fraser's exotic daughter Maureen, and Cedric's late-begotten boy. Oliver had played with Maureen now and then, before his brother took himself and his family off to the other end of the world.

The rediscovery of Fraser's one-time girlfriend meant little to Oliver. He had no recollection of her, had not been aware of the relationship at the time. He had been eighteen or so, living with his parents in the gloomy premises that had been rocked and cracked by wartime bombs, but somehow survived unchanged.

His stomach reminded him that the day was passing. He should eat. And the morning coffee had filtered down to his bladder, which was now uncomfortable. Physical needs that he found faintly irritating sent him out of the park and through Trafalgar Square. Charing Cross Station would answer his needs. He could sit there and watch passengers, almost as distracting as birds, and not entirely dissimilar, until it was time for his reappearance at the court. The big central court, where all the most notorious and sensational criminals were tried and judged and sentenced, and the press gave such great prominence to the stories that unfolded there.

It was the press that Oliver gave most heed to; it was the press, in the end, that decided him to stand up and speak – they would be his mouthpiece to the wider world, which should know precisely what had been done to him.

Chapter Eighteen

Gladwin sent Thea away, making a great effort to be pleasant, when it was obvious that she was deeply troubled by events of the past thirty hours. Two deaths in so short a time threw a glaring searchlight on her and her colleagues. If they had been simultaneous, that might have made more sense. But the chilling implications of a calculating killer picking off victims a day at a time were inescapably terrifying. 'If the Jason chap turns up, hold onto him, will you?' Gladwin asked, having elicited an account of Thea's movements since they had parted earlier. The possibility that he had hurtled down to Silk Mill Lane, slaughtered Reuben and laid him out in the alley for the others to find, was remote, but initially the only half-baked idea they had. 'It's too soon, of course, for this sort of thinking,' Gladwin admitted. 'But we obviously have to speak to him.'

Fraser and Mo were in Oliver's house, and they stood in a traumatised circle with Thea and her mother, all more or less stunned. There was no sign of Jason. 'Something is going on,' Thea challenged them. 'This whole thing is aimed at one of us, somehow.'

They all looked at her. Mo laughed harshly. Her mother put a hand flat to her chest. 'Not *me*, Thea. It can't possibly have anything to do with me.'

Thea was inclined to agree with her, before she caught Fraser's eye. There was profound doubt as to his actual connection to her mother, whether he really was who he said he was. Gladwin herself had registered this, promising to investigate the authenticity of his claims. Was it possible that Fraser was somehow orchestrating the murders in order to terrify Maureen into his welcoming arms? It seemed insanely melodramatic to imagine such a thing. But he *could* have done something of the sort. He could be using Jason as his hitman.

And Thea herself had been dragooned into the house-sitting by the Meadows brothers, with her mother liaising between them. She had been manipulated into it, not so very subtly. She had been put in position, given sight of the mysterious Melissa, and then somehow manoeuvred into finding the body in the alley. But *how* had that been done? Was it not her own idea to go that way? Nobody had steered her, and certainly her mother had no knowledge of the lower streets of Winchcombe.

Except nothing was certain. Her mother knew the alleys of Tewkesbury, after all. Perhaps she had explored Winchcombe, too, without mentioning the fact. Perhaps her first loyalties now lay with Fraser, and whatever he demanded was blindly acceded to. It felt deeply improbable, but not entirely out of the question.

Mo was capable of anything, if Thea was any judge. There was a strong sense of lawlessness about her, a flouting of any regulation that struck her as irrelevant. The sort of woman who would smoke in a public building and refuse to wear a seat belt. You had to respect a person like that, with such a solid sense of individual worth and natural human entitlement. Thea had moments when she was not too dissimilar herself; when the law cried out for contempt rather than obedience.

Jason was impossible to assess, but he appeared to have a good heart and an easy charm. In wartime he would have been a spiv, a cheerful chappie selling nylon stockings on the black market and stashing away a lot of cash into the bargain. Jason, too, might be capable of anything.

All these impressions were flooding her mind as she fondled her dog and tried to obliterate the image of the dead Reuben. It was not so difficult to do – she had already done it with the dead Melissa of the previous day. Any hauntings that the dead might perpetrate were rarely visual ones. They were obligations and anxieties, perpetual demands for attention and the righting of wrongs. Carl, dead for three years now, was a faceless presence somewhere in her bones, a black cloud where her future should have been. Any guilt accrued directly and solely to the driver of the vehicle that had killed him, and Thea had never found it easy to reproach him. She had driven every bit as badly in her time, as had Carl, and she was convinced that everybody had. The courts understood that, and gave leniency to dangerous drivers, which Thea saw no reason to challenge.

But murder was altogether different. Until the killer

was tracked down and punished, there was no possibility of order and trust. Suspicion ran like wildfire through every relationship in the victim's life. Rage and retribution blossomed and turned inwards, without an external object on which to vent it. You absolutely had to do everything in your power to assist the course of justice. It was unavoidable, as Thea knew already, and confirmed to herself again now.

Her mother might be expected to feel something the same, although they had never really talked in such terms. The events of the previous year in Lower Slaughter, involving Thea's sister Emily, had strained their mother's endurance almost to breaking point. She had been permitted to avoid direct confrontation with the truth, and only slowly, over the ensuing months, did she acquire the courage to accept what had happened in all its shame and sadness.

'That poor young man!' her mother sighed, as if to validate some of Thea's chaotic thoughts. 'I can't stop thinking about him. It's all the more dreadful because I can't say I liked him, from the little I saw of him yesterday.'

'I know what you mean,' agreed Thea, in some surprise. She had forgotten until then that she, too, had taken a mild dislike to Reuben Hardy. It added a layer of queasy self-reproach to the other emotions, she realised. When someone you regarded with aversion was cruelly killed, it was all too horribly easy to wonder if somehow you'd brought about his death. As if you might have accidentally uttered a magic spell, and the powers of darkness had misunderstood the degree of your animosity.

Fraser spoke from the armchair, where he had sat bowed and silent for several minutes. 'I imagine it was me the killer had in mind, if your thesis is correct. After all, that girl told you she was my daughter. It seems I am intended as a target of some sort.' He raised haggard eyes to Thea. 'At least that's how it feels. The way the bodies were both laid out, as if in their coffins – that is plainly no coincidence. And equally plainly, it was aimed at me.'

Thea frowned at him. 'What do you mean?'

Mo made a startled little cry as an idea struck her. 'Dad! That doesn't make any sense. You've never worked in the business. And it's not as if—' She stopped herself, with an awkward cough. 'I mean . . . somebody would have to be *insane* to kill two people just because . . .'

'You know nothing about it,' he said hollowly. 'You were never interested, never understood the implications.'

Thea looked at her mother, and raised her eyebrows in an urgent question. Maureen Johnstone shrugged. 'I suppose they're talking about the undertaker business,' she said. 'I told you that's what the Meadows family did.'

The connection hardly registered with Thea as significant. For her, the only association she could find with undertaking was Drew Slocombe and his natural burials.

Fraser spoke again, more quickly than before. 'Where's Jason? He'll be wondering what's become of us by now. Mo – can't you phone him?'

Mo laughed, a donkey-like bray that caught Thea's attention. 'Jason doesn't do mobile phones. It drives everybody mad. He says it would turn him into a caricature, whatever that might mean.'

Fraser echoed the laugh, a single nasal honk that contained no vestige of mirth. Again Thea was alerted.

'The murdered girl!' she remembered. 'She laughed like you two.' She stared hard at the old man. 'And she knew so much about you. She knew about my mother, and Mo and how this house was laid out. I'd forgotten that part of our conversation until now. She was so relaxed and open about your family, calling your brother *Uncle Ollie*. She knew where to find that memory stick. She went straight to it.' At least she had told Gladwin that part of the encounter, she consoled herself. But after Fraser's insistence that the body was not that of anyone he knew, she had not returned to the detective with her own contrary evidence. 'I ought to find Sonia and tell her,' she added recklessly.

'Shut up,' snarled Mo, her colour heightening. 'You've been duped, you silly thing. Oldest trick in the book – easier than ever these days. Just find out a few basic facts, and drop them in, and people are always convinced. She was conning you. Do you think I wouldn't know if I had a young sister?'

'I think that's quite possible, actually. She called you "Mo". How would she find that out? You must be officially Maureen.'

'I've got my own Facebook page, with family background, where I put my name as Mo. Uncle Ollie gets a mention, because he's quite a well-known photographer. There was a big book out last year, *Birds of Britain*, that he illustrated. I drop his name all the time. I joke that, as he's childless, I might inherit some of the dosh.'

'Mo!' Fraser reproached. 'I hope you don't do that. That would be . . .' He grimaced, lost for the right word.

'Tactless. Yes, Dad, I know. But that's me, isn't it?'

'They're all on Facebook,' confirmed Thea's mother. 'That's how Fraser and I found each other again. It's happening all over the place. It's a sign of the times. So that girl, whoever she was, could easily have fooled you. Mo's right about that.'

Thea was confronted by three emphatic faces, all apparently eager to persuade her. It came close to working. 'But the *laugh*,' she persisted. 'And she did look like you,' she addressed Fraser. 'Tall, fair, small ears. Even the walk was similar.'

'Again, it's easy to see similarities if you're looking for them,' said Fraser. 'If this has been some elaborate plot against my family, then just such a girl would be chosen for the job, wouldn't she?' He spoke slowly, his gaze on a corner of the carpet. Thea suspected that something else was going through his mind, as he spoke.

'And then murdered,' she said, suddenly angry. 'Employed as a spy, on the first day I was going to be here, sent to fetch that memory stick and then killed before she'd gone three hundred yards. So *who*? Who masterminded this ghastly scheme – and why kill Reuben the very next day? What did *he* have to do with it?'

'What's this memory stick you keep on about?' asked Mo. 'First I've heard of it.'

Thea clamped her lips together. It was probably very foolish of her to have mentioned it. The police routinely trusted her to keep such salient details to herself, and sometimes their trust was misplaced, she noted with chagrin. 'I probably shouldn't have said anything about that,' she explained. 'It makes things more difficult for the police if people know stuff like that.'

186

'You're a spy yourself, aren't you?' Mo accused. 'You're so buddy-buddy with that detective woman, telling her your stupid ideas about our family. Reporting every word we've said to you, I shouldn't be surprised. Poor Uncle Ollie won't know what he's let himself in for.'

'Be quiet, Mo,' ordered her father. 'Don't bring Oliver into this, for God's sake. He's got enough to worry about as it is.'

There was a key to all this, Thea told herself. Some crucial connection or motivation that would explain everything. A code had to be broken, so that the incomprehensibly garbled impressions and facts could be deciphered. It was almost within her grasp, she believed. But she was completely confused as things stood. How much did her mother understand about what had happened? How important was the absent Oliver to the story? *And who was the woman who called herself Melissa?*

Chapter Nineteen

Gladwin would be comprehensively tied up with the aftermath of the second murder, as well as the intensive efforts to identify the dead woman of the previous day. But Thea felt obliged to see her again and complete her account of everything Melissa had said to her on Saturday. The scraps she had conveyed thus far were looking more and more insubstantial, as new exchanges came back to her. Remembering everything a person had said, without prompting, was no simple task, even a day or two after the event. There had been no indication at the time that the conversation would have to be recalled. Much of it had been casual chat, routine explanations and comments that may or may not have been carefully rehearsed as part of an elaborate deception. Much of the trick of it, in that case, would be to keep it light and easy, throwing out reassurances and telling details as part of the smokescreen.

But I did challenge her, Thea remembered. *I insisted she convince me, before I let her into the house.* And she had readily been convinced. The notion that Melissa had been prepared for just such a challenge now seemed all too credible. But if that were so, then the blithe young woman had not understood how dangerous her associates were. Whoever had instructed her in the facts of the Meadows family had given her no hint that she would be slaughtered when the task was accomplished. And the task, it seemed obvious now, was the acquisition of the memory stick.

But even that made little sense. Why not just burgle the house? It was obvious that 'they' – the shadowy mind behind the entire structure – knew precisely where it was, because they had told Melissa how to find it. Why go to such lengths to construct a fake daughter and niece and fool the hapless house-sitter with elaborate acting?

Had Oliver somehow arranged it himself? He would know the exact timings, and the location of the boxes in his house. He could easily have organised an alibi for himself, wherever he was, and maintain a steadfast innocence of all that had happened. And he struck Thea as a deeply improbable murderer. He was too fragile, surely? One kick to his shin, and he would topple. And Fraser was scarcely more robust. Fraser, if guilty of anything, was likely to be the perpetrator of a far more subtle crime – a crime against her own mother.

And there was that laugh. Were laughs hereditary? Would you laugh the same as your father, even if you had never met him? Thea was sceptical of the claims of separated twins to have led identical lives, in which they choose the same colour schemes for their bathrooms and both marry men called Steve and go to a remote Cornish village for their holidays every year. Thea suspected that any two people, chosen at random, would find as many points in common, once they started to search for them.

But laughing was a peculiar thing. Her father and Damien both cackled in exactly the same way – but then Damien had grown up hearing it, and could easily have imitated it from his first months. Nobody else in Thea's family did it – and here were *three* people all braying in the same weird way: Mo, Fraser and Melissa.

She tried to guess where Gladwin might be and what she might be doing, so soon after discovering a second body. It was close to two o'clock and nobody had yet had any lunch. Any social requirement to escort her mother and the others to a local hostelry seemed to have evaporated. There was an aimless hanging about that was getting increasingly on her nerves. She remembered Fraser and her mother saying they planned to stay another night, and wondered whether the events of the morning had changed their minds. They would probably opt to stay, assuming that Thea could not be left; that at least one person must remain on guard, staying overnight again. Her mind suggested that this was in fact not a bad idea, but her feelings rebelled. She preferred to be alone. She was thoroughly accustomed to her own company, whether in Witney or one of the house-sits. She understood her own rhythms and quirks, and found another person jangling. *Two* other people comprised a crowd.

'Listen,' she began, 'we can't just mess about here, with nothing to do. I think you should all go and look for Jason, and then go home. I'll be fine. Sonia will probably want to see me before long, anyway.'

'We're in the way,' summarised Mo, with a forgiving smile. 'And I for one am hungry.'

'And where *is* Jason?' asked Thea's mother. 'Will he still be waiting for us in that pub? It's an hour and a half later than we said.'

'He'll have had some lunch on his own, and then he'll have to come back for me,' Mo pointed out. 'Otherwise I won't be able to get home.'

'You could come with us,' said Fraser. 'I imagine I could stay with you again tonight if necessary.'

Mo rolled her eyes exaggeratedly. 'Yes, I imagine you could, Pa. My home is your home now. I thought we'd established that. But I can't believe Jason would just abandon me.'

'But my car's at Damien's,' said Maureen, showing little faith in Jason's reliability. 'We'll have to go there first.'

Thea washed her hands of their complicated logistics, and wandered into the kitchen, thinking she might make herself a sandwich. Her spaniel went with her, plainly sharing her desire for some peace and quiet. 'I suppose we're being rather rude,' Thea whispered to the dog. 'But there's a limit to hospitality, don't you think?'

Hepzie gave a slow wag and sniffed idly at the table leg.

'Are you making some for us all?' Her mother was in the doorway, watching the sandwich preparations. 'I've hardly eaten anything today. I'm rumbling.'

'There isn't enough bread. I never reckoned on catering for a crowd.'

'Don't be so mean, Thea. Nothing that's happened was what we expected. You have to rise to the occasion. Can't you bake a few potatoes or something?' The older woman went through the kitchen cupboards, bringing out pasta, tomato sauce, crispbread, along with jars of honey, Marmite and jam. 'Look at all this!' she crowed. 'And there's sure to be butter and cheese in the fridge.'

Thea stood back and let her mother get on with it. She *was* being mean, she supposed, if there was an assumption that she was hostess to all the visitors. Somehow she could not persuade herself that the role was appropriate. She had been in the house for less than twenty-four hours when everything descended into chaos, and she was still trying to regain her balance. She might have been making sandwiches for a murderer – especially if Jason reappeared. The longer he was gone, the more he seemed the most obvious candidate for villainy. She might be next on his list of victims. Or her mother might. Fraser could be plotting to kill her, as revenge for her cavalier treatment of him fifty years ago. She had broken his heart and then forgotten all about him. It was not difficult to imagine that he had brooded over it ever since, intent on making her pay for the damage she had so carelessly done to him.

Maureen's efforts to provide sustenance were poorly rewarded. She carried a plate of fractured crispbreads spread with Marmite and scraps of cheese, back into the living room. 'They're a bit stale, I'm afraid,' she laughed. 'And they mostly broke when I tried to spread the butter on them.' Mo took a scrap, but clearly found it unpalatable. 'I could boil up some pasta, and put tomato sauce on it,' Maureen offered.

'Don't bother,' said Fraser tetchily. 'We'll go. We can

find something in town on the way. I seem to remember a Co-op or something, down North Street.'

'What about Jason?' asked Thea.

'He can fend for himself,' said Mo. 'He's big and ugly enough to sort himself out. Anyway, I think we'll find him out there somewhere. He could even be sitting in the car waiting for me. He does that, playing with his laptop. He loves his laptop,' she added fondly.

'The police . . .' began Thea. 'Surely . . . ?'

'What?' Mo was challenging. 'You think they think he killed that bloke? Why him? Why not any one of the five thousand people who live here?'

'Good question,' Thea realised. 'Except . . .'

'You've convinced yourself this all has something to do with our family, haven't you? You're putting down the poison against us in that detective's mind.'

Thea felt breathless at the injustice. Her thoughts lost any coherence they might have had, as she stared at the big confident woman. 'No,' she gasped. 'Not at all. But that girl – Melissa. She came *here*, to this house, minutes before she was killed. Who was she? Why did she come? She *knew* about you all. And Reuben Hardy seemed to know something, as well. He was teasing us yesterday, making some sort of hint about Oliver and the rest of you. Fraser heard him – didn't you?'

Fraser was at the door, intent on departure, not listening. 'I've had enough,' he rumbled. 'Every damned time I come here, there's trouble. It's that brother of mine – he casts a pall over everything he touches. He's a jinx – we always said so, right from when he was little. He brings it all on himself.' His eyes clouded. 'And yet . . . you can't help but feel sorry for him. He's had a rotten life, poor old chap.'

'Come on, Dad,' urged Mo. 'This isn't the time for all that. Uncle Ollie's perfectly all right, tucked away here with his birds. He'll be back in a little while, no harm done.'

Fraser heaved a great sigh. 'Cedric was never right, you know. That's where it all started. His mother dying the way she did, sent him off his rocker, and nobody even noticed until it was too late.'

'Who's Cedric?' Thea asked her mother in an undertone.

'The older brother,' was the whispered reply. 'Half-brother, actually. Inherited the business. Always been in the shadows.'

Whoever he might be, if he was Fraser and Oliver's older brother by a previous wife, he was probably well into his eighties and therefore scarcely relevant to any of the matters in hand. Mo seemed to feel the same. 'Never mind Cedric,' she said briskly. 'That's all being dealt with. We don't have to worry ourselves about it. We've gone over all that.'

'But I *should* be there,' moaned the old man. 'Not let Ollie carry it on his own. I could be lending him a shoulder, instead of playing silly buggers here.'

Silly buggers seemed to Thea a somewhat dismissive way to refer to two brutal murders, if that was what he meant. Perhaps he was talking about her mother, or Mo, or the tepid quest for the missing Jason. Whatever he meant, there was an implication that somewhere there had been a plan, a covert agreement that involved Thea and Thistledown and possibly the murdered Melissa. Or so her muddled mind suspected. Because her mind was increasingly muddled. The

Meadows family seemed to comprise a lot of very elderly men, living mainly in the past and suffering from a package of unpleasant feelings, including guilt for certain failures or misdeeds. 'Who runs the business now?' she asked. 'Or has it been sold to that American outfit?'

Mo gripped her father's elbow and pulled open the door. 'What's that to do with anything?' she demanded impatiently.

'Nothing. I'm just interested. I'd have liked to talk a bit more about it. I have a friend who's an undertaker, as it happens.'

'Well, it's still in the family. My cousin Henry runs it. He took over from Cedric a few years back. It's doing very well.'

Fraser gave the family bray. 'Doing very well,' he mimicked. 'The bloody man's making millions.'

'Hardly,' said Mo. 'That is, only if he did sell it, and he's not going to do that, is he?'

Fraser mumbled something, and let himself be pushed down the path towards Vineyard Street. Thea let them go, past caring what would become of her mother, who might find herself stranded without a car, but who showed no sign of going back with the man she arrived with. Only gradually did this strike Thea as peculiar. 'Are you staying, then, Mum?' she asked.

'I think I am,' she said slowly. 'There's too much going on. I can't just *leave* you, can I?'

Fraser seemed oblivious to this abandonment. He did not turn back to see where his friend might be. 'He doesn't seem to have noticed,' said Thea. 'Not much of a boyfriend, is he?'

Maureen smiled ruefully. 'He's not a boyfriend at all, Thea. It's not like that. He just wants to be friends and relive his youth. He's hardly conscious of what's happening in the here and now. All he cares about is the distant past.'

'Are you sure? It seems to me to be much more than that. You were full of him last week, and you introduced him to Damien. That strikes me as pretty thick.'

'Your father has only been dead a year. I'm not going to get *thick* with anybody. But it's nice to have some company. He's very interesting, once you get him started. Some of his stories about Australia are extraordinary. And he was so keen to meet you. It's a shame it all went sour.'

'Yes,' sighed Thea. 'It all went completely rotten, didn't it?' She tried to kick-start her brain and work out what to do next. 'And I've got to speak to Gladwin again. I keep remembering more about Melissa.'

'And I remember a few things about that Reuben,' said her mother, surprisingly. 'Perhaps we should go together and see if we can find her?'

It was an oddly endearing proposal, as if by simply walking up to the high street, they might stumble across a senior police detective. 'She'll be at the station by now,' said Thea. 'Trying to establish a proper course of action. Briefing the team, and so forth.'

'Well, we'll go there, then.'

'It's not that simple. For a start, they'll be setting up an incident room, if they haven't already. They'll want us there, I expect, for a formal interview. And we can't really expect it always to be Gladwin we speak to. She's quite likely to delegate us to somebody else.'

'For heaven's sake, Thea. You're not making any sense. None of that matters, does it? If we've got important facts to tell them, we should go and do it, right away.'

'I think it would be better to phone. That's what I was trying to say. I'm sorry, Mum – my head's not working very well. I can't really decide what I should do, to be honest. For one thing, I ought to go and feed Oliver's birds.'

'Too late for that. They'll have given up expecting anything by now. If you're in that bad a state, you should come home with me. We can go in your car and that will solve my transport problem.'

Thea mentally stumbled over the question of cars. Somehow, there seemed to be more vehicles than people. Where was Melissa's, for one thing? And if Fraser went back with Mo and Jason, that left his car sitting out in Vineyard Street somewhere. She imagined Gladwin trying to marry them all up with their rightful owners the previous day, in an effort to identify Melissa's. She didn't envy her the job. She knew from past experience that people could be very devious when it came to keeping their motors away from the attention of the police.

'I don't think he ever said anything about his father being an undertaker,' Maureen said, as if this was the topic they'd been discussing. 'And I certainly never knew there was an older brother, until a few weeks ago.'

'When? I mean – when didn't he say anything? You told me last week that's what the family did for a living.'

'Did I? I meant when I knew him before. I'm sure I would have remembered that, if nothing else.'

Thea was forced to accept that her mother's situation took

priority. If she wanted to talk about Fraser, then Thea would have to listen and listen carefully. 'Sit down,' she ordered. 'I'll go and put two of those potatoes in the microwave and we can have them with that sauce. The pasta doesn't appeal very much. Don't move. I'll be one minute.'

She was back within the promised time, sitting facing her mother across the hearth rug in Oliver's sitting room. 'So, let's try and get to the bottom of this. Are you at all worried that Fraser might be pretending? That he isn't the man you knew in the sixties at all? Isn't there *anything* about him that you recognise?'

The older woman pulled a face, indicating frustrated effort. 'I remember a tall, fresh-faced boy, rather shy and tongue-tied. I can't remember a single thing he ever said, but we did go to the East End. I remember the wet street and the shadowy corners where they say Jack the Ripper did his murders. It was a bit sinister, the way he relished it so much. I have an impression of talking about the war, at some point. The incredible damage it did, that sort of thing. You know – by then, people had mostly stopped talking about it in any detail. It was as if there was no more to be said. I remember thinking it was because we'd won, and were being modest about it. Not crowing or proud at all. Do you know, I'm still awkward with Germans, even now? It's a terrible thing to have beaten somebody in a war like that. Where there were no half measures. Both sides did their worst, ignoring any rules. Just burning and bombing, night after night. It leaves appalling scars.'

'Not so much modest as ashamed, then?' remarked Thea.

'Oh no, I don't think so. They gave as good as they got. It was touch and go who'd win, even though nobody would ever say that openly. We were *glad* about the bombing of Dresden and Hiroshima. Really glad. We became heartless monsters, all of us.'

'But that's not getting us far with Fraser, is it?'

'Probably not. But we've talked about this sort of thing, in the past few weeks. He makes me feel we've *shared* something, even if I've forgotten most of it. And I *like* him.'

'Do you? I wonder why. He seems very ordinary to me.'

'Yes, he is. And that's what I like. He's not interested in scoring points or showing off his wit. He's just a quiet old man who wants to be loved.'

'But Daddy didn't score points,' Thea protested.

Her mother gave her a long look. 'Not with you, of course. And not with any intention to hurt or belittle. But he did it, all the same. He always had to know best what was good for you children. He always had some better idea than mine. He manoeuvred me into my own little ghetto of housework and gardening. Everything else was his territory. He made me powerless in my own family.'

Thea felt sandbagged by this analysis. Never for a moment had she seen the Johnstones in those terms. Her father had not possessed a malign cell in his body. 'He was just a bit old-fashioned,' she protested weakly. 'He was just doing things the way his own parents had done them.'

'I know,' said her mother. 'But that doesn't really make it any better, does it?'

'So Fraser lets you take charge? He defers to you?'

'Not exactly. It's probably too late now, anyway. I don't

want to be in charge. I wouldn't know how. But I like the sensation of being needed. And consulted. He *consults* me. He wants to know what I think.'

'And you like him. You don't think there's any possibility that he's after your house and money, having seen you on Facebook and decided you were an easy target for a major con trick?'

'No, Thea. I don't think that's at all likely.'

'Or that he's held a grudge against you for his entire life, because you broke his heart in nineteen sixty-two?'

'That has occurred to me, I must admit. I do feel very bad for not remembering him properly. But he just thinks it's funny. He thinks it means we can start again with a clean slate. He seems genuinely pleased to have a second chance.'

Thea gave up. 'Well, he's gone off without you now, hasn't he? I don't think that's very gentlemanly.'

'Oh, but it is. He realised that you and I needed to have this little chat. And he knows I'm in safe hands. He explained some of it to me last night – we were going to tell you about it today. You see, he feels he's let his brother down quite badly. For the moment, he can hardly think about anything other than Oliver. That's where all his attention is, even if he isn't showing it.'

Chapter Twenty

Gladwin's mobile could offer nothing better than a promise to take a message and get back as soon as possible. 'It's Thea. I've remembered quite a lot more about Melissa. I think you might want to hear it. Let me know where and when, okay?'

Leaving a message was deeply unsatisfying. 'What if I forget it all again?' she worried. 'There's so much rushing around in my head, I can barely focus for two minutes at a time.'

Her mother had made two large mugs of tea and was slumped on the sofa, looking drained. Hepzibah had jumped on top of her, and they were enjoying a rare cuddle that made Thea feel excluded.

With the phone still in her hand, she tried to assemble her thoughts. The quest for an explanatory key was growing increasingly urgent. Loose ends and unanswered questions swarmed on all sides, with nothing to suggest a remotely credible pattern. One persistent motif came back to her: undertakers. The bodies had both been laid out as if for burial, the Meadows family were London funeral directors – a fact that suggested at least some kind of connection. And Thea knew an undertaker rather well. What better excuse – *reason*, she amended – to call him?

She went upstairs with her phone, muttering something about seeing to the beds. Her mother took very little notice and the dog stayed where she was. Holding the gadget tightly, Thea realised that her hand was shaking and her heart pounding. *Don't be so silly*, she adjured herself silently, resisting the message her body was trying to send her.

She could text him instead. Perhaps that would be safer, less of a transgression. But how could she possibly word it? The story was far too complicated, the questions too imprecise. If he was in the middle of a funeral, she might leave voicemail, inviting him to call her back. If Maggs was listening, he could pretend she was someone else. If he never wanted to speak to her or think of her again, he could be cool and unresponsive. The shaking and thumping grew worse as she considered these alternatives.

Just get on with it, her rational mind shouted. *This is ridiculous.*

So she instructed the phone to make the call with a few little motions of her thumb, and stared out of the window as she listened to the rhythmic warble as it summoned him. Outside the leaves were yellowing, the grass dry and brittle. The last gasps of summer were going unnoticed at Thistledown, which seemed to Thea another shame, to add to those already accumulating.

'Hello?' came his voice, slightly wary, slightly breathless, entirely friendly. 'I saw you on the telly.'

She wasn't sure whether to bless or curse the technology that had already told him who was calling. Wasn't it a pity that surprises had become so difficult to find these days?

'Did you? I tried to dodge the camera, actually.'

'Yes, I could tell. I've been thinking about you all day.'

Don't say that! she wanted to tell him. *You mustn't say that.* 'There's been another killing this morning. Two in two days. It's horrible.'

'Are you still in Winchcombe?'

'Yes I am. My mother's here with me. I think she's involved somehow.'

'Explain.'

She ran through the basics, relieved to discover that she could give a lucid account of the people and how they connected to each other, and to herself. 'The thing is,' she concluded, 'I thought you might know about the Meadows people. Or you can find out. There must be a directory of funeral directors.' She giggled at the phrase. 'There's something going on with Oliver, for a start. And the Henry Meadows who runs the business seems a bit of a taboo subject.'

'Thea – haven't you been following the news? It was all over the place last week. TV, radio, papers. Even I couldn't avoid it, and I can promise you I don't have much time for all that these days. If it wasn't for Stephanie always wanting the telly on, I suppose I'd have missed it.'

'What? What news?'

'There's a big trial going on at the Old Bailey. It's highly unusual, because the alleged crime took place about sixty-five years ago. The old man Meadows, who's over eighty, has been accused of abusing a dozen or more little boys, back in the fifties. It's all been brought out into the light, and apparently it was so gruesome they've realised they can't keep a lid on it.'

'And Stephanie watches that sort of thing, does she?'

'She doesn't understand any of it. But she did spot you last night. She called me in to see. I only got the final couple of seconds.' He sounded regretful.

'Okay.' She thought about his revelation of the trial. 'So I'm guessing that that's where Oliver has gone. To watch his brother standing trial. Poor old chap – no wonder he was a bit distracted. And no wonder he didn't want to tell me about it. And,' she realised, 'that explains one or two things about Fraser. He must know the whole story, as well.'

'They'll be astonished that you don't. It's all terribly public.'

'I don't think my mother has much idea, either. Maybe it's less prominent than you think, and you only picked it up because they're in the same line of work as you.'

'I doubt it. You still don't really get it. The Meadows have had an empire for generations. They're rich and famous and much loved in the East End. There were stories about how gallant and heroic they were in the war, collecting bodies from the rubble in furniture vans and giving them all a decent burial. It's the stuff of legends. The old man lived to be almost a hundred, so Cedric wasn't the boss for very long before he passed it all down to his son – I forget his name.'

'Henry,' said Thea. 'That'll be Henry. So if there was a daughter called Melissa – *grand*daughter, I suppose – everyone would know about her?'

'Probably,' said Drew doubtfully.

'Actually, Drew, I don't think undertakers are ever properly famous. They're always in the background, aren't they? People find them embarrassing or depressing.'

'Tell me about it. But, Thea, there's more. Your Oliver, the younger half-brother, was one of the abused boys. He's in London to give testimony against Cedric, not just to sit and watch. That's the best bit, as far as the media are concerned. A family torn apart, and all that stuff. I'm still amazed that you've managed to miss it all. I'm even *more* amazed that you're his house-sitter. That's fantastic.'

'Not in a good way, it isn't. I feel rather stupid, actually. But nobody has said a *word* about a trial. Not Gladwin or Mo or anybody.'

'Because it's such a nasty subject. And the victims are all so old now, people feel uncomfortable about it. As far as I can understand it, Cedric gave up his wicked ways quite early on and settled down to family and business life like the most model citizen.'

'Does that ever happen? Do men give up that sort of stuff?'

'I'm sure they do. Lots of people go through a period of being sinful, or whatever you want to call it, and then pull themselves out of it. Maybe it was the love of a good woman that redeemed him, or straightforward fear of the consequences.'

'Drew, you sound ever so animated. Are you . . . ? You know – getting over it? Karen, I mean. How has it been?'

'I might be starting to get over it, but only just. Oddly enough, I think today is the first day I've felt a bit more normal, as if my old self is still in here somewhere. We've got four new funerals today, which is a major boost, I can tell you. Maggs is a new woman, with the prospect of a bit of money coming in at last. It's been terribly tight for all of us.'

'Four! That's incredible!'

'I know. I think it's a record. And it's not three o'clock yet. There could be more.'

'Steady on!' she laughed. 'Don't get *too* ambitious.'

'You're right. We might not get anything else for a fortnight.'

'That's the other extreme. Anyway, it's good that things are busy.' She tried to inject sincerity into this last remark, despite a sense that it was not altogether good. It meant there was no chance of his joining her in Winchcombe, or dashing up to London to sit in the public gallery of the Old Bailey. 'And it's really nice to chat again,' she added, this time with genuine feeling.

'Glad to be of service,' he said, like an undertaker. 'Although I can't quite see where it gets you.'

'Nowhere, probably, but it's filled in a lot of the blanks. Thanks, Drew.'

They rang off, each feeling there had been much more they could have said.

Gladwin called back at three-fifteen, sounding stressed and impatient. 'I know, I know,' she barked. 'I have to get back to basics and talk you through it all again. We've had the post-mortem report on the girl, which helps. But there's nobody in the UK called Melissa Meadows who remotely fits her description. So she can't be who she said she was.'

'She could have been using her mother's name.'

'Of course. Yes. And how the hell are we meant to find *that*?'

'Well, all I really wanted to say now was that she definitely must have known Oliver. Anything else is too ridiculously far-fetched. And I know where he is today. I imagine you do, too, by this time.'

'Thea – it's been about thirty hours since you found her body. We've spent much of that time looking for her car, putting out calls for help with identification, examining the scene and going through her boxes. And then another killing happened and we had to start all over again with him. The wife alone has taken most of the day. She's in bits, and says she can't believe what's happened and knows nothing about anything. I've never seen such drama. She *screamed* for ten minutes.'

'Blimey. So you don't know where Oliver is?'

'It's possible that one of the team has found him and not yet told me. We can have another go at making Fraser Meadows tell us, if we have to.'

'He's at the Old Bailey. His brother's on trial for child abuse a million years ago. More than that, probably. Everybody's in their dotage, but they're trying him anyway. Oliver's a witness.'

Gladwin went silent for half a minute. '*That* trial? The one the media's been full of for a week or more? I don't believe it.' But she did – Thea could tell from her voice.

'Why should you make the connection?'

'Because it's the same *name*, damn it. How could we *not*? This team must have a collective IQ of a pigeon, to have missed it. I hate to say it – again – Thea, but sometimes I don't know how we'd manage without you.'

'It wasn't me,' said Thea modestly. 'It was Drew.'

Just saying his name felt like sucking a creamy toffee.

'So Oliver might be able to tell them who Melissa was,' Thea summarised to her mother, who was showing a keen interest in the results of the two phone calls. 'Even if Fraser has never seen her before in his life, I'm sure his brother has.'

'She could be a niece or something. Is that what you think?' Maureen pulled at an earlobe, as if trying to speed up her own thought processes.

'Well, not a niece, unless she's the offspring of big brother Cedric. I suppose that's possible. Actually, in theory, she could be the unacknowledged daughter of *any* of them. Including Fraser. She didn't call herself Meadows, which implies she wasn't born in wedlock.'

'Honestly, Thea, I don't see how she can be Fraser's. He's so adamant that she's not. I wonder what was on the memory gadget. Maybe it was the whole family tree, all neatly set out.'

Thea smiled indulgently. 'But why would she be killed? And which of the brothers could be capable of it? They're all so *old*.'

'It wasn't Fraser. He was with Mo from Saturday afternoon until he collected me from Damien's yesterday. You can ask her. And Oliver was in London . . .'

'People can get back here from London easily enough. And any of them might have paid somebody else to do it.

We need to figure out *why*. That must be the key to it all.'

'And why the other murder? What had that poor young man done to deserve it?'

'Classically, it would be because he saw something or knew something that might implicate Melissa's killer. It's the logistics of that one that defeats me. I don't see how it could have been done in broad daylight like that.'

'I suppose he couldn't have just died of heart failure or something, there in the alleyway? Or committed suicide? There weren't any marks on him, were there?'

Thea tried to conjure the image of the dead Reuben. Until then she had superimposed it onto the dead Melissa, finding them almost identical in every respect. 'I don't remember any,' she admitted. 'And he was much less *pale* than she was. Her face was a ghastly white, as if all the blood in her had drained away. He looked almost rosy, didn't he? There's something about being strangled – you can die of a heart attack, not suffocation. I can never remember it properly.'

Maureen shivered. 'It must be dreadful,' she moaned. 'Beyond words – to do something like that to another person. I couldn't do it to a rabbit.'

'Nor me,' agreed Thea. 'But apparently it comes rather easily to some.'

'No, no. I can't believe that. They must suffer terrible guilt afterwards. Or fear of being discovered. Or a kind of self-loathing that turns them into monsters. Subhuman monsters. It's such an enormous thing to do.'

Thea smiled forbearingly. 'I'm not sure that's how it is,' she disagreed. 'I'm afraid it's all less difficult than that.

People are so clever at rationalising. They'll persuade themselves it was justified, that it wasn't such a wicked thing to do, that it wasn't really them that did it at all. A powerful inner force took them over, made them mad, so they lost control. I have a ghastly suspicion that at the actual moment, it's really alarmingly easy to kill.'

'I don't want to believe that.' Simultaneously, they acknowledged the differences in their experience. Thea had increasingly intimate connections with the police, involving herself in cases where people had committed terrible acts for seemingly banal motives. She could see her mother withdrawing, anxious not to be forced to listen to stories of murdered boys and their callous killers. Even old men, who also got themselves slaughtered from time to time, made gruesome corpses, not to be contemplated. 'I think you must have a much stronger stomach than me,' her mother added, with little suggestion of approval.

Chapter Twenty-One

Oliver sat in a small room until twenty past four, when a middle-aged court official came to fetch him. 'Mr Meadows? You're to be called in a minute or two. It's rather later than we expected, so I'm afraid it'll just be the formalities today. Then, first thing tomorrow, you'll be on the witness stand and the day will be yours.'

'Just one day, do you think?' His heart was fluttering uncontrollably, as he walked beside the man down the deserted corridor. 'Is that all it'll be?'

'It's never easy to say, but from what I can see of it so far, that should be about the size of it.'

Just one day, after nearly sixty years of hatred and fear and a burning lust for vengeance. 'It hardly seems enough,' he murmured.

They made him read the words of the promise to be truthful; checked his name and address; waved a document at him which was the original statement of accusation against Cedric. They were patient and softly spoken, even the barrister defending his brother, who got up once to make a comment that Oliver could not fully understand. Raised above them all, like God, was the judge, at whom Oliver barely glanced. There was no time to worry about what he might be thinking. Several of the wigged and gowned lawyers were female, but gender seemed irrelevant. They all rustled papers and stood up and sat down in turn, like a dance. People whispered, on all sides. In the rows of the public seating, whispers seemed to go on constantly. Oliver forced himself to breathe slowly and deeply, to maintain control whatever might happen.

Because Cedric was sitting there, to one side, The Accused, looking impossibly old and small and lonely. Cedric who had frightened and hurt him so much that the injury never faded, but mutated gradually into disgust and shame, and then a burning rage. Cedric, whose face swam before Oliver's eyes whenever he came close to venturing on an intimacy with anybody, man or woman. Cedric who had told him repeatedly that he enjoyed sex with a man, that he had *loved* it. Look at how his body had responded to it. Obviously, it was something he would never forget, never know again in such vivid physical colours. Cedric had been twenty and Oliver fourteen. As far as he knew then, everything his brother said was true.

They had last met at their father's funeral, ten years before. It had been possible to avoid any direct conversation, especially as Cedric had seemed more than happy to cooperate with the estrangement. It had been a huge affair, with black horses and a glass-sided carriage, and half the population of Stepney had lined the streets to watch it pass. Prior to that, many years earlier, their mother's funeral had been only slightly less of an occasion, and again, Oliver had remained in the background, speaking not a word to Cedric, despite the absence of Fraser – claiming not to be able to afford the fare from Australia.

How was Cedric feeling, he wondered. How was he enduring the humiliation, as a slavering public lapped up the details of the case against him? There were other accusers, whose testimony Oliver was not supposed to hear. But none of them were from any later than the nineteen fifties, a fact that Oliver found troubling. He would rather his brother had continued his sinful practices throughout his life, in order to justify this public retribution. If he had stopped of his own accord, packing the whole thing away as a youthful error of judgement, it made Oliver seem to himself as unacceptably vengeful. What good could it do at this stage? Despite the consoling and encouraging words of his lawyer, it seemed perhaps that he was behaving with less than full integrity now.

Cedric had been the top man at an undertaker's that served the polyglot community to the east of the City of London. His father had taught him to adapt their services to embrace a variety of ethnicities. When it came down to it, a cremation was a cremation and a burial was a burial, and the trappings around the edges were easily accommodated. The style of coffin, the preparation of the body, the sweetmeats afterwards were the chief variants. Oliver had lived with it all for eighteen years, and remained unsqueamish about death as a result. Death was a much lesser evil than humiliation, pain, cruelty, even ridicule. Death had a dignity all of its own, and Oliver never forgot that.

Inevitably, he was forced to send his mind back through all those long decades, to bodily encounters that no longer seemed real to him. The bodies in question had changed beyond recognition. The urges and responses were long ago lost, leaving traces in the mind, not in the flesh. Perhaps, he thought, he was wrong to seek punishment now. Looking at his brother, he could not but think he was. When he ventured a glance at the avid faces of the public and the reporters, he was in very little doubt indeed.

But it was too late now. The juggernaut was rolling, and even if he backed out and refused to speak, there were others who would say the same things, and lead to the same conclusion. Cedric had, after all, been monstrous. He had raped a lad two years younger than Oliver, predating on him, terrifying him into silence. Malcolm, his name was, and a year ago he had visited Oliver and told the whole dreadful story. They persuaded themselves that they felt better afterwards, for the sharing of a secret that had most definitely ruined their lives. And there was an even more wretched victim, who Oliver had known at the time was being treated with real cruelty by Cedric. Bertie had been soft in the head, a grinning simpleton who hung about the streets hoping for casual tasks that would earn a shilling now and then. The child of an aged, arthritic mother, he was a figure that should have long ago disappeared from society, a figure classically designed for victimhood. But news headlines right up to the present day indicated otherwise. However the language might change, the pack continued to attack the weak and foolish with appalling viciousness. Cedric had thrust into the boy's uncomprehending body, telling him it was a secret brotherhood practice that would make him special. Cedric whispered of love as he wounded poor Bertie. Oliver had on one occasion been outside the sordid little shed, listening with helpless horror. He wondered, even then, whether this might be the worst injury of them all – to him, not to Bertie. To render him complicit, because he lacked the courage to even try to prevent the torture.

And then, seemingly overnight, Cedric had reformed. He had pulled himself around, with a gruesome complacency, finding Sylvia and marrying her within a few months of meeting her. If the girl looked pale and sore at times, she never made any complaint. Oliver suspected that Cedric was secretly vile to her, but she had few options but to endure, and there was money in plenty to assuage any injuries. After twelve years together, they produced a son, Henry, who was raised for ambition and respectability.

Oliver was invited to descend from the witness box and find a seat while proceedings for the day were drawn to a close. He was told to present himself the following morning, ready for the real meat of the business, with questions from prosecution and defence. He listened calmly and tried to imagine the night to come.

As the courtroom slowly emptied, he realised a young black woman was standing in front of him, blocking his way and asking if he was Mr Oliver Meadows. She drew him aside and showed him a card in a plastic holder. 'Detective Sergeant Button,' she introduced herself. 'I've been asked to speak to you on behalf of the police in Gloucestershire. Would you come with me, sir, please?'

The bloody house has burnt down, he thought. *That house-*

sitter has let me down. 'Why?' he asked. 'What's happened?'

'Let's get comfy first, shall we?' she said with a smile. She seemed terribly young, but there was steel in her eye, and a look of total purpose. She took him into a small room that had something about Police on a printed notice on the door.

'I'll come straight to the point,' she said. 'Do you know a young woman by the name of Melissa?'

'Melissa? Well . . . yes. I know a Melissa.' He was alerted instantly, his mind seizing the signals and processing them with great efficiency. 'Why?'

'Is she a relative of yours, sir?'

'I'm afraid I need to know the reason for these questions before I answer that.' Dignity had always been his refuge. He had learnt from his father that it had a very useful effect on all kinds of people. Calm, quiet dignity, even in the face of calamity, was the order of the day.

'She's dead, sir,' came the unhesitating response. DS Button was not interested in playing games. She plainly had little time to waste.

'Melissa? Dead? No, no. She can't be.'

'She was unlawfully killed in the grounds of your house in Winchcombe.'

'When?'

'A day or so ago. There was nothing to identify her, other than her first name. She collected some objects from your house, on Saturday evening, and was killed shortly afterwards.'

The woman was not reading from notes, he realised. She had a blank page in front of her, on which she seemed poised to record his replies to her questions. She had got the details by heart, presumably from someone in Winchcombe. She looked him in the eye, sitting at an angle to him, with no intervening desk or table.

'Oh, God,' he groaned, some of the dignity fraying at this news.

'Who was she, sir? I mean, what was her surname, and where did she live? And how is she connected to you?'

'Melissa Anderson. She had a flat in Oxford, but she moved around a lot. She left things at my house, and rented out the flat.'

The police officer wrote a few words. 'What sort of car does – did – she drive?' This was asked with a little frown, as if Button herself thought it irrelevant, but she'd been ordered to pose it.

'It's not a car – it's a van. A white van, actually. She'll have parked it up by the church somewhere, because she never liked bringing it down Vineyard Street. She once had trouble turning it round.'

Button made a note. 'And was she your daughter, sir? Or your niece?'

'Neither of those, Sergeant. Melissa was my sister.'

Chapter Twenty-Two

'*Sister*?' repeated Thea incredulously. 'But she must be . . . what . . . forty years younger than him. She *can't* be.'

'Half-sister, of course,' Gladwin elaborated. 'Child of a district nurse who visited the Meadows when the wife had a septic leg. Thirty-two years ago. The old man was over seventy . . .'

Thea tried to do the arithmetic. 'Nearly eighty, surely,' she concluded. 'His eldest son is eighty now. And he's been dead ten years. Wait a minute,' she jotted figures on the edge of a convenient newspaper. 'He must have been born about 1900, and Melissa about 1980. Yes, he'd have been close to eighty. How old was the district nurse?'

'I have no idea. But it looks as if Oliver was the only one who knew about it. Even the old man was never told, apparently.'

'So did Melissa really think Fraser was her father? Did she never meet him?'

'Seems not. Fraser was in Australia the whole time it was happening. We have no idea what she was told about him – or him about her. But we'll ask Oliver. There's a lot we need to ask Oliver.'

'And the older one? Cedric? Did *he* know she existed?'

'It's still guesswork, Thea. We couldn't ask the Met to go into that sort of detail for us. This is *our* investigation.'

'But you've got an identity and maybe a motive,' Thea realised. 'The family must have worked out that with all this sordid investigation into Cedric, the business is in real trouble. Somehow Melissa was seen as a threat. Maybe they thought she'd stake a claim to it and make trouble for Cedric's son. What's his name?'

'Henry. Try to keep up, love.'

'I thought you'd reproach me for running ahead,' Thea laughed.

'That too. We'll speak to Henry, of course. But there's a million miles to go before it's settled. Evidence, as you know, is the key difficulty. Without that, motive counts for nothing.'

'And there's still the question of Reuben.'

'Yes, Thea, there is. I think that should have been my line, don't you? I haven't forgotten Reuben – or his screaming wife.'

'So what now?'

'The boring stuff. Forensics. Background. Who was where and when. The pathologist's complaining because he's got a horrible cold and doesn't think he should be working. His assistant was going to do Reuben, but she's in the doghouse because she missed some bruises on Melissa's knee, or something. Patrick gave her the extremities to work on, and she said she didn't think that extended to knees.

You couldn't make it up, could you? She's been moaning to me about it this afternoon.'

Thea made a sympathetic gurgle.

'Actually, she's pretty useless. Patrick gets furious with her, makes her rewrite all her reports. She's in a major sulk now.'

'Oh dear. Nobody thinks of human interest in the mortuary, do they? Maybe it'd make a good TV series.'

'Very funny. I've got to go now. Let me know if . . . well, you know. If you stumble across a confession or something. Anything you think might come in useful. Okay?'

'Okay,' Thea agreed, feeling considerably more cheerful than she had for many a long week.

She felt for poor Gladwin, with two murders in one small town where nothing more unsettling than a prolonged pipe-laying project that had closed the main shopping street, thereby wrecking a few businesses, had happened for decades. The CID team in Gloucestershire was modest in size and not unduly eager to undertake long hours of overtime. Gladwin herself had two young sons and a husband who all enjoyed her company at home. She had transferred from Cumbria and plunged immediately into a convoluted investigation in Temple Guiting, where Thea and her then boyfriend were centrally involved. She was infinitely more sensitive and understanding than any stereotypical police officer Thea had come across. But then, so were Phil Hollis, and her brother-in-law James Osborne. Nearly all the detectives Thea knew personally were genuinely good and pleasant people. This was reassuring, since her own daughter Jessica was also a police probationer. Only

Jessica's ex-boyfriend, Detective Sergeant Paul Middleman, had manifested a number of undesirable character traits.

Gladwin would have sent officers to speak to virtually everybody on the south side of the town, as well as putting out requests for information. A police investigation like this depended totally on individual members of the public reporting what they knew. Old vendettas, squabbles between neighbours, overheard threats and invisible connections were all likely to be significant. The picture that began as little more than an amorphous grey cloud had to be given outlines and dimensions and colour in order to explain precisely *why* and *who* and *how* things had happened as they did.

Now, as Thea assembled the known facts that had emerged in the brief period since she had discovered Melissa's body, a viable hypothesis emerged. This was tremendous progress. A hypothesis could be tested. It gave direction to any questioning, and comparisons for the forensic activities. *But what about Reuben?* How did he fit the picture? She struggled to remember everything he had said on Sunday afternoon, as he interrupted her lunch and made oddly veiled remarks. He had claimed to know who she was, and to have seen her at Temple Guiting. He eavesdropped on their conversation, and admitted he had heard them talking about Oliver, and Thea's ignorance as to where he might be. Given the notoriety of Cedric's trial, it was virtually certain that Reuben himself had known full well where his elderly neighbour had gone. He had been teasing them, somehow. Her mother had reprimanded him, and none of them had liked him.

But Thea had not disliked his wife, Jenny, and she was greatly enamoured of the fabulous dog. Jenny had screamed for ten minutes when told of Reuben's death. How was that possible? It must be like singing a sustained aria in *Turandot* or something. Surely it hadn't been real actual loud screaming? The woman hadn't looked like a screamer. But shock took people in strange ways, few of them predictable.

And as her mother kept saying, Reuben had been far too young to die. And their not having liked him made it worse. Even Thea felt a pang or two of guilt, and guilt was very much not her thing. It was assuaged by the recollection of the man's deliberate provocation. He hadn't *wanted* to be liked. He had been snide and intrusive. *And*, she remembered suddenly, he had not known, at lunchtime on Sunday, about Melissa's death – unless he was a very good actor. He knew *something* had happened – probably his main reason for approaching them was to find out precisely what – but he still hadn't ferreted out the central fact, three hours or so after the event. He had been needling Thea about her reputation in the Cotswolds, implying that she was in some way the *cause* of various troubles, but he was doing it idly. Surely nobody could have taken that approach if he'd known that a healthy, happy young woman had been viciously killed in the woods a few yards from his house.

And he had been different in manner later that same day, when the truth had finally filtered through to him. He had seemed more *rehearsed*, along with his wife. They had come to the door offering protection to a vulnerable stranger, quoting their Neighbourhood Watch credentials, and been thoroughly unconvincing.

So – had Reuben killed Melissa, with his wife's knowledge, and plotted an elaborate smokescreen to throw everyone off the scent? If so, he rapidly got his punishment, as some third person wreaked revenge on him. 'No, no,' she muttered aloud. 'Far too convoluted.' She very much doubted that anybody could have acted as convincingly as Reuben would have had to, on both occasions she'd met him.

It was close to seven o'clock, and yet again, food was required. Her mother could hardly be expected to work another magic trick in Oliver's poorly stocked kitchen, but the prospect of going out to eat was deeply uninviting. 'I wonder if there's a fish and chip shop,' she mused. 'I don't remember seeing one.'

'There a Chinese,' said her mother. 'I saw it yesterday. We could get a takeaway.'

'Mmm.' Thea was unenthusiastic. 'It's probably closed on a Monday. So many places are.'

'That's what comes of pretending Sunday is just another day. The wretched creatures discover they have to have at least *one* day off, so they just shift it along to Monday. Which is a lot less convenient for the ordinary person.'

'Depends what it is, I suppose. Museums and places like that ought to open on Sundays, because people like to go at weekends.'

Her mother flapped an exasperated hand. 'My goodness, Thea, how you do *argue*,' she complained. 'Why don't I go and have a look? It's less than ten minutes' walk, and I must admit I'm damned hungry.'

Hungry enough for an expletive, it seemed, even if only a mild one. 'I'll come with you,' she sighed. 'I think we should probably keep together. I'll never forgive myself if you get bumped off as well.'

It was meant flippantly, but it seemed her subconscious knew better than that. The words sparked a flicker of fear somewhere in her middle. Somebody was out there, just beyond her field of vision, killing people. And it was already almost dark. The misery of the shortening days added another depressing strand to her plummeting mood. It would be April before there was any prospect of warm weather and balmy evenings, and even then it was far from assured. April could often be horrible.

'All right. Have you got any money?'

'Hardly any. I was planning to go to a cash machine today, and forgot all about it.'

'Well, there's one in the square. We'll pass it on the way to the shops.'

'We'll take the dog. She hates being left alone after dark.'

'Soft thing.'

They had barely closed the door behind them when a figure confronted them on the path leading to Vineyard Street. 'Hello!' it greeted them heartily. 'Just the people I wanted to see.'

It was the Heap woman. Miss Heap, no relation to Uriah, thought Thea wildly. Still wearing the corduroy jacket, it seemed, and still intruding onto delicate territory. But the heartiness proved temporary. 'I know I'm being a bore, but the fact is . . .' the voice faltered, 'I wanted a bit of company.'

'But . . . you *live* here,' said Thea daftly. 'I mean, don't you have friends or family?' It smacked of far too much desperation that the woman should seek out complete strangers.

'Friends and family are unequal to the moment,' came the reply. 'They are all bewildered or indignant, when I'm searching for some sense.'

Thea had come across women like this before. The Cotswolds in particular seemed rich with them. They were not always horsey; neither were they always reliable. But Thea liked them, and knew them to be capable of great surprises. She liked their straight talking and the sort of bone-deep courage that enabled them to live alone facing an unappealing future. She sometimes imagined that her fate was to become one of them, in about fifteen years' time.

'We're on a quest for some sustenance,' said Thea's mother, matching the woman's diction and manner with impressive accuracy. 'Do you know whether the Chinese place is open this evening?'

'It is not. But there's a sort of van arrangement in the car park that sells kebabs. I can recommend their prawn concoction. It's astonishingly delicious, and costs a mere four ninety-nine. I'll escort you, shall I? It's a bit tricky in the twilight.'

'Sounds ideal,' said Thea. 'Lead on.'

They crossed the high street and entered a smaller street that Thea had not noticed before. A sign informed them that it was Cowl Lane, and it sloped upwards. In the poor light, Thea could see no buildings of interest; nothing that might provide material for idle conversation.

Their escort threw occasional nervous glances at the spaniel, and Thea diagnosed a familiar dog phobia that she knew better than to remark on. As with many Cotswold settlements, the levels were unpredictable, and although this one was parallel to North Street, it felt higher. 'The abbey used to be just over there,' their guide informed them, waving to the left. 'It's fanciful, I suppose, but I often feel its presence, especially at this time of day. Every stone was removed, you know. There's nothing left to see. And yet it was a major centre in its day. People came from all over Mercia – and beyond – on pilgrimage. All roads led to Winchcombe at one time. Now you're lucky if anybody beyond Gloucester has even heard of it.'

'It goes like that,' said Thea. 'Reputations rise and fall.'

'Look at Tewkesbury,' added her mother.

'Indeed,' said Priscilla Heap, whose Christian name Thea had only just remembered. She added a little snort of amusement, as if belatedly grasping the point of a joke. 'Although I'm not quite sure that Tewkesbury was ever . . . ?'

'Oh, it was. King Kenulf was based there, and he was *tremendously* important in the seventh century,' Maureen asserted.

'Mother, you amaze me,' said Thea. 'I never thought you were interested in history. But wasn't Kenulf here in Winchcombe? You've got them confused.'

Maureen paused, a finger to her lips. 'Have I? I was *sure* . . .' She turned to Priscilla for support. 'Which is it, then?'

'I fancy your daughter's in the right. But there's barely ten miles between them, so I expect they all moved around a bit, and most of it's legend, anyway,' said Priscilla kindly. 'You're right that this area was very important, in any case. Up to the fifteenth century, at least. Don't forget the Battle of Tewkesbury in 1471.'

'How could I forget that?' laughed Maureen uncertainly.

'There you are, Mum,' Thea said bracingly. 'All that stuff about the war that you and Fraser have been coming out with. That's in the history books now.'

'Pity I can't remember more about it, then,' sighed Maureen. 'But let's not get started on that.'

They found the mobile kebab van with a small crowd of customers waiting for their food. 'Ten minutes,' said the small man inside. A woman was energetically chopping and slicing and sizzling onions behind him. The smells were unbearably enticing.

'I'm not sure I can last that long,' moaned Maureen. One or two of the waiting people chuckled at her. Thea hoped none of them recognised her and her mother as coming from Thistledown, and being associated with two murders. As far as she could tell, this was not happening.

The presence of Priscilla was unsettling. She was liable to come out with some treacherous remarks that might alert people. Presumably at least some of them knew her, but she had not been greeted by anybody. She moved a short distance away, the others following, and muttered, 'Tourists, most of them. They'll be self-catering somewhere locally, and too lazy to cook. Mike leaves leaflets all over the place, so they'll have decided to give him a try. His stuff really is very good.'

She had not, however, ordered a meal for herself, Thea

noted. She seemed content to wait with them, and aware of the need to hold her tongue for the moment. There was something very contained about her, Thea observed. This was not a woman who would burst out in incontinent revelations or embarrassing comments. She was tense, though; her hands clasped together and her weight constantly shifting from one foot to the other. 'Where exactly do you live?' she asked.

'Castle Street.'

'Nice. I saw some really lovely houses down there, only this morning. One in particular. And that chapel overlooking it all gave it extra character.'

'I'm just a little way down the hill from there. And my house is not regarded with much favour, I'm sorry to say. It's too new to be lovely.'

Thea laughed. 'That's ridiculous when you think about it. But I know what you mean. The stone has to weather for at least two centuries before it looks right.'

'And yet by definition it's already millions of years old. It's a pity it comes out of the ground looking so new. It's like a deep-sea creature that's never seen any light. The stone needs to gain its own version of melanin, like a suntan.'

'Is it *very* new? Your house, I mean.'

'Fifteen years or thereabouts. I've heard it called a monstrosity and an abomination, when in fact it's very well built. It conformed to all the regulations; it's perfectly in keeping.'

'Not like that blank-faced building where the silk mill used to be, then?'

'Hush!' Priscilla looked quite alarmed. 'You mustn't

criticise that. It was the town's pride and joy when it was built. You should have seen what was there before.'

'But in Blockley they simply converted the mill. That's got loads more character.'

If there was coded information in what Priscilla was saying, Thea was missing it. She had assumed that Reuben and Jenny lived in the building in question, which appeared to be divided into maisonettes or flats – hadn't Jenny said as much on Sunday? It seemed now that she might have misremembered the exact remark. There were several other possibilities as to where Jenny might live – large houses raised high above the street on the north side, and smaller ones further down Silk Mill Lane. Close neighbours to Priscilla Heap, in any event. She had not forgotten that the woman had appeared swiftly on the scene when they found Reuben's body, and had capably ushered back the onlookers. And now she was nervous and agitated, and in need of company.

They carried their food back to Thistledown. 'I've no intention of eating in the street,' said Thea's mother firmly. 'However hungry I might be.'

'Oh, Mother – you're so old-fashioned,' Thea fondly mocked.

'It's good to have standards,' Priscilla defended. 'That's what the older generation is for – to maintain standards.'

'Thank you,' said Maureen with dignity. 'Shall I take the dog, if you carry this bag?'

The food was still hot when they got back into the house, and there was no awkwardness about Priscilla not sharing the meal. She offered to make coffee while the others ate and a comfortable peace descended, which Thea could not help feeling was merely temporary and perhaps undeserved. In fact, she broke it herself, after a few minutes.

'So – did you know Reuben Hardy, then? Wasn't he a close neighbour of yours?'

'I knew him well enough, yes. Typical brash young whizz kid, off up the motorway every morning to some incomprehensible job.'

'And his wife? I met her on Saturday, briefly. With that gorgeous dog.'

'Poor creature. It only sees the people at weekends. They pay someone to take it out for a few minutes during the day, while they're both off at work. Criminal, if you ask me.'

'She seemed very fond of it.'

'How could anybody *not* be? It's the most beautiful animal you could wish to meet. Much as I mistrust dogs, I can recognise sheer beauty when I see it.'

'More beautiful than your horse?'

'My horse is twenty-five years old, with a crooked flash down her face and a tail that collects sticky burrs of its own accord. Sally-Girl is far from beautiful.'

'But you love her,' supplied Thea's mother.

'I suppose I do. She and I go back a very long way.'

'Do you ride her?'

'Of course. Her life would lack all purpose otherwise. We have our little circuit, avoiding the roads. This area has more bridle paths than anywhere I know. People have ridden to and fro for centuries, across this land. And Sally-Girl knows all the kinks and bumps for miles around. Do you ride, either of you?' She looked from face to face.

Both shook their heads. 'You should try it,' urged Priscilla. 'It's magnificent, up there, being carried along by a living animal. There is absolutely nothing like it.'

'I think you have to come to it young,' said Thea carefully. 'And we were never a horsey family. I've got two sisters, and none of us ever went through the pony stage.'

'Poor you,' said Priscilla Heap with feeling.

'It was a different sort of place to this,' defended Thea, tiring of the subject. 'So – tell us about Reuben,' she demanded. 'Isn't that why you came to see us in the first place? After all, it was only this morning we were standing over his dead body.'

'I've told you most of it. Young. Ambitious. Too affluent for his own good. That dog must have cost close to a thousand pounds, for a start.'

Thea's mother gave a shocked squawk. 'Really?' she spluttered.

'From what I hear at the shows, absolutely.'

'But he wasn't killed for his money, was he?' said Thea briskly. 'I don't expect he's got very much in hard cash.'

'Unless it was his wife, of course,' said Maureen. 'She'll get it all now, won't she?'

Priscilla gave a dismissive snort. 'How could she have carried the body up that alley? She's not very big. Besides, they're a devoted couple. Everybody says so. She'll be absolutely lost without him.'

'She screamed for ten minutes,' said Thea absently, 'when they told her he was dead.'

Priscilla blew out her cheeks. 'Gosh!' she said.

But Thea was thinking about something else. 'How do

you know the body was carried into the alley?' she asked.

'Because it was cold – been dead for hours – and even though it's not exactly a busy thoroughfare, people do go up and down it regularly. If he'd died there, someone would have found him a long time before you did.'

'That's true,' Thea accepted. 'I know it is, because I went down it myself shortly before nine this morning. And he wasn't there then. But how do you know it was cold? I didn't see you touch him.'

Priscilla lost poise for a moment, her lips working but no words emerging. 'Oh, well, I had a quick feel, remember – just the tips of my fingers on his cheek. I don't know why – just a sort of instinct, I think. Animals do it. Just a little nudge, to see if you can bring them back to life. And poor Reuben was stone cold, I assure you.'

'I believe you,' Thea said quickly. 'And somebody killed him.'

'Don't you think . . .' ventured Maureen, 'that he might possibly have died naturally, or perhaps killed himself, and then been put in the alley for some reason?'

Both the others stared at her. 'Why in the world would anybody want to do that?' Thea demanded. 'That would be insane.'

Her mother held her ground. 'Well – he might have been in the wrong place, somewhere embarrassing. Perhaps he was having a fierce argument with someone and the stress of it gave him heart failure. After all, there were no marks on him. He didn't look as if he'd been strangled, did he? Doesn't that leave obvious bruises? And the way he was laid out . . . it all looked so *careful*.'

Thea suppressed an unworthy thought that the streets of Winchcombe obviously demanded a neat and tidy murder, and focused on what her mother had said. She had to admit that there was some sense in the theory. There were clear differences between the two bodies, after the initial impression that they were identical. 'But whoever laid him out like that must have seen Melissa's body as well.'

'Or work as an undertaker,' suggested Priscilla, as if the idea was a new one, a light remark with no substance behind it. Now it was her turn to receive a hard scrutiny.

'You know about the Meadows case, then?' Thea asked.

'What? What are you talking about?'

Thea remembered that Gladwin hadn't paid much attention to the story; that she herself, despite having the news mumbling away on the radio for much of the day, had missed it. Perhaps Drew, in the business himself, had given it undue importance, assuming that everybody else in the country shared his fascination for funerals and their operatives. The reality might easily be that it had been given much less coverage than he implied, and that most people failed to be interested.

'Oliver's brother is on trial for child abuse, in London. The family are prominent East End undertakers. Oliver's nephew runs the business now. Oliver's father was—' She stopped herself. The fact of Melissa's parentage was not for public consumption. It was even possible that the girl herself had actually thought herself to be the offspring of Fraser, and not his sister. It had been a tightly kept secret, and to reveal it now felt unfair, even before the obligations to keep details of police enquiries to herself.

'What? Was what?' prompted Priscilla.

'Famous during the war, apparently,' Thea improvised. 'He was a hero, according to Drew.'

'Fraser never said a thing about that, back in the sixties,' Maureen said quietly. 'I would have remembered that sort of story. I'm *sure* I would.'

Priscilla turned to her enquiringly. 'Pardon?' she said.

'Oh, he and I knew each other, a thousand years ago. We've just been reunited.'

'Gosh! How romantic!' The thread of sarcasm was barely discernible, but Thea winced on her mother's behalf. 'Who's Drew?'

Good question, Thea thought. 'He's a friend of mine. He does natural burials in Somerset.' She glanced at her mother, aware that until that moment she had never heard Drew mentioned.

'You don't mean the Peaceful Repose chap? The one who's been trying to get a burial place going in Broad Campden?'

I might have known, thought Thea. Maybe people did take more notice of the funeral business than she'd just been assuming. 'That's him,' she said resignedly.

'How do you know him? Have you buried somebody in his cemetery?'

'No. We just . . . bumped into each other, earlier this year. His wife died a few weeks ago.'

'Thea, you've gone pink,' her mother accused. 'Is this a new boyfriend you haven't told me about?'

How was it that mothers could always regress you to fifteen, with absolutely no effort, Thea wondered. She repressed a desire to snap and snarl and retreat to her bedroom. 'Nothing like that, Mum,' she said brightly. 'I just said – his wife died. He's got two little children. He hasn't got time for anything else.' *And besides, he's six years younger than me*, she felt like adding. But that would be too great a giveaway. You didn't make those sort of calculations about somebody who was just a casual friend. Her heart skipped alarmingly. *No*, it crowed, *you don't, do you?*

'So he'll know about the Meadows family,' summarised Priscilla. 'And could be helpful to the police, maybe? If they ask him.' She smiled meaningfully, and Thea understood that the well-publicised events of Broad Campden, six months earlier, had remained in the memory of at least one resident of Winchcombe.

Chapter Twenty-Three

While Thea was gathering information and making connections, Drew was managing something similar, once the children were finally in bed, and some urgent bill payments attended to. The hours since the conversation with Thea had passed somewhat blurrily, as he tried to stay abreast of work, children, supper, Maggs and his own chaotic emotions.

This would be the fourth time since he met her that Thea had become embroiled in a violent death. The first time, admittedly, it had been less her than Drew himself, who had borne the brunt of it. Since then, they had discovered a knack of bouncing ideas and theories around, working as an informal team, or – more accurately – a mutually supportive twosome. Karen had been a serious distraction every time, and Maggs a sternly disapproving figure. But here was a clear instance where he could provide helpful inside information. Nobody could object to that. And as if to exonerate himself of any subterfuge, he had asked Maggs, shortly before she went home, whether she knew anything about the Meadows family and their undertaking business in London.

'Henry Meadows!' she exclaimed immediately. 'Yes, I met him on that conference thing you sent me to. Remember? About eighteen months ago. You thought we should make our presence felt. It cost a fortune, and I never thought it was worth it.'

'Henry Meadows was there?'

'The man himself. They treated him like royalty. Everybody wanted to be like him. There was a session on relations with the community – I had plenty to say about that, as you can imagine.'

'I remember,' he said patiently.

'Well, the Meadows chap seemed to think he'd invented the whole idea. Went on about Chambers of Commerce and Rotary and that sort of tedious stuff. I kept interrupting and talking about the WI and the local Green Party. He was furious with me,' she chuckled. 'It was great fun.'

'So he's a pompous stuffed shirt?'

'Well, no, not really. He's youngish and good-looking and quite a charmer. Not oily at all. Smiles a lot.'

'I'm impressed at your total recall.'

'I haven't given him a thought for over a year,' she defended. 'But you asked and I told you.'

'Yes, and I'm impressed,' he repeated.

'So why the question in the first place?'

He took a deep breath. 'I saw a news item on the telly. A murder in Winchcombe. Apparently it involves that Meadows brother who says he was abused as a boy, by another of the sons. His half-brother. There's a trial happening in London as we speak.'

He could see her mind whirring. 'Winchcombe? Where's that, as if I didn't know?'

'Gloucestershire, I think.'

'Come off it, Drew. It's in the Cotswolds, isn't it? That woman's involved, I suppose. And you've been speaking to her.' *When I told you not to*, hung in the air, but even Maggs wouldn't go quite as far as that.

'I can be helpful to her,' he insisted. 'So can you, if you stop being so pig-headed about it.'

She blinked and eyed him carefully. 'You do look better,' she acknowledged. 'I suppose that's a good thing.'

'It's all these new funerals,' he said warmly. 'Being busy is the best medicine. I still can't quite believe it.'

Maggs yawned. 'Well, I can. I had about four hours sleep last night. I can't wait to get to bed.'

'Get along, then,' he encouraged. 'Thanks for the info about Henry Meadows.'

'Luckily you're going to be far too taken up with the funerals to have time to slope off to the Cotswolds. I suppose a few phone calls won't hurt.'

She spoke with the air of giving gracious permission, and he knew he couldn't let it go at that. Drew Slocombe had always tried to address snide hints and innuendo wherever he found them. 'Maggs, dear friend and partner, let's get this straight. You're not my mother, sister or wife. You actually can't take responsibility for me and my life. I know your motives are perfectly pure and good, but you have to back off and let me make my own decisions. I owe you an enormous debt of gratitude for years of support and sacrifice and fantastic company. I rely on you far too much. The children even more so. It's not good for either of us to keep on like this.'

She sagged, taking the full impact of this startlingly direct speech. But Maggs Cooper was made of solid steel. Drew often imagined a Jamaican grandmother somewhere, whose genes had passed wholesale into this young cuckoo who had been raised by a quietly decent couple in Plymouth. They had valiantly risen to the challenge of a mixed-race child, who from her middle teens had wanted nothing else but to become an undertaker. She had married Drew's friend, Den Cooper, a very tall ex-policeman, who knew himself to be unworthy of her. Nobody, really, was worthy of Maggs.

'Okay,' she said. 'Fair enough. I'm not going to argue with you about it. But I'm not going to change my mind, either. There'll come a time when you'll see I'm right, and be thankful to me.'

'I'm thankful *now*. I just said so.'

'Well, that's all right then. Now let me go home to bed, will you?'

'Right. I'll see you in the morning, then. Busy day ahead.'

'Night, night, then, Drew.'

All of which left him mildly confused. Whatever he might have said to Maggs, he still found himself feeling answerable to her, in need of her permission before he approached Thea again. But hadn't she *given* that permission? And wasn't he lapsing back into the old pattern of bowing to her superior wisdom, thinking along these lines in the first place? Almost from the start, Maggs had taken it upon herself to behave as his moral arbiter. She had defended Karen's interests, working on the assumption that all men would stray and misbehave if you gave them enough rope. An assumption that Drew had almost confirmed, once or twice. Women liked him. They liked his boyishly open face and natural good listening. He met their eye and admitted to his feelings. They liked his way with children, and his easy professionalism when it came to burying the dead. And, to his own occasional surprise, they seemed to see in him a solid integrity that made him a man to rely on. That was the part that Maggs seemed to overlook. Drew was safe and much stronger than he looked. His back was straight and his shoulders square. He looked good in a suit. And he had small sensitive hands. Everybody looked at his hands, wondering with a variety of emotions just what he was capable of doing with them.

Thea had called him, he reminded himself. She had made the first move. Whether or not that was relevant was obscure to him, in his adult persona; to the adolescent who never quite disappeared completely, it was highly significant. For the girl to make the call meant the rules had changed, and the boy was expected to remain alert and serious. Karen had often made the first call in their long-ago courtship. It struck him that the pattern was unlikely to change now, whatever happened. He was required to remain alert and serious for ever, where women were concerned.

So he phoned her. He used his house phone, because it

was cheaper, and he sat in the hall, at the bottom of the stairs, automatically picking up the pen that was firmly tied to a nail in the wall. In his business, the telephone was crucial and making notes an essential part of almost every conversation.

She answered quickly, warmly. 'How's it going?' he asked her. 'Are you still in Winchcombe?'

'I am. My mother's staying another night. The others have gone. We've got an identity for the girl, thanks to you. A lot's been happening.'

'Thanks to me?'

'Absolutely. Nobody had made the connection with the London trial. I'm not sure they ever would have done, without you – unless Fraser had spoken up. He was hoping it could be kept quiet, I think. He declined to tell Gladwin where his brother was, when he was being questioned.'

'Fraser?'

'The middle brother. The one my mother's with. Or whatever the phraseology should be. Did I tell you about that? They knew each other in the sixties and he's just found her again. It's all very weird.'

'Yes, you told me. It sounds like something we should probably be worried about.'

'That's what Gladwin thinks as well. He seems to remember a lot more than she does. I'm not sure she's even convinced it's the same man.' She was speaking softly, presumably not wanting her mother to hear.

Drew considered for a moment. 'And how do we go about proving it, either way?' he wondered. 'I suppose she does remember his *name*?'

'His first name, anyway. You know – I think she might well have forgotten his surname. It was a very brief affair, and not serious on her side, at least.'

'Fraser's not a common name. If the man she knows now really is Fraser Meadows, then I suppose it must be right. Anyway, tell me about the Melissa person.'

'She's their half-sister. Fifty years younger than Cedric. Isn't that amazing! Gladwin sent a London detective to talk to Oliver, and he told them, just like that. As far as I can work out, he and Cedric are the only ones who knew about her. Fraser was in Australia when she was born. I'm not even sure *she* knew who her father was. She called Oliver "Uncle Ollie" and she told me she was Fraser's daughter. I think she really believed it. It's still very vague. Poor Gladwin's in a terrible state, with two murders to investigate. I never get a proper talk with her.'

'And the other chap? Today's victim?'

'Reuben Hardy. Early thirties, married. He lived near here but worked long hours at something lucrative. I met his wife on Saturday and him on Sunday. They've got a lovely dog.'

'God, Thea – you *met* him?'

'And I found his body. Did I tell you that?'

He snorted. 'You did mention it, yes. You told me the whole thing in about forty-five seconds. I was very impressed.'

'It's all such a *whirl*,' she complained. 'I can hardly remember who said what, and when. And we have no idea why Reuben should be killed, except that he must have seen something or known something that might incriminate Melissa's killer. We thought at first the two murders were almost identical, but now we're not so sure. There are some differences.'

'Such as?'

'Her face was terribly pale, and there was a horrible mark round her neck. He looked a fairly normal colour and I couldn't see any marks at all. Priscilla said he was cold.'

'Priscilla?'

'Oh, a local woman who knew him vaguely. She came round this evening, and we went a little walk with her. She's nice, in a horsey sort of way.'

'And she felt his body?'

'Yes. She turned up soon after we found him, and she felt his cheek. She says he was cold.'

'But he was outside, and it's what – twelve degrees or so today. He'd get cold in no time. That doesn't prove anything.'

'They were *arranged*, Drew, both of them. Laid out, like statues on top of a tomb. Hands folded, eyes closed. That alone shows it was the same killer both times.'

'I suppose it does,' he agreed. 'So what happens next?'

'I have no idea. I imagine Gladwin will wait for Oliver to give his testimony, whenever that happens.'

'That's tomorrow, I think. According to the news, anyway.'

'So then she'll bring him back here for a proper interview.'

'Maggs has met Henry Meadows,' Drew remembered to say. 'That's what I called to tell you. She says he's youngish, charming, self-confident. I forget exactly what she said, now.'

'Charismatic, probably. I wonder whether Cedric is the same. And I wonder what this trial is doing to Henry. It must be excruciating for them all. They must really *hate* Oliver.' Somehow she had failed to fully grasp this aspect of the story until now. 'And I have no idea how Fraser feels about it all. He manages to keep everything calm, with no sign of any emotion. Even when he was told his daughter was dead, he kept his head.'

'Thea, stop. I thought I was keeping up, until now, but you keep throwing in bits I haven't heard before.'

'Sorry. I suppose it would take all evening to tell you every single thing. Melissa said she was Fraser's daughter, so that's what I told the police. Then Fraser showed up here with my mother, and the police asked him to identify the body, and he said he had never seen her before in his life. And he did it all with very little sign of emotion. Does that cover it?'

'It certainly helps.'

'So, I'll tell Gladwin what you said about Henry. She'll probably have some ideas, and maybe some forensic findings or something. At least they won't have to do a DNA test now. Anyway, I should go. My mother's going to feel neglected at this rate.'

'Keep me posted, okay? Tell me if there's more I can do.'

'Thanks, Drew.'

When he put the phone down, a little voice floated down the stairs. 'Daddy? Have you been talking to that lady? The one on the telly? I heard you saying her name.'

He sighed and turned to reply. 'Go back to bed, Steph.

You should have been asleep ages ago. There's nothing for you to worry about.'

When had his own daughter turned into a miniature version of Maggs, he wondered?

Chapter Twenty-Four

Oliver assured the Button person that he would be perfectly all right to get himself back to Norfolk Square. She had insisted on knowing where he was staying and how he could be contacted.

'I'll be here again in the morning,' he said. 'Isn't that enough for you?'

'You've just had a shock, sir, in the middle of something that must already have been extremely stressful. You need to be gentle with yourself. Have an early night. It's unfortunate . . .' She tailed off with a little frown, before starting again. 'It's a pity you have to stand witness again tomorrow. Perhaps your counsel could get it deferred, in the circumstances.' She spoke uncertainly, as if on shifting ground.

'I wouldn't dream of it,' he said with feeling. 'I've waited far too long already. There's nothing I can do for Melissa now. She was a good girl, with everything ahead of her. It's a terrible thing for someone to have done. But I can get through another day of this before I let myself dwell on that.'

But he found he couldn't. He found himself comparing the evil done to himself with that done to Melissa. For all the good he'd achieved in his life, for all the value he'd been to anybody, he might as well have been murdered in his youth, just as she had been. He had behaved like a dead man for much of his life. If it hadn't been for the birds and the technical challenges he'd set himself in photographing them, he might have permitted himself to slide into some chronic sickness and early death, purely by abandoning all interest in living.

He supposed there must be a bus that traversed the route from the Strand to Paddington. There were probably several. Somewhere in his memory he knew which they were, if he made the effort to recapture it. The streets of London had been stencilled onto his mind as a boy and would remain there for ever. He knew the way without thinking about it, the diagonal clear before him, cutting off Oxford Circus and bringing him out at Marble Arch, from which it was a short stroll to the hotel. A bus would find itself snarled up at Piccadilly Circus, and then crawl jerkily along Oxford Street, even with the reduced traffic wrought by the congestion charge. He had been surprised at how little change that had made to the progress of the buses, when it first came in.

He did not even consider the tube, despite the easy Bakerloo run virtually from door to door. He had never liked the underground and the strangers who stared blankly just past your shoulder. People were less uncomfortable to be with on a bus.

So he set out on foot, scarcely lifting his gaze from the

pavement in front of him, not even thinking in any coherent way. He felt old and unnecessary. His effect on other people was to embarrass them at best and humiliate them at worst. His wretched brother was facing retrospective contempt and disgust that would overshadow his lifelong reputation as a caring professional. The one person who had genuinely enjoyed his company from time to time was now dead, killed within hours of his turning his back on Winchcombe. Poor Melissa, he kept thinking. That poor, poor girl.

He avoided Regent Street, which he had always found to be tiring, with its insidious long incline, and instead wove his way through the smaller streets and squares that he would normally relish seeing again. He had never lost his affection for London, with its constant cosmetic changes which only served to emphasise its permanence. Shopfronts modernised, and evolved into coffee bars or expensive restaurants; the method for disposing of rubbish swung from bins to bags to boxes, and back again, stacks of discarded materials of every sort cluttering the pavements. He had noticed this especially in Norfolk Square and Sussex Gardens, where the hotels evidently created daily mountains of refuse which were noisily collected at first light. But he was still some way short of Marble Arch, and everywhere lights were on, as evening took hold. It was close to seven o'clock, he realised, and he ought to eat something. He would go to one of the small grocery shops in London Street, a minute away from his hotel, and eat it in his room. He tried to increase his speed, looking up at the street names at each junction, still aware of the glamour with which some of them were imbued. Grosvenor Square conjured indelible images from the sixties, with the anti-American protests, as he walked around it and into North Audley Street. Again, it had changed in many respects, and yet was essentially the same. He had taken no part in the Vietnam marches, but many of his contemporaries had, and he recalled the songs and the slogans quite vividly, despite never voicing them himself.

He emerged onto the western end of Oxford Street, with the cacophony of traffic and the complexities of scaffolding around the eternal remodelling of various buildings. Something massive and futuristic stood just to his right, which had certainly not been there last time he looked. But across the street the buildings were reassuringly familiar, especially the upper floors. He had often wondered what lay inside those third- and fourth-storey windows – did people live there, or were they merely storerooms for the shops below? In other cities, they would all be dwellings. In Lisbon people lived in the very heart of things, keeping the place alive all day every day. He had liked that aspect of the place more than anything, on a rare moment of adventure when he was forty.

He passed the Marble Arch tube station, and turned right. Edgware Road had been stretched, it seemed, and strangely mutated into a small piece of Arabia. Women in long black burkhas, men smoking hubble-bubbles, the signs in Arabic – it came as a welcome distraction to observe this particular alteration to the London he remembered. Idly he wondered at the process by which it had happened, and what the area would turn into next.

Star Street was his goal. He had made a particular note of it as the most direct route to take. The instant change of atmosphere, with the absence of traffic and the houses with their deep basements and yellowing plants outside, was a relief. If he ever came back to London permanently, he thought, it would be perfectly acceptable to live in Star Street.

His feet grew heavier as he reached Norfolk Square and the big inviting garden in the middle. He could see the door of his hotel welcoming him with a bright light over its name, and he began to fumble in his pocket for the key they had given him. The prospect of buying food seemed suddenly burdensome, and he decided against it. He would eat the free biscuits in his room and drink coffee and survive quite well till morning.

When the figure came out of the shadows of the public garden, he barely even saw it. 'Oliver!' came a voice, and he stopped. It was an old woman, hair silvery blonde in the streetlights, neat figure corseted and straight. 'Oliver, it's me, Sylvia.'

'Sylvia?' He had no idea who she was. 'What do you want of me?'

'You don't remember me.' She sounded sad. 'Cedric's wife. Your sister-in-law.'

'Good God! Sylvia!' He peered at her, searching for any familiar features. 'I would never have known you.'

'We only met a few times, after all. Weddings, funerals.'

'How did you know where to find me?'

'You're a predictable man, Ollie. It was easy enough to guess you'd come here for a room. You stayed here when the old man died.'

'Did I? Are you sure?' He could not recall any of the organisational details at that time, ten years earlier.

'Henry drove you back here afterwards. I've been waiting for hours. You took a long time to come back.'

'I walked. And the police . . . Did you know about Melissa?'

'What? Melissa who?'

'Our sister. Thirty-one years old. Murdered on my land at the weekend. They couldn't identify her until they asked me. They caught me at the end of the trial business.' He swayed on his feet, suddenly unbearably weary. 'What do you want, Sylvia?'

'Come and sit down, for heaven's sake. You look ready to collapse. There's a seat just inside the garden. It's nice in there. This is a much more pleasant part of London now. Funny how it changes. I remember Paddington as awash with prostitutes and homeless drug addicts. Everyone seems quite respectable now.'

'I was thinking something along those same lines,' he agreed. He still couldn't reconcile this person with the girl his brother had married so long ago. It was like a fairy tale, where the princess appears disguised as a crone. 'Are you *really* Sylvia?' he demanded pettishly. 'I don't recognise you at all.'

'You'll have to take my word for it. Sit down, Ollie, please.'

The relief was almost frightening. Surely he wasn't so old that his legs could no longer manage a stroll through the West End? 'You shouldn't be being so nice to me,' he objected confusedly. 'You must loathe the very sight of me.'

251

'It's got beyond that,' she said, sounding almost as tired as he felt.

'So you're not here to ask me to withdraw my accusations? To nobble me somehow, so I can't testify tomorrow?'

'Not really, no. It's rather late for that. I wanted to try to make you understand that the whole business has come far too late. Cedric is unlikely to live more than another year. He's got prostate cancer, and his lungs are in an awful state.'

'Why? He never smoked, did he?'

'He had pleurisy about four times, in his forties. It left them damaged. Nothing to do with smoking.'

Oliver absorbed this information without emotion. 'So he doesn't know about Melissa?'

'I don't expect so – no. How would he?'

'I think it's been on the news.'

'We don't watch the news these days. You probably can't imagine how it feels to see yourself and hear what they say about you, when it was all sixty years ago. It's literally like the worst sort of nightmare – where everybody gets you completely wrong and you can't do a thing about it.'

'He did look very . . . shrunken,' Oliver acknowledged. 'But he's eighty. What does he expect?'

'And you're not so much younger. Neither of you is the same person as when all that stuff happened. Your mother was useless; the war had knocked everybody sideways. Your father was a local hero and pretty well ignored you boys. Cedric went off the rails. It was horrible, what he did, but it wasn't regarded as the unspeakable evil that it is now.'

252

'It was by the victims,' Oliver protested, while knowing this was not entirely accurate. It had all been so very much more complicated than that. Evil was beside the point. 'And not being able to speak about it made it worse. You talk about nightmares – that's exactly how it was. Homosexual rape was regarded as completely unmentionable, even as a joke. Everybody pretended that such a thing could never happen, except perhaps in the most vile of prisons. Even the Nazis were never accused of that. They might bayonet babies and roast them on a fire, but the idea that they might rape young boys never even occurred to anybody. It was utterly taboo.'

'Yes, all right,' she shrank a few inches away from him. 'That's all true, I know.'

'You *don't*, though. You have no idea. You wouldn't want to know what happens, what it does to an unwilling body. And that's only a small part of it. Bodies heal. Minds very often don't.'

'Stop it, Oliver. Stop dragging it all up again. What good can it do? Cedric is ruined. He's dying. What more is there to say?'

'Nothing more. But it needs to be said loudly and often. Other men need to be deterred from doing it. I can't afford to care about Cedric. As you say, it's too late for that. He has been a dark shadow across my whole life, and yes, I really do dream about him, even now. The things that happen to you when you're fourteen get branded into your brain for ever. They form the person you are for the rest of your life. That's Cedric's bad luck, as well, as it's turned out. But he lived his life in the world, a success, admired by everyone, with a family and all the trappings. While I . . . well I've been a hollow shell for sixty years. He did that to me. It's no small crime, Sylvia, and it shouldn't be hidden any longer.'

'The shadow stayed with him, as well. That's what I want to say to you, really. He was damaged by it, too. He married me in an attempt to change his nature and it worked up to a point. He was thrilled when Henry was born. A son was the outward sign that he'd achieved normality. He put everything that was decent and normal in himself into that boy. I think Henry was his atonement. That's how he saw it. And now that the secrets of the past have been exposed, Henry has cut him off. He won't speak to him. He's appalled by the whole thing.'

Oliver had never considered his nephew's reaction. He had come close to forgetting the man even existed. If he did think of him, it was as an adolescent who might be at some risk from his predatory father. 'How old is he now?' he asked.

'Forty. He's getting married in January. Or he was. He's afraid his fiancée might change her mind, with the Meadows name so sullied. It's taken him all these years to find a girl who didn't object to being married to an undertaker.' She sighed. 'I'm not blaming you, Ollie, but I do want you to see what the damage is. How many people are being affected.'

'It doesn't change anything. What if I'd done this thirty years ago? When our father and mother were still alive, and Henry just a young boy? Would that have been better or worse?'

'I don't know. I just wish you hadn't done it at all. Most people don't, even now. It's the *publicity* that's so unbearable. I feel everybody's looking at me. I want to move away – go to live in the Canaries or Florida or somewhere. And Henry thinks he won't be able to keep the business going. Nobody's going to come to Meadows & Son after this.'

Oliver hadn't heard the family business referred to like that for a very long time. The '& Son' referred to a family relationship that went back a century or more. But it still carried a resonance for him – his father had been Francis Meadows, Cedric his son, and Henry *his* son. The chain had continued unbroken, and now Henry had found a girl who might well produce another male Meadows to carry it on.

'I hope that isn't true,' he said, genuinely shocked. 'I must confess the publicity came as a surprise. It never occurred to me there'd be so much interest.' In fact, he had been partly pleased by it, hoping that clandestine abusers would read and shiver with fear at this stark example of what could happen to them. The prospect of that had made the embarrassment worthwhile.

'It's not so bad for you, hiding away in the Cotswolds,' she accused. 'And besides, what do you have to lose?'

It was a fair question. 'Less than you,' he conceded. 'Now, anyway.'

They both realised the conversation had run its course. She put a hand on her smart leather bag, and gathered herself. 'I'd better go,' she said.

'Does Cedric know you've come looking for me?'

She gave a harsh laugh. 'Cedric and I seldom speak. He's brought home every evening, and collected again every morning. Every day he seems a little bit smaller, a little bit more silent. I stay out of his way as much as I can.'

Oliver could not imagine it. Nor did he want to. The image of a dead Melissa still persistently intruded into his thoughts. The entire conversation about Cedric had felt like a distraction from the more important matter. 'Melissa was murdered,' he said loudly. 'Somebody killed that poor girl, the moment my back was turned. She kept her things at my house. She came and chatted to me, every few months. And you hardly even registered when I told you.'

'I never met her. I had entirely forgotten she existed. Somebody told Cedric when she was born, and he helped to get it hushed up. His mother never knew about it. We didn't know where she was, or what she was doing. Why should I care about her now? What does it have to do with any of this?'

Oliver stood up shakily. 'She was a Meadows, and the Meadows family is the object of public loathing. I dare say there's a connection.' His mind began to form lucid links and theories that were startling in their clarity. 'If Henry gives up the business, one of the next generation might be tempted to take it on. That means Fraser's Mo – or Melissa. Meadows & Daughter.' He savoured the thought. 'They'd both be free of the taint that people associate with Cedric. Perhaps the idea had occurred to Henry. Perhaps Mo has already said something to him.'

'Stop it, Oliver!' Sylvia ordered. 'This is ridiculous talk.'

'I wonder,' he said. 'You know, in the past year or so, I've come to understand that there's a great world of difference between what people will acknowledge in open conversation, and what they'll do under cover of darkness and secrecy. The trouble comes when those two worlds collide.' He lifted his chin defiantly. 'And I have to say I rather relish being part of it.'

'Then God help you,' she spat, and walked quickly away towards Paddington Station.

Chapter Twenty-Five

In Oliver's house, Thea and her mother were having an oddly parallel conversation to that taking place in Norfolk Square. They had pooled their knowledge of the Meadows family, and made inspired guesses as to the state of mind of Henry Meadows, current proprietor of the undertaking business. 'He won't be popular, will he?' Thea suggested. 'The whole operation will be tainted by this child abuse case.'

'Maybe Mo will offer to run it instead,' said her mother, semi-seriously. 'Although I can't really see people talking to her about coffins and hymns with very much confidence.'

'Maybe *Melissa* was a more likely proposition. You know – she was an insurance assessor, covering a huge area down the western side of the country. Oliver told the police about it. It involved living out of a suitcase and moving around a lot.'

'So . . .' said Maureen slowly, 'what if Melissa wanted to change and settle down? Perhaps she was positioning herself to oust Henry, and he got to hear about it.'

Thea watched her mother's face as she reran this hypothesis for flaws. 'That does sound alarmingly feasible,' she concluded. 'But surely Henry wouldn't come here and do it himself? He'd pay somebody to do it for him. A hitman.'

'Do people really do that?' Maureen queried. 'How could you ever trust the person to keep quiet? You'd have to pay them an *enormous* sum of money to be sure. If it was me, I'd rather take the risk and do it myself.'

'But you were saying earlier that only a depraved monster could kill someone.'

'And you said I was wrong about that.'

Thea smiled at the ludicrous image of her mother as murderer, while knowing it was not that simple. Even ordinary women, elderly housewives, would kill in certain circumstances. 'It might seem easier in the short run,' she said. 'But could you live with yourself afterwards?'

'Good question,' nodded her mother.

'I'm still not clear how much you knew about the family business from Fraser, before you came here yesterday. I've been assuming you knew most of it, having met Mo already. But it's all a bit hazy. I'm not even sure how long ago you two rediscovered each other.'

Maureen spluttered at this direct questioning. She had always preferred a more circumspect approach when seeking information. 'It was about six weeks ago now,' she said. 'I told you – he contacted me on Facebook.'

'So you put your maiden name on there, did you? Otherwise he couldn't have worked out that it was you, could he?'

'Yes, I did. I was wondering whether there was anybody from my schooldays who I might contact again. You know how you always wonder how people turned out. Looking back now, you can see the whole span of their lives, and it's fascinating. There was a girl called Susan Bradford who emailed me. We sat next to each other in class for years.'

'And has she had an interesting life?'

'I'm not sure. She just listed her children and said her husband was in a nursing home. I assume not. But then, neither have I, when it comes to it.'

'But something was different about Fraser? He persuaded you to meet him, and now you're practically an item.'

'Is that what you call it? I can't explain it, Thea, so stop trying to make me. He's good-looking, interesting, attentive. He doesn't seem to find me boring. And to answer your question – no, I had no idea about the child abuse case being anything to do with him. I don't remember noticing anything about it on the news. These things just trundle on, don't they – just background noise.'

'What I mean is – did he list all his relations? Cedric and Henry and any cousins or in-laws? People do usually talk a lot about their family, especially when you first meet them.'

'I knew about Mo. I don't think he did mention Cedric or Henry specifically. Of course, I eventually got it out of him that his father was an undertaker. We argued about whether he told me that when I knew him before. I'm *sure* he didn't. I would definitely have remembered that. He says he talked about it when we did our Jack the Ripper walk, but if he did, I've forgotten. And I've been thinking about what's happened here, and I'm quite certain that Fraser never even knew Melissa existed. I believe him completely. He couldn't have just gone on pretending he knew nothing about her, if he actually knew full well she was his sister. Besides – what would be the point?'

'I'm not sure we used her name in his hearing.' Thea struggled to recall an instance where they might have done, but her mind went cloudy with the effort. 'Did we?'

'I don't know. But even if we didn't, he'd have made the connection. He must have just thought she was some waif Oliver had picked up somewhere.'

'But, it would fit with him being a very good actor, wouldn't it? Pretending to be your old boyfriend, when he's not.' Thea felt soiled by this deliberate attempt to undermine her mother's faith in the man. She assured herself it was for the best, that he could not be permitted to swindle and betray such a trusting woman, but just the same, it was not kind.

Her mother, however, showed no sign of wobbling. 'But he *is* Fraser Meadows,' she insisted.

'Yes, I suppose he is.' Thea felt the frustration of going over the same ground again, while at the same time feeling sure there were details still to come, with enough clues to establish once and for all whether Fraser Meadows was who he said he was, and if not, what his intentions were. 'And your boyfriend's name was definitely Fraser, was it?'

Maureen laughed uncomfortably. 'Yes, it was. It was in my diary. But . . . actually, I was quite silly. I gave a little list on Facebook of people I hoped to find, and of course anybody could have *pretended* their name was Fraser, based on that.'

Thea forced herself to concentrate on the logical thread of this. 'No, but this man's name really *is* Fraser. That much is certain, surely. The question is – is he the *same* Fraser that you knew?'

'Oh, he *is*, Thea. He *must* be. Anything else would be too horrible.'

'Yes it would. And I still can't see how in the world we can ever prove it, either way. Unless you've got something from nineteen sixty-two with his DNA on it. Then we could get Gladwin to run a comparison.'

'Well I haven't,' said Maureen with an emphasis that suggested the opposite.

'Of course not. How would you?'

'Except . . .'

'What?'

'He gave me this silly little locket in the shape of a heart. It was pretty. I've still got it somewhere.'

'So?'

'It had some bits of his hair in it. I imagine it still has. Would that work, do you think?'

'Gosh! It probably would. How amazing, if so.'

Maureen shivered. 'It's awful, really. I don't want to do that. I'm not entirely sure that it *matters*, you see. The Fraser that's here now is a perfectly respectable, pleasant person, and I like him. I'm sure he likes me.'

'But that's what conmen *do*. They make you like them, and then they take your house and your money and disappear. Why else would he go through all this charade of pretending to be someone else?'

'He isn't like that,' Maureen maintained. 'I know he isn't.'

'Tell you what,' Thea began, 'we could test him. You could leave that locket somewhere he'll see it, and if he remembers it and gets all romantic about it, that'll prove he's the real original Fraser. But if he's never seen it before, and you show him the hair, he'll panic and try to take it on some pretext, and then you'll know he's a fake. Simple.'

'Not simple if he's as good an actor as you think. He knows I can hardly remember anything, so he'll weave some tale about how much in love he was, and how poetic it seemed, and leave it until some later time to spirit it away. All he has to do is change the hair, come to think of it.'

'Well, obviously, you take the hair out first, before you show it to him. That would be a better test, actually. If he asks where it is, without any prompting or hints from you, that'll confirm he's real.'

'Yes, Thea,' said her mother patiently, 'I can see it would be easy to prove that he *is* real. But far harder to prove he isn't. I mean, even if he seems to fail the test, there could be an explanation. I'm not sure I'd be any the wiser.'

'So we should go ahead and get the DNA test done now. That would settle it.'

'Let me think about it for a bit.'

Since the first mention of Fraser, there had been one burning question that Thea had been unable to ask. The taboo against enquiring into your parent's sex life was ridiculously powerful, and she found herself unable even to frame the words. Her mother was averagely prudish, changing clumsily under a large towel on the beach, and fumbling for a suitable response when her daughters started their periods. Their big brother Damien had been their informant as to how babies were made, for which their mother appeared to be thankful. There had been a hugely embarrassing period during which their mother had plainly conceived a strong liking for one of the teachers at school, during a trip on which she had been a volunteer parent. Thea had been forced to witness her own mother flirting with Mr Lewis. Afterwards, she had grabbed any excuse to turn up at the school on the off chance of seeing him. The transparency of it had been the worst thing. Not even a lovelorn teenager would have been such a fool about it. Their father, fortunately, had seemed oblivious, and the children had all taken great care to keep it that way, scarcely even mentioning it amongst themselves.

Mr Lewis had been Jocelyn's form teacher, so she bore the brunt of it. Not until the following September did it start to fade away. The entire episode came back to Thea now, complete in all its detail, startling her in its clarity.

'Do you remember Mr Lewis at school?' she asked recklessly. 'How you had that crush on him.'

'I was menopausal,' came the ready reply, 'and not responsible for my hormones. I expect it was very embarrassing for you.'

'It was. And for him, probably.'

'Oh, he didn't mind. He thought it was tremendous fun. It *was* fun. You don't get that sort of experience very often in a lifetime, more's the pity.'

'But it wasn't like that with Fraser?'

'I was young and single. There wasn't much to lose, other than my virginity.'

Thea's instinct was to stop her, to put a hand over her

mouth to stem the excruciating words. But it had been what she was aiming for, all along, and she needed to hear it. 'So you did? Lose it, I mean?'

'Actually, not quite. There was another boy before Fraser, in the summer after I left school.'

'But you *did* sleep with Fraser?'

'Oh yes, of course I did. That's all I can really remember of him – his skin, and his . . . parts. If I could see him naked again now, that might clinch it. Although I imagine that changes through life, like everything else.'

'I'm not sure,' said Thea faintly. 'Possibly not. So you haven't seen *this* Fraser naked, then?'

'Definitely not. It seems that at our age courtship can take an awfully long time. I think we're both terrified of revealing our wrinkles. Understandably, in my case, I promise you.'

'But you'd like to? I mean – you'd still enjoy it?'

'Of course I would. It's only been a year since your father died, but in that respect it's been a very *long* year.'

In Thea's own case, it had been about a year, as well. There was something unjust about that, she couldn't help feeling. At her age, she was *supposed* to still get lots of sex. Both her sisters had husbands, and her friend Celia had a new boyfriend. And here was her mother complaining about deprivation, in her seventies!

An association reminded her of the murdered Melissa, child of an old man, proof that the sap kept rising for an astonishingly long time. 'Well, if Fraser is his father's son, you've got plenty to look forward to,' she said. 'He's still a few years short of his father's age when he fathered Melissa.'

Maureen laughed. 'You've worked it all out, have you?'

'More or less. He must have been close to eighty. I don't know how old the district nurse was. Anything from eighteen to forty-six, I suppose.'

'Let's hope she was forty-six. That makes a far nicer story.'

For the first time, Thea wondered where the woman was, and whether she knew her daughter was dead. Had Gladwin efficiently tracked her down and notified her, in the few hours since discovering Melissa's identity? It seemed unlikely. If she'd been forty-six when she produced the child, she'd be in her late seventies now. Perhaps she was dead. Melissa had seemed like a person with no close ties, no parents to store her possessions for her. 'It would,' she agreed. 'The older the better.'

'Preferably dead,' said Maureen sagely. 'That would save her the heartbreak.'

They were off the impossible subject of sex, Thea realised with relief. Murder was much easier to deal with. They now had a theory to explain the killing of Melissa Anderson. Presumably Gladwin had arrived at a similar hypothesis, given the same set of facts and relationships. In the morning, they would speak again, filling in more details, dredging up more snippets of conversation. But now it was almost time for bed.

'Better take the dog out for a widdle,' said Maureen. 'Do you want me to come with you?'

Thea went to the back door and pulled it open. Everything in the woods beyond was silent, the sky to the south pitch-black, but the lights of Winchcombe casting a

266

glow in other directions. 'We'll be all right,' she called back. 'I don't think we'll go far.'

Hepzie squatted on a patch of grass lit by the light from the doorway. Thea applauded with the obligatory 'Good dog!' and thought about Oliver's neglected birds. First thing next morning, she would go to the hide and feed them again. In a day or two they would return, she hoped, as if nothing had happened. The nervous woodpecker might take longer, and the opportunistic tits could have found a better bird table somewhere else, but no great harm would be done. Oliver could step back into his routines easily enough. Except his friendly young sister was gone for ever, and his humiliated older brother might prey on his mind, especially if he was ending his days in prison. And Fraser would take her mother to bed, which was a terrible thought.

'Come on, then,' she called the dog in, and closed the door.

They went to their separate beds at ten, conceding to each other that it had been a tremendously long day. Thea's final waking thought was, 'But why kill *Reuben*?'

Chapter Twenty-Six

Tuesday morning was drizzly and autumnal. Although the leaves in the hedges were still almost universally green, the grass was rapidly losing its colour. Across the allotments there were wilting stalks and a sense of everything bracing itself for the first frost. Dahlias and tomatoes alike would blacken and die the moment the temperature dipped below zero. The bright Cotswold gardens would lose much of their colour, sinking into winter dormancy more or less tidily, according to the diligence of their owners.

'I'll have to plant some bulbs next week,' said Maureen, over the breakfast toast. 'I like to do it in the middle of September.'

Thea thought about her own neglected garden, back in Witney, which was forced to fend for itself for far too much of the time. She had, however, given it a concentrated week of attention recently. 'I put some tulips in last week,' she said. 'I really like tulips.'

'Everybody does. The squirrels take the bulbs, though. It can be very disappointing.'

'Hepzie sees them off, when she's there. And next door's cat is very helpful. I think it'll be all right.'

'I had a dream,' Maureen remembered. 'Damien and Jason were fighting. It was quite nasty.'

'Have they ever met?'

'Fleetingly. I don't know why my unconscious should see them as enemies, though. They've got nothing to fight over.'

'What was it in the dream?'

'The locket – sort of. Damien was only about twelve, and Jason was big and angry. Damien stood up to him, and held the locket behind his back. When Jason tried to take it, he kicked him.'

'Damien kicked Jason? Gosh! What did *you* do?'

'Nothing. I was just an observer. You know how it is in dreams. You often don't get to participate.'

'We've been forgetting Jason,' said Thea thoughtfully. 'Which is odd when you realise he was gone just at the time Reuben was being dumped in the alley.'

'Thea! Jason couldn't have killed him. He was *cold*. Priscilla said so.'

'I didn't say he killed him.'

'So what do you think he did? Found the body somewhere and took it into the alley for safekeeping?'

'I had a dream as well,' Thea remembered. 'Something about Reuben and Oliver's brother Cedric.' *And Drew*, she recalled with a sudden flash. 'There was a funeral. It's all very hazy.'

'This time yesterday we were sitting here, Fraser and me, wondering what you were up to with that detective woman. Fraser was saying she seemed very unconventional, and I said you liked that sort of person. He ate all the biscuits and said you'd fallen short as a hostess, not cooking bacon and eggs for us.'

Thea laughed, taking no offence. 'I don't regard myself as your hostess. It isn't my house.'

'That's what I told him. He wasn't looking forward to Mo and Jason arriving. Poor old boy – he finds everything very hard, you know. He gets very agitated at times.'

'Really? I'd have thought the exact opposite.'

'He hides it well.'

'He said he'd never seen Melissa in his life. Do you really think that's true?'

'Oh, yes, I'm sure it is. He was in Australia, remember. There's all sorts of things he's lost track of here. Sometimes he seems quite adrift. He doesn't know Mo very well, actually. He missed out on most of her growing up.'

'So you think he's trying to make up for lost time? With you *and* her? Isn't that rather futile?'

'No, I don't think so. It's never too late – I hope you'll learn that for yourself eventually. He'll always be her father, and they obviously like each other. She's got very protective of him.'

'But he didn't want her coming here?'

'It didn't seem right to him, everybody invading Oliver's hideaway. And it made rather a nonsense of persuading him to have you here. He was all for leaving the birds to fend for themselves for a bit. We said there should be somebody to keep things going.'

The familiar sense of being manipulated washed through Thea. 'Why?'

Her mother flushed. 'I thought you might need some distraction. You always seem so *aimless* when you're there in that cottage in Witney, with nobody but the dog. At least the house-sitting is a change of scene.'

'Thanks, Mother,' said Thea dryly. 'So all this is your fault. I might have known.'

'Don't be silly.'

A knock on the door saved the moment. 'I bet that's Gladwin,' said Thea, in some relief.

She was right. The detective was alone, and almost ran into the house as soon as the door opened. 'This'll have to be quick,' she panted. 'We've got a busy day ahead. Wall-to-wall interviews all morning. All the important people seem to be in London, which is a real pain.'

'Coffee?' Thea offered.

Gladwin shook her head. 'I'll explode if I have any more. Look at me.' She held out a quivering hand. 'I'm a wreck already. Forty-eight hours exactly, since all this began, and I've had practically no sleep. Two murders is more than we can cope with, let's face it. The townspeople have woken up to it, as well, so the phones are red-hot. You wouldn't believe the number of people who see it as a personal affront.'

'Who are you interviewing?'

'Melissa's mother, for one. She's as bad as Mrs Reuben, apparently. Worse, probably. We tracked her down last night and somebody went round to give her the news. She's got some sort of chronic illness, and practically dropped dead on the spot. All very unpleasant, but we've got to ask her some questions, if we can.'

'Like why her daughter lived out of suitcases and kept so much of her stuff here?' Thea suggested.

'Right. And how close she was to the Meadows family in London. Did she even know who her father was – or did she really think Fraser was her father?'

'Tricky,' Thea agreed.

'To say the least. Then there's that Jason chap. He hasn't turned up, you know.' She gave Thea's mother an intense look. 'It would have helped to have Fraser and his daughter still here, actually.'

Maureen almost shrugged. 'Not a lot we could do to keep them, if they wanted to go,' she said. 'You've interviewed Fraser, anyway, haven't you?'

'Not since we found Reuben. And that's another thing . . . a very big other thing.'

'Tell us,' Thea urged.

'The post-mortem was done this morning. Started at half past seven, would you believe? I went along myself. He wasn't strangled . . .'

'I *said* there were no marks on his throat,' Thea triumphed. 'What was it, then?'

'Overdose, by the look of it.'

'*What?* So he wasn't murdered at all? But surely . . .' This was so shocking that Thea sat down heavily on a kitchen chair. 'He didn't seem the type. He was *here*, on Sunday, with his wife, all charming and greasy. People like that don't kill themselves.'

'Thea, we've talked about this before,' Gladwin reminded her. 'Stop making assumptions.'

'You think somebody *poisoned* him, then? That'd be

his wife, if so.' The one who screamed for ten minutes, she remembered.

'Stop it! We have to keep to the facts. You haven't told me properly *why* he came here on Sunday. What did he want?'

'He'd heard about Melissa, sometime during the afternoon. When we saw him in the pub, he obviously didn't know what had happened – just that there was a disturbance here in the woods.'

'That doesn't seem very likely,' Gladwin interrupted. 'His bedroom window looks over the very spot. He could practically have seen the body.'

'Wait a minute!' Thea tried to visualise it. 'That can't be right.'

'Well, it is. He's got a flat at the top, and if he leant out and looked to his right, he could see most of the land belonging to this property.'

'But could he see through the trees to the hide and the bird feeding station?'

'I think so. Most of it, at least. In any case, he'd see the police tent and the yellow jackets and the general activity. Anybody with half a brain would realise there'd been an unexplained death. Most would assume it was a murder.'

'So you think he was lying to us in the pub? Hoping to trick us into giving something away? You think he knew it was Melissa?'

Gladwin was not sitting down, but jittering on the spot. It made Thea feel restless and anxious. 'I don't know. But he wasn't just an innocent local, was he?'

'He might have seen it happening,' Thea realised. 'If he

was awake and looking out of the window, he might have seen her being killed. That's what we thought all along – that he had to be killed because he'd seen too much.'

'Except—'

'Except he wasn't killed in that sort of way,' supplied Thea's mother, who had been quietly following the conversation. 'If it wasn't suicide, it must have been carefully planned. And it was all so *quick*. It doesn't make much sense, as far as I can see.'

'And why put the body in the alley? That seems so crazy,' Thea persisted. 'How long had he been dead – do you know?'

'Something like four hours. Not more than that.'

'About the same time as we were walking down there, then.'

'Down the alley, and right past the silk mill building where he lived. Precisely.' Gladwin's expression was anguished. 'We were in full view, looking at the stream, admiring those houses, chatting about Melissa. Anybody might have heard us. I can hardly believe I was such a fool.'

'Why?'

'I'm the senior investigating officer in a murder enquiry. You found the body – *both* the bodies – you're a major witness. There we were like any two gossipy women, for all the world to see. It looks bad. It looks unprofessional.'

'Since when did you care about that?'

Gladwin snorted. 'They're going to *make* me care, if I don't clear this up quickly. The boundaries have been blurred, and they don't like that. Your role has always made them nervous; and now they see me as almost as bad.'

'So you're here now as a professional – right?'

Gladwin sighed. 'Not entirely. If I'm to interview you according to the book, we need another officer, a recorder, a closed environment where we can't be overheard, and you can't be influenced. And so forth and so on. The waste of time is phenomenal if you do everything properly.'

Thea shook her head as if to clear it. 'Henry Meadows,' she said. 'We were talking about him last night. Have you seen him yet?'

'Of course we haven't,' said Gladwin crossly. '*We* aren't likely to see any of them. The people in London will have to do it by proxy, at least initially. That trial is confusing everything. Either it's the whole explanation behind what's happened here, or it's a major distraction that's just getting in the way.'

'Henry's likely to be badly affected by it, isn't he? A business like that relies on being respectable and trustworthy. Even if he's pure as pure himself, he's bound to be tainted. His father and grandfather have always been pillars of the community, according to Drew.'

'You're still ahead of me on all that,' Gladwin admitted. 'I've never known an undertaker socially. I can't believe it's quite like the stereotype.'

'It is, I think, even now,' Thea observed. 'But surely you must have met several of them, in your line of work. Socially as well as professionally. Don't you invite each other to the Christmas party?'

'Oddly enough, no. The coroner's officer is the kingpin, the go-between. *He* gets to every party there is, not to mention being top banana at the Freemasons. But I've never been at a party with an undertaker, to my knowledge. I gather they don't go out very much, as a rule.'

Thea laughed. 'I really don't know, either. Drew's not at all traditional or conventional. We'll have to ask him how the more orthodox ones behave.'

Gladwin looked at Thea's mother, strangely conspiratorial. The sort of look one woman gives to another when romance is in the air. 'Have you met Drew?' Gladwin asked.

Maureen shook her head. 'I'm still not really sure who he is. She mentions him quite a lot, though.'

'He's good-looking, clever and kind, from what I've heard of him. Which is very little, I admit.'

'Sounds promising.'

'And his wife has just died,' said Thea, too loudly. 'He's struggling to keep his business going and he has two small children.'

'Poor man. He obviously needs a lot of help and support,' said her mother, with another smile at the detective.

'Stop it, you two. I can't bear to be teased.'

'I remember,' sighed her mother. 'You always were far too serious for your own good.'

It wasn't the way she thought of herself, and the maternal pulling of rank felt unfair. 'What does this have to do with anything, anyway?' she demanded. 'I thought it was a police interview.'

Gladwin moaned. 'Slave driver!' she protested. 'So where were we?'

Neither mother nor daughter responded. The thread, if there had been one, seemed irretrievably lost. Thea tried to think. 'There were some bits and pieces I thought I should tell you, about Melissa and Reuben, but I'm not sure they matter now. We know she was close to Oliver, and he can fill in any gaps about how much she knew of her family. Reuben and his wife came here on Sunday, once they'd caught up with who'd been killed. Did I tell you that?'

Gladwin dipped her head, and threw a reproachful look from beneath her straight black fringe. 'Thea Osborne, you know you didn't.'

'Sorry. I never really got the chance. It was all such a shock, so soon after Melissa. And then everything got rather out of control for all of us.'

'So you saw him in the pub at lunchtime on Sunday, and then he came here with his wife? When, exactly?'

'About five or half past, I suppose. They were both rather *pushy*. Offering us their help or protection against monstrous criminals lurking in the bushes. I thought they must be from some peculiar church, the way they talked. Like evangelicals, trying to make you like them. His face was positively shiny, and she stood behind him, sort of egging him on. The dog was with them.'

'That makes almost no sense at all,' Gladwin concluded. 'Do you think they knew Melissa?'

'I couldn't tell for sure. They might have been telling bare-faced lies. Reuben must have known something, surely, to have died so soon afterwards. Mum sent them packing in the end.'

'Oh?' Again Gladwin gave Maureen a long look.

'I didn't like them,' said Thea's mother simply. 'Neither of them. I thought they were unwholesome.'

'That's an excellent word,' Gladwin applauded. 'I must remember that.'

'It's true,' Thea realised. 'Him especially. Something in his eyes, I think. She wasn't so bad. And she obviously loved him, if she's in such a state about him dying.'

'Right,' said Gladwin slowly, her mind patently elsewhere. 'That's the first link of any sort between the two victims. Up to now, they've been like two magnets turned the wrong way. No amount of force would bring them together. Mrs Hardy flatly insists they never saw Melissa or knew anything about her existence. They very rarely saw Oliver Meadows either, according to her.'

'And yet they live so close by,' said Thea. 'If you use the back way from here, you're almost under the Hardys' window.'

'But they don't have a back way. And if you used the front in both cases, they're really quite a distance apart.'

Thea mentally walked the route from door to door: up Oliver's track, turn right, along Vineyard Street to the square they called Abbey Terrace, past the pub in the high street and right again down Castle Street, before turning left into Silk Mill Lane. 'That's true,' she agreed. 'But I met the wife in the Sudeley grounds, so she obviously comes this way with the dog.'

'But, Thea, you know what people in villages are like,' put in her mother. 'Especially if they've got busy lives. They might know each other by sight, but they often have no idea of names or personal details. How many people do you know in Witney?'

'A lot, actually.'

'Winchcombe's a bit bigger than a village,' said Gladwin. 'And if Melissa just paid flying visits, it's quite likely that nobody knew who she was. That's what we're picking up from our enquiries, anyway. Oliver was a recluse and his visitors were a complete mystery to everybody we've asked about it.'

'Reuben knew who I was!' Thea suddenly remembered. 'In the pub. He was quite unpleasant about it, in fact, making innuendoes. That's why I disliked him to start with. After that, he just seemed to dig himself deeper and deeper.'

'But how—' Gladwin began. 'Do you mean he'd heard about your house-sitting exploits in other places?'

'Apparently so, yes. Temple Guiting specifically. It is only a few miles from here, I suppose.'

'Which implies that he knew Oliver had gone away and taken on a house-sitter.'

'More than *implies*,' said Maureen. 'Proves, surely?'

'Okay. And that *suggests* there was more than a casual connection between them, if Reuben was taking so much interest.'

'It also suggests that Reuben knew about the Meadows trial, and that Oliver was going off to testify.' Thea had a sense of threads coming together to form at least a faint picture. 'He hinted he did know, when we were in the pub. There's a key in here somewhere,' she insisted.

Gladwin's mobile interrupted them imperiously. She automatically moved to the door before answering it, walking restlessly down the hallway and back as she spoke. It seemed she was receiving significant information, to judge from the staccato responses she was making. Thea wondered whether to offer pencil and paper on which to take notes.

The detective was almost dancing by the time she rang off. 'They've had another look at Melissa's body,' she reported. 'There's something written on the palm of her left hand. Would you believe they never noticed it before! It's that dim-witted assistant, of course. She's such a liability.'

'So what does it say?' Thea demanded, sharing the excitement. 'Surely not the name of her killer?'

'Sadly not. At least – it seems to predate her death by quite some time. They can't read all of it. Looks a bit like B-E-N, apparently. And something else before that – possibly numbers.'

'So if she was meeting a man called Ben, he could have killed her?'

'It doesn't say *Reuben*, does it?' suggested Maureen. 'Was he known as Ben for short?'

Gladwin spread her hands impatiently. 'We don't *know*,' she said. 'Everybody's trying to answer those very questions. I'll have to go. Thanks for the chat. Always a treat.' She threw Thea a warm smile, and was gone in a flash.

Chapter Twenty-Seven

It was only nine-thirty, and the damp day stretched uninvitingly. 'I should try and get hold of Fraser,' said Maureen half-heartedly. 'And find out what all this business with Jason is about. I should have phoned him last night, really. He'll think I don't care.'

'And do you?'

'Yes, I do.' The emphasis was surprising. 'I really do. I've been worrying about him ever since I woke up. I don't think he wanted to go back with Mo yesterday. She just bundled him off without giving him a chance to think.'

'I should walk the dog.' Thea peered out at the sky. 'It'll probably brighten up in a bit.'

'I hate September. Always have. I hated you children going back to school, worried about new teachers and new timetables. It always seemed so cruel to me.'

'You must be the only mother in the world who felt like that. Four kids under your feet all summer must have been dreadful.'

'No, it was nice. And look at Jocelyn. She's got five, and

she says the same thing. She really finds the new term a pain. All those new shoes and packed lunches. It's a nightmare.'

They contemplated the imagined chaos of Thea's sister's domestic arrangements. 'It must be rather a scramble,' Thea agreed.

'And there's always somebody in trouble, these days. Especially the boys. The poor little things can't do anything right in the eyes of those silly, soft, female teachers. Did you hear about poor Noel, at the end of last term?'

'Sort of.' Thea wasn't interested in an analysis of modern education. Her own child had sailed through the experience with very little difficulty. The only children she had spent time with recently were Drew's, and that had been quite a brief acquaintance. She knew nothing about their attitude towards school.

'You've got me terribly confused about Fraser,' Maureen complained, changing the subject. 'I just keep going round and round it, all the time.'

'We've said everything there is to say about it, for now,' Thea cut her off. 'Just so long as he isn't planning to kill you, I suppose there's no great urgency about it.'

'But what if he is?'

It was the sort of question that you either had to dismiss completely, or treat with utter seriousness. Thea hovered between the two. 'I expect he would have done it by now, if that was the case. If he did intend to at first, it looks as if he's grown to like you now. It's very difficult to kill somebody you like.'

The words echoed around the room. Thea conjured the cheerful Melissa into her mind's eye, and wondered who in the world could possibly have hated her enough to kill her. She herself had found her faintly irritating, she recalled, for no very good reason. But dislike was ten million miles from a murderous loathing. Reuben was different – she could already name three people who found him obnoxious. But that wasn't good enough. A murderer needed to convince himself that his own happiness, reputation, prosperity or stark survival depended on this person being dead. Somewhere, somehow, Melissa Anderson had threatened another person's well-being, and had been viciously punished for it. Thea felt a sharp pang of sympathetic pain for the elderly mother, hearing the annihilating news about her girl.

'Let's go out,' her mother said. 'We're depressing ourselves in here. We might find a person called Ben and solve the whole case for your nice detective lady.'

'Have you got a mac? It's still quite wet.'

'I can borrow Oliver's. There's one hanging on the back of the kitchen door.'

'He's at least eight inches taller than you. It'll look silly.'

'No, it's a short one. And he's so thin that I'll fill it well enough. It hasn't got a hood, though. I need something for my head.'

They found a somewhat greasy black scarf hanging with the coat, and Maureen wrapped it gingerly around her head. 'It's one thing to borrow someone's coat and quite another to wear his scarf,' she observed. Thea fetched her own waterproof anorak and they set out with the dog for a walk in the Sudeley grounds. Hepzie pulled annoyingly at her lead, so Thea released her before they reached the park. There was little enough traffic on the lower end of the street, and the dog was reasonably sensible with cars anyway.

The drizzle was invisibly fine, misting the trees and grass in a way that could only suggest autumn. In summer it would evaporate away; in winter it would turn to ice, or at least heavy droplets on the bare boughs. Swelling chestnuts still hung on the large handsome trees, reminding Thea of the words 'mellow fruitfulness' in a poem she had always loved. The flat grey light cast no shadows at all.

'Pity we can't go around the castle,' said Maureen. 'That would have been just the thing for a day like this.'

'We wouldn't be able to take the dog,' said Thea automatically. She had been prevented from indoor exploring on more than one occasion by this difficulty. When necessary, she would leave Hepzie shut inside whatever house she was looking after, but she preferred not to do it. Idle sightseeing did not constitute necessity, to her mind.

'It isn't open to the public anyway.'

'Right. Although they do tours now and then, at significant cost. I can't say I'm tempted.'

There were very few people around, unsurprisingly. A play area for children stood deserted, and a handsome old bridge over a small lake, which had attracted people on Thea's first excursion, was now unoccupied. 'We'll turn back at the bridge,' Thea decreed. 'I don't think any of us are enjoying this very much.'

They stood gazing at the water below for a minute or two, trying to work out whether the lake was man-made or natural, and whether it was fed by a stream or simply by rainfall. They reached no conclusion, and turned to retrace their steps. 'Oh, look,' said Maureen. 'There's Priscilla.' She spoke as if it was her best friend who had suddenly come into view.

'So it is,' said Thea, with considerably less enthusiasm. 'She looks a bit cross.'

Hepzie bridged the substantial space between them and Priscilla by running up to the woman and jumping at her knees with wet paws. She was swiped away with scant ceremony – something she was quite accustomed to. 'Sorry,' said Thea insincerely, when they got close enough for conversation. 'Don't jump up, Heps. How many times have I told you?'

'I've just had the police questioning me,' Priscilla Heap burst out. 'Was that *your* doing?'

Thea and her mother froze under this unexpected attack. 'What? Of course not,' said Thea, after a pause. 'We haven't even mentioned your name. Have we?' she asked her mother to confirm.

'Not that I can recall,' said Maureen. 'And what if we had? Why does it matter? I expect they want to speak to everybody.'

'You do live near the Hardys,' Thea remembered. 'It must have been a routine house-to-house.'

'No it wasn't. It was because I was there yesterday when you found his body. I deliberately melted away before they could get my name. But somebody gave it to them anyway. Are you *sure* it wasn't you?'

'Why does it matter so much?' Maureen asked again.

'Do you have something to hide? Don't you *want* them to find the murderer?'

'I think you told them that I touched his face. They knew about that. They kept asking why I'd do such a thing, and did I have special feelings for him. It was most unpleasant.' She shuddered. 'They made me feel guilty, when I haven't done anything against the law.'

'It wasn't us who told them. Perhaps it was Fraser or one of those people at the top of the alley. There were three or four watching, weren't there? Someone amongst them must be more public-spirited than you.' Thea spoke sharply, annoyed by the woman's attitude.

'Could be, I suppose. The town is full of busybodies.'

'And I get the impression that you're not very popular,' Maureen observed. Then she addressed her daughter. 'It wasn't Fraser, though. We'd gone by then.'

'What makes you think I'm unpopular?' Priscilla demanded.

'You came to us when you wanted someone to talk to, even though you've lived here for years. Why haven't you got friends to turn to?'

'Be quiet!' Priscilla snarled. 'How dare you?'

Thea felt a vague sadness that things were turning out so unpleasantly. For herself, she had rather liked the woman, and felt some sympathy for her apparent isolation. Not everybody wanted to be bosom pals with the people next door. 'It wasn't us,' she said again. 'And I know what you mean about being under suspicion. It happened to a friend of mine earlier this year, and I know it's horrible.'

'It is.' Priscilla visibly mellowed. 'And they've got it

hopelessly wrong, of course. I didn't care a fig for Reuben. I never could see what Jenny saw in him, to be honest. Oily little beast, he was.'

'I hope you didn't say *that* to the police?' Thea smiled.

'No, no. I've got more sense.'

Thea was burning to reveal the news that Reuben had apparently died of a drug overdose, and therefore probably had not been murdered after all. But she too had enough sense to remain silent. She cast a quick look at her mother to reassure herself that there would be no revelation from that quarter, either. Maureen showed little sign of wanting to divulge anything.

'Nasty weather,' she said, greatly to Thea's amusement. The past few days had caused her to revise her assessment of her mother, based on a lifetime of family myths and assumptions. There was a lot more spirit inside her than Thea had ever discerned until now. To her credit, Priscilla Heap similarly appreciated the gesture, and gave a little smile.

'And showing no sign of improving,' Thea added. 'I thought it would have done by now.'

'Rain before seven, fine by eleven,' quoted Maureen. 'Your father always said that.'

'So did Carl. It's generally true.'

'Well, it's got another forty minutes,' said Priscilla, having consulted her watch. Harmony having been restored, the three walked together, back towards Vineyard Street.

'Funny how quickly a place becomes familiar,' said Thea. 'I feel I know Winchcombe rather well, already.'

'You don't, though,' Priscilla argued. 'You have no idea of how people are with each other, on a daily basis. It's got its share of miscreants – some of them with very unpleasant dogs. Look what one of them did to me last year.' She proffered her forearm, which sported a jagged red scar. 'Twenty-seven stitches,' she boasted. 'Nearly bled to death. And I didn't do a thing to provoke the bloody animal.'

Thus was her antipathy towards dogs explained, realised Thea. 'It must have been dreadful,' she said.

'Did they put it down?' asked Maureen.

'They did – at my insistence.'

'You can't blame the dog,' said Thea automatically. 'I suppose it was a pit bull or something?'

'Or something. Bull terrier of some sort. It was doing its best to kill me. The owner was pathetic. All he did was kick at it and shout.'

'Well, Hepzie wouldn't bite anybody,' said Thea with perfect confidence. 'It would never even cross her mind.'

'That's what Jenny says about that handsome puppy of hers. I quite liked dogs before that happened,' said Priscilla wistfully. 'Perhaps one day I'll get over it.'

Again Thea felt the shadow of an unfocused sadness pass over her. Despite the effort to be brisk and witty the previous evening, this woman was leaking misery and anxiety. Lonely, antisocial, clumsy – whatever image she presented, these underlying traits would soon emerge. She had antagonised neighbours with her new house, favoured her horse above people, and very possibly let Reuben Hardy know what she thought of him. But she had been genuinely shocked by his death – Thea was sure of that. She had surreptitiously stroked his dead cheek, after all. Or perhaps it had been a gesture very far from affectionate. Perhaps she had simply needed to satisfy herself that he really was gone for ever. Perhaps she had hated or feared him, and could scarcely believe her luck when he'd died. Perhaps . . . perhaps . . . There was no real evidence for any of these suppositions – the only sure thing was that the death of a healthy young man was a sorrow that affected them all.

'When did the police question you?' she asked.

'First thing this morning. Two of them, at half past eight. Made me late for poor old Sally-Girl.'

'It wasn't Gladwin then?'

'Who?'

'The detective superintendent. She came to see us at nine.'

'No, it was two men. I don't remember their names.'

'You know the Hardys quite well, don't you?' Maureen accused. 'Both of them. That must be why you were questioned.'

Priscilla flushed. 'Not especially. What makes you think that?'

'You use the wife's name so casually. You know their routines. You were appalled by his death. It's obvious.'

Again, Thea was impressed by her mother. 'You like her, but not him – is that right?' she asked Priscilla, starting to feel as if they were playing some sort of party game. At the end of all these questions there lay an answer that might be the key to all that had happened.

'For heaven's sake!' the woman burst out. 'This is exactly what they asked me this morning, and I'm not going over it again. What business is it of yours, anyway? Can't I have an opinion of people living across the street from me without being suspected of killing one of them? I don't imagine I'm alone in finding Reuben Hardy difficult to like. He was too charming to be real. He was selfish, greedy, rich and insincere. Like a lot of men around here, in fact. He took what he wanted, with no concern for other people's feelings. His wife had to make the best of it. She got her nice home and a lovely dog out of it, and seemed happy enough. I make no claims to understanding what happens in a marriage. That way is far too fraught with confusion for my simple mind. She's going to have to start all over again without him. And I think there might be a baby on the way, as well. Her waistline has expanded over the summer.'

'But she hasn't said anything?'

'Little hints, that's all. Having the dog for practice, and thinking of moving to a larger place – that sort of thing.'

'She talks to you, it seems.'

'She talks to *everybody*.'

'She even talked to me,' Thea remembered. 'In this very spot.'

'Did you like her?'

'I liked the dog,' laughed Thea. 'I didn't take a lot of notice of the woman. When they came to the door on Sunday, it was mostly him I focused on. She seems pretty ordinary, at first glance, except for her hair. It's a rather dramatic colour, isn't it?' *And she screamed for ten minutes*, ran the line in her head.

Priscilla showed no sign of wanting to accompany them back to Thistledown. 'I'm going that way,' she said firmly, tipping her chin towards the castle. 'I need the exercise, and I like this weather, to be honest. I find it restful.' Her colourless hair was frosted with drizzle, and there were damp patches on the shoulders of her jacket. 'I can circle round along the footpath, and over to the bridge at the top of town.'

Thea was lost. 'Oh?' she said. 'Another bridge?'

'It's the main one over the Isbourne. That's the name of our esteemed waterway. The footpath, river and road all converge there, which is handy.'

'Right,' Thea nodded vaguely. 'I might go that way later on, if it stops raining.' She glanced at her watch and wondered what they might profitably do for the rest of the day – the rest of the *week*, probably. Sightseeing was the obvious answer, admiring the endless glories of Cotswolds towns and villages, but that depended on the weather being at least dry. Sunshine would be a nice bonus. There was a little museum in the middle of Winchcombe, and another one beyond the church. She approved of such local enterprises, usually run by dedicated eccentrics who could spend most of their time knitting or reading, lucky to receive more than two or three visits a day. 'Or we might go to the museum.'

Priscilla snorted. 'That won't take long. It's one and a half rooms of jumble. Most of it's devoted to a display of old police stuff.'

'Fascinating!' crowed Thea. 'Just my line. Several of my friends and relations are in the police, you know.'

'Oh,' said Priscilla sourly. 'I might have guessed. Now, I'm on my way. Goodbye.' She gave a formal little nod and strode away.

'We don't have to go to that museum, do we?' muttered Maureen. 'I've never really liked museums.'

'What else do you suggest?'

'I want to go home, Thea. I want to see Fraser and find out how he's coping with this horrible trial. I want to know where Jason's gone, and if he's under police suspicion. Mo will have something to say about him going missing, and she'll probably take it out on her father. He lives with her, in case you've forgotten.'

Thea had a sense of events taking place beyond her capacity to keep track. On the face of it, Jason had behaved very suspiciously by disappearing shortly after the discovery of Reuben Hardy's body. The complications of who had used which car still eluded her, but she supposed Jason had heartlessly driven off without his girlfriend and her father. Fraser had taken Mo home in his vehicle, and her mother was now stranded without transport. The notion of Jason as murderer was both feasible and ridiculous. He was a strong man, engaged in shady property dealings, superficially bluff and amiable, but probably capable of all sorts of dodgy doings. But the timing didn't work. When Reuben died, the man had either been in the car with Mo, or at home in his caravan park. It could only be that Gladwin had worked this out already and dismissed him from her list of suspects. Any attempt to unearth a motive looked doomed to fail, not to mention a convoluted theory whereby he was in Winchcombe in the early hours of the morning, then fled home again, collected Mo and made the return trip to Thistledown, looking perfectly relaxed. Unless, of course, Mo was actively involved, and had conspired to lay a false trail. It was, after all, possible that they had both arrived in Winchcombe before dawn, or even the previous evening, and somehow killed Reuben with pharmaceuticals and hidden his body. Then Jason could have laid it in the alley at half past ten, not long before it was found by the little party, subtly led there by Mo.

She ran it through again, slowly. Had Mo actually arranged for them to go that way? It seemed possible. There had been very little deliberate steering on Thea's part, although she had regarded herself as the party leader. The most difficult part to square was the actual killing. Could Reuben have been forced to take the overdose – or could it be injected into a vein? Would the pathologist find the place on his skin, if so?

And *why*? Only the original suggestion that Reuben had seen something he shouldn't offered itself as an answer to this central question.

'You've gone very quiet,' her mother remarked.

'Sorry. I'm thinking.'

'About murder, I assume?'

'Right.' She gave a quick outline of the direction her thoughts had been going. 'It would mean Mo being part of it,' she concluded. 'For some reason.'

'And that would take us back to the question of who, if anyone, is going to continue the Meadows funeral business?'

'Yes,' Thea nodded, 'I hadn't got that far. I keep forgetting about them. All I can get my head around is what happened here in Winchcombe. I'm being very parochial about it.'

'You won't get to the bottom of it like that. It seems obvious to me that it's all about the people in London, with Oliver as the link. It'll be that Henry. I've been thinking as well, and it keeps coming back to him. He killed Melissa at the first opportunity after Oliver was out of the way, and somehow Reuben got himself involved, so he killed him as well.'

'Hmm. Maybe. But that leaves a lot of unanswered questions. Like – was Reuben actually murdered at all, and if so, why was he dumped in the alley?'

'That's the bit we don't know,' Maureen agreed. 'Can we go in now? It must be time for some coffee.'

They were a few yards from the turning into the Thistledown track. Hepzie was plainly of the same opinion as her mistress's mother, and veered to the right on the assumption that they could get out of the rain. 'All right, then,' said Thea.

'That dog is awfully wet. We can't let it onto any of the furniture like that.'

'It's only water. She's not muddy.'

A woman stepped in front of them, from behind a wall. 'Thea Osborne? I've been waiting for you,' she said.

Chapter Twenty-Eight

Thea stepped back, recognising the woman as somebody she had previously exchanged heated words with. 'How did you know where to find me?' she blustered.

'It's a small town, and Oliver Meadows is in the phone book. You're fairly conspicuous, too, with that dog.'

'So what do you want this time?'

'To apologise,' said Maggs. 'To throw in the towel and try to make amends.'

'Gosh!' said Thea faintly.

'Who *is* this person?' asked Maureen.

'It's Maggs,' Thea introduced inadequately. 'She works with Drew, in Somerset. But I thought you were dreadfully *busy*,' she added. 'Lots of new funerals all at once.'

'We are. I left him organising four new graves and lining two coffins. It's raining there, as well, and there wasn't enough space for me in the workshop. It's very small, you know. I'll have to be back by one. He can cope without me until then.'

Thea was familiar with the journey from the North

Staverton burial ground to the Cotswolds. It could not be done in less than two hours. 'What time did you leave?' she asked.

'Eight. I was up before six. It's not as bad as it sounds – I went to bed really early last night. I'm using the motorbike. I've had it for years, and it comes in useful sometimes.'

'Not much fun in this weather,' remarked Maureen.

'What do you *want*?' Thea burst out. 'Surely not just to bury the hatchet? You could do that by phone.'

'I had an epiphany,' said Maggs seriously. 'After talking to you, Drew's a different man. I've been a fool about the whole thing. He told me off for trying to run his life for him.' The dark-skinned young woman looked bewildered and far more subdued than the last time Thea met her.

Thea opened and shut her mouth, lost for words. In the presence of her mother, the conversation had no chance of getting anywhere. 'Mum,' she said, 'would you mind very much taking Hepzie back to the house, and leaving us to have a quick chat? I know it's rude, but we won't be very long.' A glance at her watch showed barely fifteen minutes before Maggs had to leave again.

Maureen acceded to the request with reasonably good grace. 'Come on then, dog,' she said. 'I'm going to rub you thoroughly with a towel before letting you into the living room.' The spaniel hung its head and trailed reluctantly behind the determined woman.

'We can go to the pub,' Thea suggested. 'It'll probably be open.'

'No time. Is this your car? Can we sit in it for a bit?'

It seemed rather foolish, when they could have gone to

the house, but Thea understood the instinct behind it. A car was a perfect place for intimate revelations, especially as the windows were sure to steam up within moments, making them invisible as well as inaudible to anyone outside. 'All right, then,' she said.

'You're involved in another murder, I gather,' Maggs began, almost before the car doors had closed. 'Drew's told me some of it. He asked me about Henry Meadows. I saw something about the trial of his father. He's desperate to help somehow, but he can't get away.'

'I see,' said Thea, not entirely truthfully.

'No, you don't. You haven't seen him since Karen died. He's been in bits, a real wreck. He wouldn't have her buried at Peaceful Repose – did you know that? It was terrible. I was furious with him. I probably made it all a lot worse.' Her black eyes grew shiny, and she clasped her hands together. Thea thought she had lost some weight since they last saw each other, six months previously.

'Hard for you,' she ventured. 'Being so fond of him.'

'Yeah. It was as if I'd never really known him at all. I mean, I just *assumed* that's where she'd go. He said I didn't understand what it was like. I was so *angry* about it. It was so bad for the business. He *betrayed* the whole basis of it. For weeks I couldn't think of anything else. And that meant I was much less use to him than I ought to have been. And it all got tangled up with you, so I blamed you for it. I thought it showed he felt guilty towards Karen and didn't want her constantly there to remind him.'

'I didn't know,' said Thea. 'I thought the grave was right there, just outside the house.'

'It's in another alternative burial ground, twenty miles away.'

'But you've kept it all going – the business, I mean. And helped him with the children. He'd never have survived at all without you.'

'He would, but the business might not have done. And there's this Broad Campden angle, as well. That's never going to happen, is it? How can it? We'd need to employ somebody – two people – full-time. We'll never afford that. It's hopeless.'

'And you associate that with me as well,' Thea said.

'Right. And I blamed you for it. I've been seeing you as an evil interloper, making everything worse. But that wasn't right. I guess I knew, deep down, how it was really. And I suppose I got carried away, seeing you as a threat to the kids and the whole set-up. But Drew really loves playing detectives. He always has. He wants to get to the bottom of things and make sure it's all fair. When he met you in March, that was seriously bad news at first – even you must admit that. He nearly got prosecuted over it. That daughter of yours – is that who she was? He only told me afterwards, in a garbled sort of way, just how scared he'd been.'

'You're being a bit garbled yourself,' Thea said, feeling very much older than this tormented young woman at her side. 'Does this visit have anything to do with the murder that happened here, or is it all about me and Drew?'

Maggs rummaged in a roomy shoulder bag, and extracted a buff folder. 'I found this,' she said. 'On the Internet early this morning. I printed it out for you.'

'What is it?' Thea leafed through four or five sheets

of apparent newspaper reports, some with photographs.

'All I could find about the Meadows family. See – there's a family group from 1960, with the three brothers and the old man and his wife. Plus one of Oliver, much more recent – when his bird book was published. And I tracked down Fraser as well, because he seems rather a dark horse. Lucky it's an unusual name. He had his own website when he was in Australia – did you know? It's still floating around, the way they do. He put his graduation picture on there – and look! There's another one from way back when – with a girlfriend. Drew said something about your mother, and I thought this looked a bit like you, so I added it in. Have a look.'

Thea peered through the steamed-up murk at the small smudgy picture, dated 'March 1962' and clearly recognised her own youthful mother, standing next to a tall and perfectly identifiable Fraser.

'Well,' she said, with heartfelt relief. 'That solves one mystery, anyway.' She looked at the clock on the dashboard. 'You should be going.'

'Yes.'

'Thanks, Maggs. You don't know what this means.' As she leant over to embrace the younger woman in an awkward hug, she had no doubt that Maggs knew precisely what she was talking about.

Her mother was in the kitchen, washing up a single mug in a bowlful of hot, soapy water. 'What a waste!' said Thea.

'Habit. If you don't wash everything as you go, it quickly gets sordid.'

Housework had never been an interesting topic of conversation for Thea, less than ever now. 'I have news for you,' she said.

'Oh?' Her mother turned round warily, drying her hands on a tea towel. 'What?'

'Fraser is who he says. Look at this.' She proffered the picture. 'This is on his website.'

Maureen took it slowly and gave it a long examination. 'That *is* me, isn't it? I look like you.'

'Do you remember it being taken?'

'No. Who can have taken it, anyway? We didn't know any other people. I don't remember a camera. I don't remember this place.' She looked almost panicky. 'It hasn't triggered anything at all.'

Thea's confidence wavered. Could the picture have been faked? Photoshopped somehow? 'But you recognise yourself. Have you ever seen that picture of you before? Without Fraser?'

Her mother shook her head. 'I would remember that. We always take great notice of ourselves in photos, don't we?'

It was true, Thea realised. A picture from another person's collection featuring you was deeply fascinating, providing another angle on your self-image. She remembered being shocked to discover that one's image in a mirror was not what others saw – not what the camera saw. She was still trying to work out why that was.

'There's a date, look. You can check your diary and see if you went anywhere with him. It doesn't look like London to me. That's a sort of lay-by you only get in small towns.'

'And isn't that a seagull?' Maureen indicated a faint

smudge in the background. 'Oh! It was Worthing!' she cried suddenly. 'Yes – we got a train to Worthing for the day. It was windy and freezing cold. And that scarf – I lost it. It must have blown off while we were walking on the seafront. Fraser went to look for it, but never found it. But we didn't have a camera. I'm *sure* we didn't.' She puckered her brow in the effort of recall. 'The train was empty and we joked about it being specially provided for us – and I said perhaps it was a ghost train taking us to the other world. I got myself quite frightened, and he explained very seriously that there were no such things as ghosts. There was a man just outside the station with a camera, and Fraser gave him five shillings to take a photo and send it to us when it was developed. We argued about whether he would ever do it. This must be it.'

'Blimey,' said Thea, rocking back on her heels. 'That's got you going, hasn't it?'

Maureen's eyes were bright with excitement. 'This is amazing – everything was in here all the time.' She tapped her head and laughed. 'You can't imagine how wonderful it feels.'

'I can see.' She could feel the delighted relief herself. There was something richly reassuring about the whole episode. Not only was her mother probably not developing Alzheimer's, but she was savouring the recollection of that day at the sea with such evident relish that it was catching. 'Can you remember more about him now?'

Maureen's eyes closed as she inspected her memory. 'Hardly anything,' she admitted. 'But this is enough for the time being. He'll be so glad when I tell him.'

'And it's all down to Maggs,' said Thea, wonderingly. 'I thought she was my lifelong enemy, and instead here she is bringing all sorts of good news.'

'I still don't understand who she is.'

'Come into the sitting room and I'll explain,' said Thea.

Chapter Twenty-Nine

In London, all three of the Meadows brothers were in Court Room Four, together for the first time in thirty years or more. Oliver's heart had lurched alarmingly at the sight of Fraser, sitting tall in the heart of the public gallery. His voice had faltered in the middle of answering the first real question of the day, keeping his eyes on the prosecuting barrister and fumbling for words to describe what had happened between him and Cedric a lifetime ago. He had lifted his gaze for a moment, searching for release from this excruciating ordeal, and found himself looking into the eyes of his brother. Fraser, who had failed him repeatedly in those early years. The gangly, dreamy, self-absorbed brother who managed to ignore events around him. Fraser had been in love, successively, from the age of sixteen, a Romeo who only had to see a girl to fall for her. Immersed in his terrible memories from that time, Oliver saw a young Fraser sitting there and struggled to make sense of his presence. Why turn up now, when it was all far too late?

'Mr Meadows?' the barrister prompted gently. 'You were saying?'

'Ah, yes ...' He had lost the thread completely. 'I'm sorry. What *was* I saying?'

The barrister could not suppress a sigh. 'I know this is very difficult for you, sir. It would be hard for anybody. But if you could just finish your testimony. Perhaps we could read the last few words back . . . ?' He cocked his head at the judge for permission. The judge nodded, and the stenographer read back 'I was forced repeatedly to have sexual relations against my will' in a flat voice.

'Did I say that?' Oliver had no recollection of uttering those words. 'Well, yes, it's true. He forced me. He was six years older than me, in many ways a stranger, after Fraser and I were evacuated. Fraser and I went, but Cedric didn't, you see.'

'Thank you, Mr Meadows. Now, just a few more questions . . .' The drama continued, with Oliver choking out the horrible details, appalled that Fraser was there to hear them. Until then, Fraser had been a kind of refuge, a haven of decency and distance that had nothing to do with Cedric and his ghastly abuse. He steadfastly avoided looking at his brother again. Nor did he look at the accused, his other brother, the man who shared half his parentage only. Fraser and he were the real brothers; he had always felt that.

But it hardly mattered any more. His voice trailed away, as he saw the futility of what he was doing. He had been manipulated yet again, by these punitive forces. Everything they had told him, all their persuasive arguments, fell to dust. He remembered Sylvia from the evening before, having successfully pushed her image away so far that day. He could not afford to give attention to what either of them had said. It was too late for that, as well. He had made a case for his own behaviour, in good faith, only to have it collapse at some point during the night.

It was too late because Melissa was dead. That terrible fact was amongst so many pushed into a corner of his mind for later. The mental box containing this and much more now exploded open, and made him sag at the knees. 'I can't,' he whispered. 'I can't go on with this. There isn't any point to it now. Look at him.' He pointed a wavering finger at Cedric. 'It was all too long ago. What's done is done.' He sat down, almost missing the chair that had been provided in consideration of his age. He had resolved not to use it, some twenty minutes ago.

Mutterings in the court grew louder, and the judge cleared his throat warningly. The prosecuting barrister wiped his brow. All was not yet lost. Order was being maintained. Oliver watched him with a dispassionate sympathy. This must be a very rare experience for the wretched man. 'I'm sorry,' he said. 'I truly am. But this is enough. Cedric has been humiliated and exposed. I thought it was for the best, but I was wrong. He has been a model citizen for sixty years now. He has very little time left. *And Melissa is dead!*' He added this last as a howl, emotion breaking through like a river bursting its bank. 'Somebody killed Melissa, my little sister. That's what all you people should be thinking about – not punishing a poor old man for crimes that happened in another world, and another time.' He was gasping for breath, his heart pounding, his eyes wet.

'Get him down from there,' hissed the judge. 'The man's on the point of collapse.'

Strong hands helped him down, but then nobody seemed to know quite what to do with him. Magically, he found himself being supported on either side by his two brothers, although there were confused cries of protest at Cedric's desertion of his place as the person undergoing trial. There had been a token effort to keep him under guard, with a police officer stationed close at hand, but when he moved, nobody felt it necessary to use force to restrain him. He was an old man, who had been slumped in a state of almost comatose indifference since the trial opened. Nobody worried that he would suddenly wreak havoc or run amok.

'Court adjourned,' shouted the judge. 'Clear the court!'

Nobody was in any hurry to leave. The drama being played out in front of them fascinated the reporters and idle observers alike. Those who had come along in the hope of hearing salacious sexual details were only mildly disappointed by this turn of events. Many of them had begun to squirm inwardly at the way the accused simply took it on the chin. It was hard work to maintain the outrage and hatred against him. And there was clearly some sort of subplot going on. Who was Melissa? Had she really been murdered? The sibilance of her name was to be heard all around the room.

Already people were asking each other if that was the end of the trial. There had been other accusers, all of them elderly and quavering, none of them especially inviting of more than a fleeting sympathy. Even before Oliver's collapse, there had been a feeling that the trial was ill-advised, that some things were simply best covered over and forgotten. The events had taken place in the nineteen fifties, for the Lord's sake. After the initial burst of enthusiasm for justice, however long after the event, doubts had begun to set in. The damage was severe, admittedly, but it was also irreparable. There had been whispered references to 'political correctness' and such a thing as going too far. Even the newspapers had begun to carry more thoughtful passages about the good sense behind the statute of limitations, where it was deemed that too much time had passed for a meaningful prosecution to be brought.

Eventually the court officials took control and people filed out, looking back at the three old men as if hoping to memorise the image. A few of them were doing just that, Oliver supposed dimly, for those pastel sketches they showed on the news. No cameras allowed in court, even these days. He leant against Fraser and heaved a deep sigh.

They were taken to a room, where Oliver's solicitor waited. Cedric sat on a chair against the wall, and Fraser stood beside him. Of the three, he was by far the most stalwart, showing no signs of the disintegration that was evident in the other two. 'Why are you here?' Oliver asked him. 'It was seeing you that finished me. I'd have been all right, if it hadn't been for that.'

The solicitor eyed Fraser reproachfully, and tapped a pen irritably on the top of the table in front of him. 'This is a real mess,' he said. 'What are we going to do now?'

'If it depends on me, then I want to drop the charges,'

said Oliver. 'I think we've been through enough.'

'It's not that simple. There are others involved.'

'I believe they will agree with me. They've had their say, and they know as well as I do that there's no real prospect of retribution at this late stage.'

'Sylvia saw you – last night. Didn't she?' Cedric spoke directly to his younger brother for the first time in a decade. 'What did she tell you?'

'That you're ill. You haven't got long to live. One or two other things.'

'I hoped she wouldn't. It seemed to me like cheating.'

Nobody responded to that for a minute or so. Then Oliver replied, 'It didn't work. It wasn't because of her I stopped. At least . . .' He looked at Fraser, 'I don't think it was.'

Fraser went to him and put an arm round his shoulders. 'It was Melissa,' he said softly. 'You remembered her when you saw me. She told people she was my daughter. That house-sitter – Maureen's daughter. That's what Melissa told her. She said she was mine. I didn't know about her at all. She's not mine, though, is she?'

'She's our sister. You were in Australia,' said Oliver simply. 'You didn't know and Cedric didn't care. And now she's dead. I suppose it was Henry who killed her.' The words brought a thick lump to his chest, which swelled into his throat and sent a sob escaping into the room. 'She could have saved the business for you and your son,' he told Cedric.

The oldest of the three brothers raised his head, and stared furiously at Oliver, out of the same dark eyes that had made him quail and beg for mercy, sixty years before. 'Henry did no such thing. Don't be such a fool,' he said forcefully. 'He'll carry on the business just as always. He's not such a weakling as to let this business affect him.'

'That's not what Sylvia thinks,' Oliver disagreed.

'It's the truth, just the same, whatever Sylvia might say. He's marrying that girl of his, and there'll be more Meadows to come. Nothing can change that. Some by-blow of a sister was never going to make any difference. Why in the world do you think Henry would go to the trouble of killing her? The idea is ludicrous.'

A court official came to the door. 'Excuse me, gentlemen, but I'm afraid you'll have to leave now. There'll be a consultation as to what happens next.' He looked at the solicitor. 'You'll be informed.'

Outside the room was a large crowd of reporters, many with cameras. In the twenty minutes or so since Oliver's outburst, word had gone round that there was a bigger story emerging and connections had been made with the murdered girl in the Cotswolds. The moment the brothers appeared, they were mobbed. Oliver shrank back; Fraser likewise. But Cedric stood firm. He permitted the TV cameras to linger on his craggy face, with impressive dignity. 'I have a statement to make,' he said in a voice just low enough to quieten the clamour. The mob hushed each other and gripped their pencils tighter.

'I wish to express my regret at the death of my young half-sister, Melissa. I was not aware of it until now. It has been suggested to me that my son, Henry, could somehow be responsible for this crime. I wish to state here, publicly, that this is nonsense. Whoever might have killed her, it had nothing to do with my family. The business is not changing hands, as some people might have thought. As for my aborted trial, I dare say I am forbidden from commenting. Suffice it to say that I hold no hard feelings towards my brother Oliver for the humiliation he has brought down on me. What remains to say will be said privately between the two of us. Thank you. I have nothing further to add.'

A barrage of questions was steadfastly ignored, as Cedric's solicitor belatedly forced a way through the jostling crowd. Oliver and Fraser shambled after the main player, trying in vain to conceal their feebleness. Their brother, they silently acknowledged, had more backbone than they did.

Headlines were already being composed, Oliver assumed. He imagined such examples as: 'Trial Erupts in Chaos as Witness Collapses'; 'Link Between Meadows Trial and Gloucestershire Murder'; 'Sex Offender Undertaker Denies Involvement With Murder'. *Clumsy*, he thought wryly. They could probably come up with something snappier than these. Perhaps, he hoped forlornly, there would be a far bigger story during the day about the economy or a small earthquake somewhere which would eclipse his own family's sordid little activities. But meanwhile, the twenty-four-hour-news culture would probably see him on TV by lunchtime, with all the embarrassment he had hoped to avoid.

Chapter Thirty

'Do you think we'd be welcome if we paid Jenny Hardy a visit?' Thea suggested. 'Would she think we were out of order?'

'She might,' her mother judged. 'But so what? I don't suppose anything is normal for her at the moment. We might be a welcome distraction.'

'I'm not sure exactly where she lives.'

'I thought we said it was that building that is a sort of conversion of the old silk mill? At the top somewhere?'

'Yes, I think that's right. But are they flats or maisonettes or what? It's not obvious from looking at them.'

'We can ask somebody when we get there. Of course she might have gone away. People do that. She's probably got a mother she's gone back to for consolation.'

Thea was gratified by her mother's eager cooperation. It had never occurred to her that here might be another fellow detective. She was still feeling warm from Maggs's capitulation, secure in the knowledge that Drew's partner had abruptly changed allegiance, and thereby given the future a far rosier glow. Whatever happened in Winchcombe over the next few hours or days was secondary to this. She felt reckless and carefree in her approach to helping Gladwin solve her murders. A shadow had lifted and the sun was beaming down on her. The same sunbeam was favouring her mother, as well, after the flood of seaside memories featuring Fraser. They were both smiling more readily than they had for a long time.

'Let's go and have a look.'

It was half past eleven – not a terribly good time for a visit, if Jane Austen was anything to go by. 'After all, we *did* find his body,' Thea said, doubtfully. 'She might want to talk to us, to be assured he didn't look as if he'd suffered.'

'Is your police lady going to be in favour of this?' her mother questioned. 'Are you allowed to go and talk to close relatives of dead men?'

'She hasn't objected yet. She trusts me, I think. She uses me as a sort of unofficial liaison person, now and then. I can get under the skin more easily – just being an ordinary bystander, so to speak.'

'I doubt if people see you like that,' smiled her mother. 'If Reuben knew something about your reputation, his wife must have done as well. She could take against you. That's if she's there at all, of course.'

'Priscilla is probably ministering to her already. She seems to be rather fond of her.'

'I'm not so sure. That woman is not what she appears, to my way of thinking. She's clever with words, and makes people think she's all bluff and straightforward – but she kept a lot close to her chest, don't you think? I keep remembering how she suddenly appeared in that alleyway yesterday. Wasn't that a bit coincidental?'

'Gosh – do you think *she* put him there? That hadn't occurred to me.'

'She's strong enough.'

'But . . .' Thea tried to visualise it, with partial success. 'Do you think that links her to Melissa as well?'

Maureen shrugged. 'It's all a complete mystery to me, Thea. I try to think about it, and get a few ideas, and then it all goes murky on me. I've never been anywhere near a murder before, and it's been rather a shock. But in spite of myself, I do keep having these ideas.' She frowned exaggeratedly, mocking herself.

'That happens,' Thea nodded. 'It must be a sort of instinct.'

'The search for an answer, you mean? Or seeing that justice is done?'

'More the former, I think. Justice can get so complicated.'

'That's what Fraser says. He's been trying to ignore this business with his brothers, but he can't, of course. He knows he should be on Oliver's side, and he hasn't even met Cedric since he went off to Australia – but he can't help feeling sorry for the poor old chap.'

'Did you phone him?' Thea remembered that this had been the plan.

'I tried, and got Mo. Fraser went out early this morning, wearing a suit, and she's not at all sure where he's gone.'

'Did Jason turn up?'

'Not yet. She doesn't know which one she should be more worried about.'

'Were you going to tell me about any of this?'

'Possibly not. I think we've said all we need to about Fraser, for the time being. I'd rather discuss your undertaker friend and his exotic partner.'

'She's not exotic,' said Thea automatically. 'She's just mixed race.'

'That's what I said. Anyway, she seems nice. Coming all this way to tell you something to lighten your heart.'

The antiquated turn of phrase struck Thea as exactly right. 'She did that very thing,' she confirmed. 'She said she had an epiphany yesterday, talking to Drew. Last time we met she was screaming at me to leave him alone.'

'I won't enquire,' said her mother, with self-conscious restraint. 'But if you'd like to tell me . . .'

'Not just now. Let's go and find that grieving widow. We might even manage to make her feel better.'

They set out with the spaniel, which Thea said would play with the golden retriever and make everything go more easily. 'It's my belief you're going more to see the puppy than the widow,' said Thea's mother.

'I admit it's an attraction. I'd never have stopped to talk to Jenny if it hadn't been for that. It really is a lovely creature.'

'There have been times over the past three years,' said her mother, 'when I worried that you were going to spend the rest of your life with dogs, rather than people. I hope this Drew person is planning to change all that.'

Thea's heart gave a lurch. 'Don't say that. That's an awful thing to say.'

'Is it? Why?'

314

'Because . . . things aren't like that between him and me. We just want a normal friendship, to get a chance to know each other. You probably wouldn't like him, actually. He's not terribly manly. He's younger than me and only about five feet nine. Nothing like a romantic hero in the movies.'

'He sounds perfectly all right to me. Your father was five feet nine.'

'Carl was only five feet eight, now I come to think of it.'

Maureen sighed, as she always did when Thea's husband was mentioned. Everybody had liked him, the family embracing him unreservedly, despite the precipitate marriage when Thea was barely twenty-one. She had to admit that her loss had been wholeheartedly shared by all her relatives.

'I wonder whether Jenny has much family,' she said. 'The poor thing. She must be only thirty or so.'

'And I wonder whether she really is pregnant. That'll be so strange – all those confusing emotions. That poor baby.'

Immersed in oceans of sympathy, they took the short way to Silk Mill Lane, through Oliver's woods, expecting to be there in ten minutes.

But they never got as far as Jenny's home. The lower part of Castle Street was blocked by a very large horsebox, attached to a powerful truck. It had jackknifed spectacularly, with the trailer painfully twisted on its tow bar. Alarmed equine cries were coming from inside. A man was dancing furiously around the vehicles, clearly at a loss as to what he should do.

'What on earth happened?' asked Thea, trying to make sense of the scene.

315

'I was trying to avoid that bloody dog,' came the tight response.

'Oh, Thea – look,' cried her mother, pointing at something under the wheels.

It was literally a bloody dog. The enchantingly lovely golden retriever puppy was bleeding and whimpering and dying before their very eyes. 'We've got to get her out of there,' Thea instructed. 'For God's sake – why haven't you done it already?'

'What do you suggest?' the man grated. 'The wheel's on top of her.'

Thea's heart expanded to breaking point at the realisation that this was true. The dog's pelvis was taking the weight of the horsebox – which contained at least two horses, from the sound of it. The truck's nose was wedged into a wall on one side of the street. If it tried to reverse, the jackknifing would only get worse, and no progress was likely. 'We have to do it,' Thea repeated.

'Get the horses out and unhitch the trailer,' said Maureen, urgently.

'She can't possibly survive, can she? It would be best to call a vet and have her put down.' Thea felt tears gathering rapidly behind her nose.

'I've got a shotgun,' the man said. 'In the back of the truck.'

The three-way dilemma paralysed them all, until Thea knelt by the puppy's head and gently stroked it. Above her, heavy hoofs were stamping, rocking the unstable horsebox. 'Get out of there,' said the man. 'It could all tip over on you.'

'What in hell's name is happening?' came a new voice. Nobody explained. The facts would quickly speak for themselves. 'Patrick? Is that you?'

'Cilla,' he acknowledged. 'We've got a right old mess here. Can't decide what to do for the best.'

'For heaven's sake, man. Get the horses out – tie them to the gate over there, look. Then we can unhitch the trailer and get the dog free. She might not be as bad as she looks.'

'Do you know what this thing weighs?' grumbled the man, who Thea was beginning to understand wasn't the brightest spark in Winchcombe.

'Come on.' Priscilla was already rattling at the fastenings of the ramp at the back of the horsebox. 'Have they got headcollars?'

'Yeah. But they're big, mind. And not happy.'

'Who can blame them? Take a corner here, will you?'

Together, Patrick and Priscilla lowered the heavy ramp, and climbed in with the horses. Thea winced at the thought of yet more weight crushing the wretched puppy. Alarmed for herself as well, she crouched lower, half beneath the trailer. Her mother seemed to have disappeared from view.

Providentially, another man materialised from somewhere, who added further calm efficiency to that of Priscilla. He took one horse, and attached it to the gate, hurrying the lifting of the ramp with brief orders. Then the two men manipulated the twisted mechanism connecting the two vehicles, and within moments had heaved the trailer backwards and off the trapped dog.

Release made little difference, however. The flattened hips and back legs were plainly useless. Beyond pain, the eyes were filming over, and the head flopped onto Thea's lap, as she ducked away from the slowly rolling horsebox. 'She's dying,' she said.

'Oh, darling,' came her mother's voice. 'What a terrible thing.'

It was disproportionately terrible. It seemed to Thea at that moment like the greatest tragedy there could ever be. She felt a helpless rage against the dim-witted Patrick, and his useless horses, flashing him a venomous look. Tears dripped onto the yellow head, as the final breath was heaved: a long sigh of release, followed by an involuntary stretching of the front legs as the muscles fought one last time for oxygen.

'I couldn't help it. The stupid thing dashed right under the wheels. I was only going about twenty. They get confused by trailers, that's what it is. I swerved as best I could.'

The truth of this was unarguable. 'I'm sure you couldn't help it,' soothed Maureen. 'It was only a puppy. Can't have had much sense.'

Only then did Thea remember her own dog. She had dropped the lead to minister to the retriever, and left Hepzie to her own devices. Now, as she looked around, she saw the spaniel sitting patiently unconcerned, well out of the way of all the activity. The heartlessness did something to bring Thea back into balance. The spaniel was trusting everything to come right, accepting that there was nothing she could do. *Even so*, Thea sniffed, *she might have come to offer me some sympathy*. A cuddle from a warm living dog might have been consoling.

'Who's the owner?' asked Patrick, of nobody in particular.

'She's called Jenny. Her husband's just died,' said Priscilla. 'Typical, the way things always come together like this. One thing after another.'

'That's true,' said Maureen. 'She must be too distraught to watch out for her dog properly. It should never have been out on its own.'

'Who's going to tell her?' Thea quailed. 'She's going to be absolutely flattened.'

'She's flattened already. There's no further down for her to go,' said Priscilla. 'I've just come from there, as it happens. I'll go and tell her, shall I? If somebody can move the body and wrap it up in something.'

The nameless man who had turned up to help went back to his car that nobody had noticed. He had apparently been trying to drive up to the main street, and finding his way blocked, decided the best thing to do was hasten the removal of the obstacle. 'I'll be off, then,' he called over his shoulder. 'I think I can just about get through.'

Watching him, Thea realised that several other cars were waiting for the blockage to clear, from both directions. The news of the accident would soon spread around town, she supposed. The handsome bay horses tied to the old gate added picturesque detail to the scene. The small dead dog would very likely escape notice, especially if it was quickly covered up.

'If you've just come from there, why didn't *you* watch out for the dog?' asked Maureen accusingly. 'You didn't let it out, did you?'

Priscilla flushed, but said nothing. A scenario flitted through Thea's mind, whereby the woman had carelessly opened the door, hardly noticing the departure of the puppy. Or perhaps it had been following her when it was hit. Perhaps she had shouted at it and pushed it away, so it had been bewildered and vulnerable to a confusingly large motor in its quiet little street.

'She hardly suffered,' Maureen said quietly to Thea. 'It was all over very quickly.'

'I know,' choked Thea. 'It's just—'

'Come on. We can go and have a drink and pull ourselves together. They don't need us here any more.'

It was the best and obvious course of action, and Thea got to her feet clumsily, brushing at her grubby clothes. There was blood on her trousers. 'I'm a bit dirty,' she said childishly.

'That doesn't matter. You need a few quiet moments somewhere, to get over the shock.'

Slowly, Thea noted once again how competent and effective her mother could be. No distracting hysterics or helpless hand-wringing – she had been the first to spot the practical solution to the problem, even though nobody had acted on her words until Priscilla showed up and repeated them. 'Thanks, Mum,' she said. 'I'm so glad you're here.'

'Come on, then.'

They walked up to the main street and turned left, instinctively seeking the near-familiarity of the Plaisterers Arms. 'It's such a *waste*,' Thea burst out. 'A waste of a beautiful dog, I mean.'

'Yes, it is. But animals die every day, lovely animals. It's always there, in the background, even for me. I've never lived on a farm or even had many pets, but I feel it, just the same. All those cows and pigs, killed for us to eat. And badgers and rabbits on the roads. You know – I think that's the single most dreadful thing about life on this planet, the way we torture animals. It's the one we can't bear to face up to.'

'Gosh, Mum,' Thea laughed shakily. 'Where did that come from, all of a sudden?'

'I've always thought it, from a girl. Hunters shooting bears and tigers; men on boats harpooning whales; Italians shooting little birds out of the sky; it just goes on and on, an endless list of cruelty and killing. It makes me hate the whole human race.'

'Horses in the First World War is the one that gets to me – and I don't even *like* horses very much.'

'You don't have to like them. What about rats in laboratories, and being poisoned because they eat the cattle feed? And those poor cane toads in Australia. I don't expect they're very nice, but people think it's fine to be unspeakably cruel to them.'

'Stop it. It's too depressing to think about.'

'My point exactly. We can't bear to face our own wickedness.'

The drift into philosophy had managed to divert Thea from the specific anguish over Blodwen and her surely distraught owner. 'I don't feel up to seeing Jenny,' she admitted, after walking a short way in silence, Hepzibah trotting discreetly at her heel, dimly aware that she was not in her mistress's best books, for some reason.

'I wouldn't think she'd want to see us, either. It perhaps wasn't such a good idea, anyhow.'

It was a little after midday when they entered the pub, and the place was deserted. Thea looked down at herself again and flinched at the sight of her messy clothes. 'I'm not sure . . .' she began, but her mother had already started talking to the man at the bar.

'I've ordered you a brandy,' she announced. 'And we'll sit here in this cosy corner. Nobody's going to care about your clothes.'

Thea was forced to concede that this was undoubtedly true – since there was nobody else in the place *to* care. Only when sitting down did she become fully aware of how shaken she had been. Her spaniel put both front paws on her knee, gazing into her face with large liquid eyes. 'Down, Heps,' said Thea feebly. 'There's a good dog.'

She briefly stroked the soft head, and flipped a long black ear through her fingers, in the old automatic gesture. Hepzie seemed satisfied, and slumped onto the floor with a sigh.

'Brandy seems terribly decadent,' she protested. 'In the middle of the day.'

'It's what you need. That horsebox might easily have crashed down on you. My heart was in my mouth.'

'So *you* need a brandy as well.'

'I certainly do,' agreed her mother. 'Possibly two.'

'It couldn't have tipped over, though. Not while it was attached to the truck. I wasn't in any danger.'

'Fraser would call it a "ute",' said Maureen, with a fond smile. 'That's what they have in Australia. Huge great things, apparently, that cost a fortune to run. People take them into the outback, with very luxurious camping stuff.

It'd be nice to see it. He says it's incredibly beautiful down there. He showed me some slides he took when he first went out. It does look wonderful.'

'Phil Hollis has been to Australia,' said Thea. 'Queensland. He didn't like it much.'

'Fraser says it's much better in the west. Less conformist, apparently.'

The idle chat was soothing, and combined with the brandy was serving to settle Thea's nerves. The sadness over the dog was already more bearable than it had been fifteen minutes earlier. But she found that any thought of food was repugnant. 'We're not having lunch here, are we?' she said. 'I don't think I could face it.'

'Leave it a little while, then. There's no rush. We don't have to be anywhere.'

It was true, and yet Thea felt uneasy at the idea of spending hours in a pub, when outside there was murder and misery swirling all around. She patted her pocket, reassured to feel her phone still in place. If anything drastic happened, somebody might phone her, she thought, pulling it out and switching it on. 'What's that for?' asked her mother.

'I just thought . . . Gladwin might want me.' *Or Drew*, she added silently.

'I've got mine as well.' Her mother prodded the shoulder bag she'd brought with her. 'Lucky I put my purse in, or we wouldn't be able to pay for the drinks.'

There seemed to be nothing to say. It was like being at the eye of a hurricane, waiting for the next onslaught. Except that it was an erratic sort of storm, coming and going unpredictably. Only an hour ago, she and her mother had been so happy, never guessing that a dog was about to die and plunge them into sadness.

Maggs wouldn't be back yet. Would she tell Drew about her meeting with Thea? What would his reaction be? Did he resent his partner's influence over his life, needing her permission before he did anything? Or was it not like that at all? Would he collapse completely without Maggs at his side?

And Gladwin? What was she doing at that precise moment? Thea felt a sense of obligation towards the detective, a need to be available at a moment's notice, just like any paid employee.

There was a small television behind the bar, which had been switched off when they arrived. Now the barman, apparently in an effort to add some cheery distraction to the place, turned it on. A news reporter was speaking, from in front of the Old Bailey. The name 'Meadows' crashed into the quiet bar like a small bomb.

'Oh, my goodness,' said Maureen, her hand to her mouth. 'What's happened now?'

It took them a few moments to decipher the story. An old man was speaking to camera, with a quiet dignity that had plainly magnetised everyone around him. 'Whoever might have killed her, it had nothing to do with my family,' he said.

'He means Melissa, of course,' said Thea. 'But how does he *know*?'

Maureen slowly caught up. 'That must be Cedric,' she realised. 'He doesn't look much like the others, does he?'

'Oliver's collapsed – is that what they said? The trial's been suspended. So what happens now? He'll come home, I suppose, if he's well enough.'

'I must go to Fraser,' her mother announced urgently. 'I really must go to him right away.' She stood up, her face pinched with worry. 'I *told* him to stay away from all that nastiness. It's got nothing whatever to do with him.'

'That's what Cedric just said,' Thea remarked. 'And yet surely it can't be true.'

Her mother was unstoppable. Thea followed her out of the bar, into a town square that was suddenly bright with sunshine. 'But how will you get there?' she protested. 'What's the hurry? Do you want me to take you to a station? The only one I know is at Moreton. It isn't far away.'

'Yes, yes. A station.'

'To London? Are you going to London?'

'Yes. No. I suppose so. Wherever Fraser is.'

'We don't know where he is. He might have gone home to Mo's by now. Calm down, Mum. Stop and think for a minute.'

But at that moment the storm came back, and there was no time for thinking.

Chapter Thirty-One

It began fairly quietly, with a minor kerfuffle in the pub doorway, in which a man tried to step around Hepzie and got entangled in her lead. 'Sorry, sorry,' Thea apologised, trying to unwind them.

'For God's sake,' snapped the man. 'Get out of the way, will you.'

'Just stand still a minute,' Thea ordered, as if to the dog. But since the spaniel was meekly waiting for release and the man was hopping and twisting, he rightly assumed the instruction could only apply to him.

'Don't tell me what to do,' he shouted.

'We're in a hurry,' put in Thea's mother.

The man jerked roughly and Thea dropped the lead. Aware of her freedom, Hepzie darted forward into the square, where cars were parked. Cravenly she scuttled underneath a silver Peugeot and crouched quiveringly out of reach.

'Satisfied?' snarled Thea at the man, and ran to retrieve the dog.

It was accomplished without much difficulty, Thea's mother eventually snatching at the trailing lead and hauling the dog out from just below the number plate. 'Come here, you silly thing,' she said. 'There's no time for this.'

Thea found herself staring at the car's registration. 'RE08BEN' she read aloud. 'And look what somebody's done to the zero – added a screw or something, to make it more like a U. Look, Mum! Is it just me, or is it trying to look like REUBEN? With two Bs, though. That rather spoils it.'

Maureen stood back for a look. 'I would never have guessed,' she said. 'Aren't you being rather fanciful?'

'Don't you think it could be what Melissa had written on her hand, though? I wonder whose car it is?'

'It must be Reuben's – but why is it parked here, when he only lives around the corner?'

'Hmm. It's got something stuck on it – see. A parking ticket, presumably. Which means it must have been here . . .' Thea peered more closely at the plastic-encased missive. 'There's a date – the sixteenth. That was yesterday.'

'Wouldn't it have been towed away by now? I thought the police were checking all the cars, anyway.'

'Yes, that's right. They were. And this must surely have attracted their notice.'

'Especially if it does belong to Reuben.'

'But you don't have to pay to park here on a Sunday, so it might just have come up as belonging to a local resident, when they ran the check, so it escaped their notice. Once Reuben's body was found, they went on to something else and stopped worrying about cars.' Thea was hypothesising wildly, her detective instincts suddenly activated. 'It's possible,' she finished, rather lamely.

'Well, never mind now. I want to get moving.'

'No, Mum. I have to call Gladwin, and tell her about it. I can't believe it's not important.'

'Afternoon, ladies,' came a voice from the pavement behind them. 'Can I be of service?'

'Jason!' gasped Maureen. 'What are you doing here?'

The man grinned cheerily at her. 'Mo sent me. She thought you might be in need of some wheels. And the old man's pining for you, so she says.'

'Where did you go on Sunday?' Thea challenged him. 'You just disappeared. The police—'

He spread his hands ingenuously. 'Tell me about it. The phone's been red-hot. How was I to know you'd fall over a dead body the minute I let you out of my sight?'

'Come on, Jason. I'm not that stupid. You made yourself scarce for a reason. Nobody had an idea where you'd gone.'

'Listen.' He put his face close to hers. 'There were a few things in the back of my car that I didn't want people to see, okay? I got back to the high street here after looking at the trains, and saw the rozzers gathering, so had a quick look to see what was going on – just walked down to the end of that Silk Whatsit Street. I saw you two and the uniforms and thought I should keep my head down. When Mo didn't show, I reckoned she'd get a ride with her dad, no trouble, so I went off on my own. No great mystery to it. Don't know why you set the law on me like you did.'

'They found you, then?'

'As I said, only on the phone. Seems I wasn't near as suspicious a character as you made them think.' He turned to Maureen. 'Now, milady, can I drive you to a reunion with your beloved? That's what I came for. I was just about to turn down your road when I spotted you here. Couldn't miss that pretty doggie, could I?'

Thea struggled to find further flaws in his story. Whilst having no real fear that he had committed murder, or even behaved violently, she could still not believe him. 'Did something happen?' she asked. 'After you left us to go to the museum?'

'Not a thing,' he said forcefully. 'I told you.'

'I will go with you, if it's all right with Thea,' said her mother. 'It's rather a godsend, actually. We were going to have to find me a train, otherwise. Where is Fraser now?'

'Back at Mo's. Silly old lad went off to London first thing, and upset his brother so much they had to stop the trial. It was all over by ten, as far as I can see. He got home somehow – from Paddington, I s'pose – and phoned from the station. Mo says he's in quite a state.'

'But it's only half past twelve now. How did you get here so quickly?' Thea could not help but question.

'There you go again. I was on the road, Burford way, when Mo called me. There's such a thing as mobiles now, you know. Sent me over here asap.'

'But she told us you never use a mobile.' It was Maureen's turn to doubt him. 'Said you thought it would make you into a caricature.'

Jason rolled his eyes. 'Blimey! Spanish Inquisition's got nothing on you two, has it! I keep one in the car, all right?

Hands-free, ten years old. Only works when it's in the right mood. Only two people even know the number, and one of them's Mo.'

Thea refrained, with difficulty, from asking who the other was. He told her anyway. 'And the other is Janice, my assistant. She handles the caravan park, bookings and so forth. About three times a year she needs to check something with me, so she calls me. Otherwise she can manage it all herself when I'm not there. Just like in the olden days.'

Thea laughed. There really was something very endearing about the man. 'All right, you win,' she said. 'Take my mother off with you, if you must.'

'You trust me with her, then, do you?'

'She's old enough to look after herself. We'll walk down to the house and meet you there, shall we?'

'Um . . . yeah, okay.' It was the rapid glance to his rear, and then across the street that alerted Thea. All her reluctant faith in him evaporated in an instant. He was afraid of being seen; afraid of spending another minute in Winchcombe. But she said nothing, feverishly calculating what her next move should be.

'She'll have to pack up her things. Give us fifteen minutes or so. Have you had any lunch?'

He shook his head. 'I thought we could stop somewhere on the road.'

'Okay. Well, we'll be as quick as we can. You can wait outside for us. It'll only slow us down if you come in and we get talking.' It sounded feeble in her own ears, but he seemed to accept it.

'I'll get the motor and find somewhere to park, then,' he nodded. 'Might be further down, by those big gates.'

'We'll find you,' said Thea.

The moment they were around the corner, Thea called Gladwin, hoping desperately that she would respond quickly. The countless possibilities as to where she might be and what she might be doing were dizzying.

But the detective answered on the second ring. 'Thea? What's the matter?'

'Jason's here. He says he came to fetch Mum and take her to Fraser, but he's acting oddly. I don't think I should let her go with him.'

'Hey!' protested Maureen. 'What are you saying about me?'

'Where, exactly?' asked Gladwin.

'We're in Vineyard Street, going back to Oliver's house. We said we'd meet him in fifteen minutes. I don't know what he'll do if we don't show up.'

'Are you scared?'

Thea hesitated. 'Not exactly. I just don't think we should let him get away again. He says the police haven't seen him, just spoken on the phone.'

'That's true, but it's not the whole story. We haven't had *time*, do you see? It's all happening so quickly.'

'So . . . ?'

'Stall him as long as you can. I can't come for a bit yet, but I'll send Jeremy. He can keep him talking until I get there. I'm working on something at the moment . . .' A faint voice apparently spoke to her in her other ear. 'Yes . . . I'm coming,' she said before returning to Thea. 'Do you know what his car looks like?'

Thea removed the phone from her ear and asked her mother. 'What sort of car does Jason drive?'

Maureen's eyes widened helplessly. 'Goodness, I don't know. We should have asked him, shouldn't we? I think it's black, and fairly old.'

Thea reported these scrappy details, and added that he was planning to wait by the gates into Sudeley Park.

'Jeremy will find him,' said Gladwin. 'See you in a bit.'

She was never to know just what DI Jeremy Higgins said to Jason, what he threatened him with, or how he appealed to his better nature. But the two of them appeared at Thistledown within half an hour of the phone call to Gladwin, and asked if they could come in.

'Mr Padgett and I will wait here, if that's all right,' said Higgins, with a quick smile. 'The DS is going to want to talk to him.'

Jason was a shadow of his former self. His head hung heavy and he could barely raise his gaze from the floor. 'Oh,' said Thea. 'Oh, dear. What has he done?'

'One thing at a time, Mrs O,' said Higgins, deftly reminding her that the two of them had a bit of history; enough for a certain degree of informality, but not enough to warrant any breach of protocol. 'Least said the better, for the moment.'

Thea's mother was less forbearing. 'But I want to *go*,' she insisted. 'Jason said he'd take me. I've been ready for ages.'

332

'Why don't you phone Fraser and tell him you'll come as soon as you can?' Thea suggested. 'I don't expect this will take long.'

Her confidence was far less stalwart than she made it sound, but the prospect of her mother nagging and chafing for the rest of the afternoon was too grim to ignore. There was a chance that Fraser would reassure her that he was in good hands and could easily wait another day if necessary before they were reunited.

The phone call took place upstairs and took a long time. Before it was finished, Gladwin had arrived. In stark contrast to her previous visit, she was composed and collected. 'Ah, Mr Padgett,' she greeted Jason. 'Just the man I've been wanting to meet.'

Jason shuffled his feet like a teenager and mumbled, 'Don't know why.'

'Yes you do, sir. Don't let's be silly about it. Now, I think the best thing would be for you to come with us to see Mrs Hardy, don't you? You can tell her what happened on Sunday morning, and we can get it all straight, in one fell swoop, so to speak.'

Thea's ears pricked up at this, and she took a step forward. 'Um . . .' she said. 'Does this involve me at all?'

Gladwin gave her a look. 'Not really, love. That is . . . you *were* at the scene, of course. I'm guessing you'd like to be in on it, if that's possible.' She glanced at Higgins. 'What d'you think, Jeremy?'

'Mrs Osborne might well have a contribution to make,' he said. 'And I dare say she'll know when to keep quiet.'

'Mum – can you stay here with Hepzie? Is that okay?'

'Doesn't seem as if I've got any choice,' said Maureen ungraciously. 'Does it?'

'Won't take long, with any luck,' Gladwin breezed. 'Come on, then. We may as well walk.'

They followed the identical route to that taken earlier by Thea and her mother – the walk that had been aborted by the horrible death of Jenny's puppy. Thea wondered whether she should try to tell Gladwin about that, before turning up at the Silk Mill Lane house. It seemed unkind to all concerned to remain silent, but she had been obliquely warned not to talk, and the story was too raw to simply spill out in a few words.

Jeremy remained in the street outside, while they walked up to the Hardy residence. Jenny opened the door warily, her eyes swollen and red. 'What do you want?' she asked. 'Can't I have *any* peace?'

Thea had not seen the woman since Sunday evening, when she had turned up with Reuben. She wasn't sure that she would have recognised her, except for the hair, and even that seemed to have faded and flattened during the intervening days.

'Mrs Hardy, we have here a witness to your husband's final moments, and we thought he should come and tell you about it himself,' said Gladwin.

'What's *she* doing here?' Jenny glared from Thea to Jason. 'If this bloke's your witness. Who is he, anyway? I don't know him.'

'His name is Mr Jason Padgett, and he was in your street yesterday morning. If we can come in, he'll tell you all about it himself.'

Jason was somehow urged forward, and the four of them collected in the small living room. Thea edged herself towards the large window and found herself looking straight down into the woodland surrounding Oliver Meadows' hide. It only required that she angle her head slightly to get a perfect view.

'Go on, Mr Padgett,' Gladwin encouraged. 'I'm sure Mrs Hardy is anxious to hear what you have to say.'

'Right. Well . . .' Jason coughed. 'Well, I was planning to go and see the railway museum, on the Greet Road, and I *did* go, just so people there could say they'd seen me, if it came to asking questions, and I only stayed ten minutes or so.'

'You wanted an alibi,' Gladwin said flatly.

'No, no. Not really. I mean . . .'

'Mr Padgett, you'll need to start from the beginning. Where did you go when you left Thistledown House?'

'To get my car. I'd parked it down a narrow little street. It turns out it was this one – Silk Thingy – up the far end.'

Everybody nodded, even Jenny, who was on the edge of her settee, eyes fixed on Jason's face. He sat forward in an unconscious imitation of her, but avoided her gaze.

'So, it was at the far end, as I say, and before I reached it, I'd come across this geezer, staggering round like a drunkard. "Steady on, mate," I says. "You'll fall down if you carry on like that." He was in that little alleyway by then, wheeling about and holding his guts.

'"I'm not drunk," he says. "I've taken something, and I want to be left alone."

'"No, no, old son," I tells him. "That's not the ticket,

now is it?" If I'd had a phone on me, I'd have called an ambulance there and then. 'Course I would. But he looks right at me, and tells me it's too late, he knows what he's about, and his liver would never stand a chance after what he'd taken. Scared me rigid, I can tell you. There wasn't a soul to be seen, and I didn't like to shout for help, not understanding the situation at all. And then, all in a minute, he folds up on me, right there on the floor, and breathes his last. Just like that.' His pale face and quick breathing added further horror to his fantastic tale.

'And you never called anybody?' Jenny stared at him in disbelief. 'How could you be so callous?'

'He was dead, love. Dead and gone. I didn't see much sense in shouting about it. And I wasn't too keen to be involved, truth to tell. As I said before to Thea, I had a few reasons for keeping my car out of sight. Besides, it wasn't going to matter if he stayed there a bit longer. I never did anything wrong, not really.' His face acquired an earnest expression of appeal to their better feelings, clearly wanting them to agree that he was guilty of nothing more than a piece of selfishness. 'He'd pegged it before I could have got through to the ambulance people, it was that quick.'

'Did he say anything else?' Gladwin asked. 'Anything about why he'd done such a thing?'

Jason ducked his head and gave her a shifty look. 'Not that I can recall,' he muttered.

'All right. So then what did you do?'

'It's daft, I suppose, but I laid him out tidy, and closed his eyes for him. I knew I was wrong, just to leave him there like

336

that, but someone was sure to find him soon, and as I say—'

'Yes, yes. So then you drove away?'

'No. I went and sat in the car, up at the far end. I was too done up to drive, tell the truth. Must have been there half an hour or so, just sort of stunned. Nobody went past in all that time. Never known such a quiet place, and that's an honest fact. Then I went to the railway place, which was daft, I know. Wasn't ever going to make a difference to anything. I wasn't thinking straight.'

'What time was it?' Gladwin wanted to know. 'When you first met him?'

'Dunno. Half ten, maybe.'

'Because you see, sir, the times are puzzling me. When the police doctor examined him at one-thirty or thereabouts, he thought he must have been dead for about four hours.'

Jason bristled. 'I'm telling you God's honest truth, so help me,' he protested. 'How could I make up something like that? Besides, those doctors never get it right, do they? The poor bloke was shivering, said he'd been out most of the night – he was *already* cold when I found him.'

At the window, Thea silently agreed with him on all counts. The sheer strangeness of his story served to make it credible. But it must have been later than ten-thirty when Jason first saw Reuben, all the same.

Gladwin cleared her throat. 'We are, as you know, investigating the murder of Miss Anderson, sometime during Saturday night. Could you help us, Mr Padgett, in resolving that case?'

'I guess he did it. He was mumbling her name, sobbing about it.' He threw an agonised glance at Jenny.

Gladwin's eyebrows met in a glare of acute severity. 'Mr Padgett, are you telling me now that you let the police waste two days of their time in an investigation that you could have resolved for us on Sunday morning? That's a criminal offence, let me tell you. Obstructing the course of justice.'

To Thea's surprise, Jason hung his head in a sheepish acceptance of the detective's tirade. 'Right,' he muttered. 'Sorry.'

But it's hearsay evidence, Thea inwardly protested. *It would hardly have affected anything.*

'All right,' Gladwin took a deep breath, having flashed a warning glance at Thea. 'Then we can proceed on the clear assumption that Mr Reuben Hardy, at some point between six pm and midnight on Saturday evening, did unlawfully kill Miss Melissa Anderson by means of strangulation. His name will be officially and publicly registered as her killer.'

'*No!*' howled Jenny. 'No, no, no. Reuben didn't kill her. He *loved* her.' She jumped up from her seat and stood face-to-face with the detective.

A deep silence enveloped them, as all three stared at her. 'Pardon?' said Gladwin, eventually.

'Reuben loved her. They were having an affair. He bought me the puppy as a guilt offering.' Tears began to stream down her face – more for the puppy than the errant husband, Thea suspected.

'So he killed her because . . . ? Was she trying to finish with him, perhaps? Or threatening to tell you?' Gladwin spoke gently, persuasively.

Jenny's head moved heavily from side to side. 'Of course not. They were going to go away together. I found it on his phone, the bloody idiot.'

'So it *was* his car outside the pub!' Thea burst out, unable to contain herself any longer. 'He was waiting for her there. She said there was someone at the pub. But why was she in the woods?'

'She was early. I sent her a text from his phone, saying to meet at seven instead of six, but I'm not sure she ever saw it. And I tried to make him late by insisting we watch something we'd recorded, before going out.'

'You knew he was going out?'

'He said it was to play poker with some mates.'

'So he met Melissa sometime before seven, in the woods?' Gladwin repeated carefully. 'Is that what you're saying?'

'No, no, of course it isn't.' She wiped her sodden face with one hand, and threw herself back against the cushions. 'Won't you even *try* to understand?'

'All right,' Gladwin said patiently. 'You made him watch something you'd recorded, because you wanted to make him late.' She looked briefly at Thea, with an expression that said *I don't know about you, but I'm not convinced this makes any sense.*

Jenny nodded. 'Yes. Priscilla was coming here at seven, to watch *Doctor Who* with me. She often does. We both love it,' she added with a defensive glance around the room, as if aware that her fractured shards of information were seriously lacking in coherence.

'When *did* Reuben go out, then?' asked Gladwin.

'That doesn't matter, does it? He took the car up to

the high street at about six, and came back here, when he should have been waiting at the pub. He thought they were due to meet at six, you see.'

'And you were here then, as well?'

'No.'

'Where were you?'

'Isn't it obvious?'

'You have to tell me, Mrs Hardy. Either here or at the police station. Well, both, actually.'

'Reuben must have seen me going into the woods from here. See – the window looks over most of it. But he didn't understand, at first, what he'd seen. It was getting dark, and there are trees in the way. But he did see enough to know something had happened. It took him until Sunday to work it out. He came back here on Saturday evening, when Priscilla and I were watching the telly, saying he'd changed his mind about the poker. He just wanted a quiet night in. I suppose he thought Melissa had stood him up. He was very quiet and distracted, obviously upset and confused, but no more than that. He went to bed early.'

Thea remained by the window, looking out at the place where Melissa had died. She could see little of Winchcombe, looking to the south across the fields and woods and a few dotted houses, but she was aware of the fairy-tale town at her back, with its useful little river and the other-worldly gargoyles. She remembered the varied house frontages and their deliberately preserved roofs, free from modern technology. She wondered what effect, if any, this messy weekend of death would have on the people. Finally, she thought about Reuben again. 'We saw him at Sunday lunchtime,' she interrupted, both her own diversionary thoughts and Jenny's disjointed confession. 'Did he know by then that Melissa was dead?'

'He hadn't the slightest idea. I was careful to keep him busy all morning, with shopping and stuff. We took the puppy out in the car, for a run. Then he insisted on going to the Plaisterers for some lunch, on his own. I couldn't think of a way to stop him.'

'But if he'd *seen* it happen, why didn't he go straight to the police when he realised they were in the woods investigating something terribly serious?' Thea knew she was meant to keep quiet, but the questions exploded out of her, beyond her control. 'And you came to Thistledown late that same afternoon. What was that all about?'

Jenny made an awkward shrug. 'Smokescreen. I wanted us both to seem ordinary and innocent. Of course, he'd realised by then that it was Melissa, and he was trying to behave normally with me, as well. He was already in meltdown, though. He'd seen me more or less where it happened, and something gave him the idea that I might have found out about him and the girl. I don't know what that could have been.' She swallowed painfully, putting a hand to her stomach, turning her face into a cushion for a few moments, before turning back again.

'When we were coming back here from that visit to you, he told me. He said, "It must have been you. I saw you," and then he ran off somewhere. I never saw him again.'

Fresh sobs racked her, and for the first time Thea

remembered that she was probably pregnant. If she lost the baby as well, that would be a horrifying threefold loss for a woman who had acted out of the most classic and predictable emotion of them all.

'You have to say it,' Gladwin pressed her. 'Get it over with.'

Jenny looked up, her face completely ravaged. 'All right! I strangled that girl in the woods, and left her there, for Reuben to find. I *wanted* him to find her. They used to meet there, in that hide. He would have gone there to look for her. Except he didn't. I still don't know *why*.'

'Perhaps he came back here to watch for her from the window? Didn't you think of that?'

'He was supposed to be at the *pub*. And Priscilla was going to vouch for me. I was only out for about fifteen minutes. I left Blodwen here . . .' The sobs escalated, making her words barely audible. 'Poor darling Blodwen. Priscilla says she died instantly, but I can't *bear* it. She was so sweet. She was my only true friend.'

Thea began to feel sick with pity. It swirled inside her like porridge, heavy and thick. 'She did die quickly,' she said. 'She was shocked, but not in any pain.'

Jenny tried to focus her blurred eyes on Thea's face. 'How do *you* know?'

'I was there. She died in my lap.'

Jenny sniffed and said nothing, but she gave Thea a despairing look.

'All right,' said Gladwin. 'I think that's enough. Mrs Hardy, will you please come with me? I have a car waiting . . . or I will have in a few moments. Mr Padgett, you're free to go for the time being, but I'll need you again, so don't go missing, will you? Thea, you'll almost certainly be needed as a witness at some point.'

'But she's confessed, hasn't she? There won't be much of a trial.'

'Let's hope not. Even so . . . you might be needed.'

'She's pregnant, you know,' Thea said in a whisper. 'Apparently.'

Gladwin wiped her brow in a masculine gesture. 'Oh, God! How do you know that?'

'Her friend Priscilla told me. I suppose it might not be true.'

Jenny remained on the settee, looking drained of all emotion. 'It went completely wrong, you see,' she muttered, almost to herself. 'I thought Reuben would come back to me, and we'd have the dog and the baby, and perhaps move away, closer to his work, and it would all be fine, without that Mclissa seducing him away. It was easy enough to kill her.' She looked up and gave a ghastly smile. 'I used the strap of her bag to do it. It was already on her shoulder. All I had to do was loop it over and pull it tight. When you hate someone as much as I did – it was really very easy.'

'Mrs Hardy . . . Jenny . . . you'll need to see a doctor,' said Gladwin.

'Oh Christ,' said Jason, who had retreated to the edge of the room. 'She's bleeding, look.'

Jenny's pale blue trousers were tight around her groin, which was visible as she half lay on the settee. A purple stain was spreading as they watched. Thea realised that

Gladwin had already seen it. 'Oh, no!' she cried. 'We have to call an ambulance.'

'I don't care,' Jenny moaned. 'Why would I want it now? They wouldn't let me keep it anyway, would they? Not in prison.'

The unorthodox interview was plainly concluded. Gladwin called Jeremy to go and fetch the car and summon an ambulance. 'Threatened miscarriage,' she said. 'Just to complicate everything.'

Thea had only a few more questions, and she knew they would have to wait, perhaps for ever. She could phone Gladwin in a few days, when the paperwork had been done and all the statements taken. For the time being, she left them to it, dragging herself miserably back to Thistledown the long way. She didn't think she could face going through Oliver's woods again. Winchcombe's main street was quiet, a knot of people clustered outside the big Methodist chapel the only sign of activity. Nobody took any notice of her, as she passed the Plaisterers Arms and turned down Vineyard Street. She would leave soon – perhaps the next day. Oliver would be coming back, his own private anguish lanced, or so she hoped. The death of his young sister was a fresh sorrow, of course. He would miss her visits and the sense of being of use to her. But in some complex way, it might give him some comfort, or at least a validation of his solitary life. See what happens when you get involved, he might think.

But Thea could not rid herself of the memory of that girl, so blithe and sure of herself. A girl who drove a white van, moving from town to town in it, helping people with their disasters, listening to their tales of fire and flood and loss. A girl who was never supposed to have been born, but who had earned her brief place in the world, and had not deserved to leave it so soon.

Epilogue

Four people gathered at Richard Johnstone's grave, the following Saturday. 'Funny place to meet, I know,' said Thea. 'But oddly appropriate, I suppose. Mum, Fraser, this is Drew. He's my friend.'

Fraser reached out and shook Drew's hand, with a melancholy smile. Maureen gave him a little pat on the arm. 'So pleased to meet you,' she said.

'So I missed the whole Winchcombe story,' said Drew. 'I still don't quite understand what happened.'

'It's simple enough,' Thea said. 'Jealous wife kills husband's girlfriend. But husband happens to see her on the way to doing it, and can't take the consequences, so kills himself.'

'But there's a lot I still don't understand,' complained her mother. 'How could they possibly have seemed so normal on Sunday evening, knowing what they knew? She'd done a murder, and he'd found out about it. Nobody could behave as they did, after that.'

'They were doing it for each other,' Thea explained. 'She had no idea that he'd been watching from the window. And he didn't know that she knew about his affair with Melissa. So they were both fighting to keep everything as usual, hoping to keep each other in the dark, and they were sort of practising on us. And they wanted to check up, probably, on how much the police had discovered. They thought we might tell them.'

'So how did he work it out?'

'Must have been something she said or did. Or he couldn't deceive himself any longer. After all, he knew she was out somewhere, leaving him alone in the flat. Any fool could have worked it out eventually.'

'So what was on that memory stick?' Drew asked. 'That seemed like the biggest clue of them all to me. I've been desperately trying to guess what it could have been.'

Thea laughed. 'Nothing. There was nothing on it. It was new, never been used. She must have simply wanted it for work or something. She lied to me about it, anyway. I can't think why. They found it in her bag, which Jenny had thrown into a big clump of brambles.'

'Oh,' said Drew, rather crestfallen.

'It's Jason I feel sorry for,' said Fraser.

'He was an idiot,' said Thea heartlessly. 'What did he think he was doing?'

'Playing at being an undertaker, maybe,' said Drew.

'What?' Thea and her mother said simultaneously.

'It's a sort of repressed instinct, I think, to make a body look tidy. And with him, it was maybe a sort of penance. He'd let the chap die at his feet, and was too selfish and scared to do the right thing and call the authorities. So he did what he could. I think it shows he had a basic decency.'

'Oh, he has that all right,' confirmed Fraser. 'Jason has

always been very kind to me.' His eyes lost focus, and he smiled faintly. 'But that's another story.'

'You must tell me all about it,' said Maureen, squeezing his arm. Then she turned to her daughter. 'Have you any work coming up? Any more house-sitting in the diary?'

'Actually, yes. Somebody emailed me yesterday. The week before Christmas, in a village called Stanton. It isn't far from here, but I've never seen it. I gather it's amazingly beautiful.'

'Aren't they all,' sighed Maureen, with a visible mix of emotions.

Thea changed the subject. 'I like the headstone, Mum.' She examined her father's name and dates, with a sense of detachment. So many other deaths had overlaid that of Richard Johnstone, in the intervening year. Her mother was here in some muddled sort of quest for permission to begin a new partnership with Fraser. Fraser Meadows, who was going to need solicitude and reassurance as he caught up with the facts of his family's past, and their ongoing implications.

And it was, in a way, a sort of prelude to a similar scenario in the next generation. One day, she and Drew would have to stand over Karen's grave, and seek a similar sanction on whatever new relationship they might construct together. Whether as colleagues, lovers, friends or mere acquaintances still remained to be seen.

REBECCA TOPE is the author of three bestselling crime series, set in the stunning Cotswolds, Lake District and West Country. She lives on a smallholding in rural Herefordshire, where she enjoys the silence and plants a lot of trees, but also manages to travel the world and enjoy civilisation from time to time. Most of her varied experiences and activities find their way into her books, sooner or later.

rebeccatope.com